Another Fawcett Gold Medal Book
by Peter Corris:

THE DYING TRADE

WHITE MEAT

Peter Corris

FAWCETT GOLD MEDAL • NEW YORK

A Fawcett Gold Medal Book
Published by Ballantine Books
Copyright © 1981 by Peter Corris
First published 1981 by Pan Books (Australia) Pty Limited

ISBN 0-449-13027-4

Manufactured in the United States of America

First Ballantine Books Edition: September 1986

for Elizabeth Riddell

I'd seen him a couple of times on the flat at Randwick racecourse—six foot four and eighteen stone of expensive suiting and barbering with jewellery and shoe leather to match. I'd given him some of my money and he'd put it in a bag. I hadn't liked him much but it's hard to like people you lose money to. I suppose we'd exchanged twenty words, not more, on the course, so I was surprised when he rang me at the office.

He was lucky to catch me. I had an appointment that afternoon and had called in to check the mail on a whim—private detecting is slow in the winter and I wasn't expecting any notes in invisible ink or bundles of currency. Turned out it wasn't just luck. I thought briefly about ignoring the phone but couldn't do it.

"Hardy?" The voice was rich, pickled in Courvoisier. "Ted Tarelton, I've got a little job for you."

"Good, I'm free. Tomorrow do you?"

"Today'll do me. Now!"

He could take my money but not my pride.

"Sorry, Mr. Tarelton, I can't make it, I've got an appointment."

"I know, with Tickener in Newtown. I heard. That's why I called you, you can kill two birds with one stone. Get over here first, you've got time."

I hung onto the receiver and thought. Tickener had called an hour ago asking me to meet him. He didn't say why and he'd been secretive about the whole thing. But Big Ted knew. Interesting.

"All right. Where's 'here'?"

"Paddington. Armstrong Street. Number ten. Make it quick." He hung up. We hadn't discussed fees or anything like that but then that wouldn't be Ted's style. Eighty dollars a day would be a flea bite to him and my expenses wouldn't come up to his cigar bill. We also hadn't discussed the job but I'd never heard that Ted was a villain so he probably didn't want me to kill anyone. Maybe he'd lost a horse.

I could have walked to Paddo at a pinch and it would have been good for me. Also the car wasn't going too well and it would have been good for it. To hell with doing good. I drove. Armstrong Street was long and curvy and you could see Rushcutters Bay along most of its length if you stood on tiptoe—that meant the view would be fine from the balconies. And balconies there were plenty of. Almost every house in the street had been restored to its former glory with glistening black iron lace standing out against the virgin white paint jobs. The gardens in front were deep for terraces and there was enough bamboo in them to build a *kampong*. Number ten was really numbers ten to twelve; Ted had belted down a three story palace like his own to give himself some garage space. Two great roller doors faced the street beside his garden like giant sightless eyes. Say two hundred thousand all up.

I parked the Falcon between an Alfa with some dust on it and a spotless Volvo and went up to wipe my feet on the mat of number ten. The gate swung open in a way you could never get them to in Glebe where I live, but I thought I could see a small chip out of one of the ornamental tiles on the steps. The bell was a black button set inside several concentric rings of highly polished brass. I pushed it and something deep and tuneful sounded inside. While I waited I picked lint off my corduroy coat and brushed down the pants that almost matched. A quick rub of the desert boots against the back of the pants legs and I was ready.

2

The heavy panelled door was opened by one of those women who give me short breath and sweaty palms. She was thirtyish, about five feet ten inches tall and she wore a denim slacks suit over a white polo neck skivvy. Her hair was black and it hung over her shoulders, framing a long olive face with a proper arrangement of dark eyes, strong nose and wide mouth. Her lip gloss was plum-coloured like her eye shadow. If she was carrying an extra pound or two it didn't look as if it'd get in the way.

"I'm Madeline Tarelton," she said. "You must be Mr. Hardy."

"That's right, Madeline Tarelton. I don't suppose you're his niece, going spare?"

She smiled understandingly. "Wife. Come in."

I followed her down a hundred yards of polished cedar planking in which the nail marks were black the way they always are—something to do with chemical reaction between the metal and the wood I suppose. I'm sure it's no problem. A cedar staircase ascended to the stars on the left before we reached a living room with an acre of Persian carpet on the floor and several tons of brass weapons and shields on the walls. Ted Tarelton was sitting on a silk upholstered chair reading a form guide and making sure that his cigar ash hit the enamelled dish at his side. He raised an arm in greeting, which I could understand, given the effort it would have taken to lift the whole carcass. He pointed to another chair done out in flowered silk and I sat down. Madeline murmured something about drinks and moved off with a rustling of denim and a light tapping of high cork heels.

"You met Madeline," Tarelton asserted. "Married her two years ago. She fixed up the house."

I nodded and rolled a cigarette and waited.

Tarelton folded the form guide this way and that and put it down on the chair beside him. He picked up his cigar from the tray and took a long pull on it. I lit my smoke and breathed some of it in and out and waited. After some

3

tapping of cigar on dish and fiddling with the form guide, Tarelton looked directly at me.

"I want you to find my daughter."

"OK," I said. "Is she in Newtown?"

Tarelton gave me a sideways look to see if I was kidding him. He decided I wasn't and displayed some of his intelligence.

"Oh, that. No mystery. I rang one of my mates on *The News* to get a line on a good private man. He heard Tickener talking to you and told me about it. I remembered you from the track."

I nodded. "Newtown?"

He put three big fingers into a pocket of his tweed waistcoat and pulled out a card. He flicked it across to me with the practiced gesture of a card player. It had been white, but was white no longer, closer to grey. It hadn't been folded but it hadn't been pressed inside the family Bible either. The words "Sammy Trueman's Gymnasium" were printed across the card and an address and a phone number were in the opposite lower corners.

"I found this in with some of Noni's stuff," Tarelton said. "It seemed out of . . ."

"Character?"

"Yeah. Out of character. That's after this James bloke tells me she's missing."

"Hold on." I drew on the cigarette and wondered if I'd heard right when I thought drinks had been mentioned. "Let's get it clear. You've got a daughter named Noni and she's missing. How old is she? How long's she been gone?"

"Twenty-five. Been gone a week, I think."

"Who's James?"

"Saul James. An actor she . . . lives with."

"She's on with him?"

"Yeah. In a funny way, seems to me."

"Tell me about it."

"Well, Noni's my girl from my first marriage. Her mother died eight, ten years ago. I didn't see her for most of

4

her young life but she came to me when Ingrid died. Finished school and started acting. That's when she met this James. She moved out and set up with him a couple of years ago. I only see her from time to time. I pay a lot of her bills, though."

The cork heels came clicking again and Madeline's husky voice broke in.

"Too many."

"Yeah, well, she's my kid and I can afford it."

Mrs. Tarelton was carrying a tray with three tall tinkling glasses on it. They were amber and had little bubbles rising through the liquid. Looked for all the world like Scotch and soda to me. I accepted one and looked at the gargoyle clock on the mantel—eleven o'clock, quite late.

Tarelton sipped his drink and then put it on the arm of the chair beside him. Madeline frowned so he lifted it up and held it close to his body like an undischarged grenade.

"Well, I got this bill to do with Noni's car and I phoned James because I wanted to talk to her about it. Hell of a lot of money. She wasn't there. James said she was with us but we never saw her at all around then."

"How often did you see her?"

Once in a blue moon," Madeline chipped in. "When she wanted money."

Tarelton sighed. "Right. Turned out James thought she came over to stay with us regularly, every month. That's what she told him and he believed it. You'd reckon he'd ring or make contact some way but he says he never did. He sounds like a silly prick to me."

"Don't be coarse, Ted."

"Well, he does. What sort of man lets a girl go tripping off for a week a month and doesn't check on her? Bloody idiot."

I didn't want to be coarse but I had to agree, it sounded odd. A lot of things could go on in a week a month over a couple of years.

"When did you speak to James?"

"A week ago—no, four days—and she'd been gone for a few days then."

"Tried him again?"

"This morning. Nothing."

"All right. What about the card?"

"She left a bundle of clothes here for some reason on her last fleeting visit," said Madeline acidly. "Ted looked through them and found the card."

"It's rough country," I said and reminded myself of just how rough by taking a long swallow of the drink. Not too much of that brand in Newtown. "Did James know anything about this connection?" I flicked a fingernail against the card.

"Yeah, strangely enough he did. He said she'd mentioned a boxer a couple of times, guy named Ricky. It was some sort of joke with them, apparently. I don't get it."

"I think I do." Madeline moved off her chair to stand in the middle of the room between her husband and me. She stood well and Tarelton seemed to get uncomfortable from just looking at her; he started fidgeting again and crossed and uncrossed his legs. I couldn't blame him.

"I think Noni and James had an understanding," she said, "—what's called a sophisticated relationship, if you know what I mean."

"I think so," I agreed. "It's going to make her hellish hard to find. Too many trails to follow."

Ted decided to take offence; he had to do something. "That's crap," he barked. "Noni's a bit wild but . . ."

"You wouldn't know, Ted," said Madeline. "Let Hardy here find it all out."

The bookie sat back in his silk chair, picked up his Scotch and downed half of it. "Right, right," he muttered. He was half a foot taller than her and twice her weight but she had him on toast. I finished my drink and stood up.

"Could I see this bundle of clothes?"

"Why?" Tarelton growled.

"Just to form an impression. I'll need a photograph, too."

Mrs. Tarelton set her barely touched drink down on a coaster on a darkwood table. "Come upstairs. She has a room, her things are there."

I followed her up the stairs to the second story. The shag pile was so deep I felt I needed snowshoes. Her jacket came down just below her waist and I had an almost irrepressible desire to slide my hand into the pocket stretched tight across her left buttock. I fought it down. We went into a room at the back of the house which looked down onto a leafy garden. There was a low narrow bed and a few bits of pricey furniture. Otherwise it was a rather bare room, not welcoming to anyone.

Madeline opened a couple of drawers to show me an array of female clothing. I ran an eye over it. Expensive stuff, not hippy—dressy. She opened a built-in cupboard and reached down a cardboard box. She flipped a few things inside it over and came up with a six by eight glossy photograph. It showed a girl in her early twenties standing in a street. The passers-by were washed out and the girl dominated the scene. She was shown full-length and looked to be tall with a high waist and long legs. It was hard to tell because she was wearing an enveloping cloak over a long dress.

"Some kind of publicity shot," said Madeline. "Good likeness though."

I looked closely into the picture. There was no sign of Ted's fleshy features in the face. This was a tight, bony structure with high cheekbones and a Slavic look. A strand of what looked like blonde hair was draped across the face.

Madeline drummed her fingers impatiently on the chest of drawers as I examined the picture.

"You'll know her if you see her," she said tartly.

"You don't like her?"

"She leeches on Ted. Doesn't give a . . . damn for him. Still, you'd better find her. He's in a state about it."

We went downstairs. Tarelton had finished his drink and the cigar was dead in the tray beside him. He was reading

7

the form guide again. I told him my fee and he brushed the matter aside. Then I told him I needed a retainer and he reached back to his hip pocket. He stopped the action and produced the wallet from the breast pocket of his jacket. It bulged and he detached four fifty dollar notes from it without a thought. He handed them to me.

"This do?"

"Yeah."

"Get on it, eh? Newtown, I don't get down there much these days."

You wouldn't, I thought. You're a long way from book-making in the lane beside the pub and the sly-grog joint at the weekend. You're in the silk department but the price is high.

"I'll be in touch," I said.

Madeline walked me to the door and I smelt some kind of apple fragrance on her as she moved. She opened the door and was bathed in a beam of ruby light from the stained glass pane above it. She knew it too. She always stood just there when the light was like that. I said goodbye and headed for the torn leather and faded duco and the clutch that slipped.

2

I met Harry Tickener outside Trueman's gym in Newtown. We crossed the street and had a beer in the bloodhouse opposite while we waited for Trueman to open the place up for the afternoon loungers. Tickener had put on a bit of weight since I'd first met him a year ago on the Gutteridge case, and I ribbed him about it. It didn't worry him.

"I've been living better since I got off the errands and into the real stories. Even got an expense account of sorts."

I put my money back in my pocket and let him pay for the drinks. We sipped the beer and he told me about the offer he'd had from another paper which he turned down. I told him about a few of the less dull jobs I'd had recently. Private detecting is mostly about missing people who may or may not turn up, guarding people and money and putting asunder those whom God hath joined together. I'd been doing a bit less of the latter lately which suited me fine although I never knew when I'd have to go back to it as my mainstay. The new divorce laws were cutting down on the old *in flagrante delicto* stuff somewhat, but there were always people around nasty enough to want it that way.

A clock above the bar, old enough to be the missing link with the sundial, struck two and we let the barman take our glasses away and mop up our puddles. Outside a fine rain was falling and we turned our collars up and dashed for the doorway across the street.

"Why did you bring me out in this?" I asked him. "I was drinking at home, you could have come over."

"You said you were interested in fighters," he sniffed. A drop of moisture that wasn't rain hung off the end of his long, thin nose.

"You're getting a cold, Harry, you shouldn't be out. Yeah, I was interested in fighters, when there were some."

Tickener blotted his nose with a tissue. "There's one here, I want to get your opinion on him."

"Why? And why the hush-hush?"

"Might put some money on him next time he's up, might do a story on him."

"Well, your security's lousy and I thought you were above all that now, the sports page?"

I told him about Tarelton's grapevine but he shrugged it off.

"I like to keep my hand in. Come up and have a look at him."

We went up three flights in a building which had probably served a dozen different purposes since it was built in the middle of the last century. There were signs that it had been a stables on the lower level with living quarters above and it had been a sweatshop factory and a rooming house at different times and probably a brothel. Now the ground floor was a dry-cleaning plant, the second floor accommodated a dental technician and a small instant printing joint that looked dodgy. The top floor was taken up by Sammy Trueman's gym.

The room was about a hundred feet square and neon lit because the grimy, cob-webbed windows let in practically no light. A bank of lockers stood along one wall and a partitioned-off section contained a changing room, a toilet block and Trueman's office. The ring was in the middle of the room on a metre-high platform. The canvas was stained with sweat and blood. Incongruously the ropes were new, bright yellow, and the padding over the hooks and post tops was pillar-box red. In one corner a battered heavy bag hung from a hook in the ceiling and a punching ball on a stand stood a little to the left. The light bag in the opposite corner was red and shiny like a tropical fruit.

A big man, thick in the waist and shoulders, with a neck like a bull and frizzy white hair on his head and arms, came out of the changing room, plodded up to the bag and began pounding it. He danced a heavy one-two, one-two on the thin canvas mat. The noise was like a tattoo on a snare drum played a bit slow. Sweat started to roll down his pink shoulders and seemed to trigger off all the latent odours in the place. A stink of liniment, resin and cigarette smoke blended in the air, asserted itself and then faded to become an atmospheric background. A dark-skinned youth limped out, took a rope off a peg and started skipping; he had one slightly withered leg and he was clumsy on every second swing.

Sammy Trueman had been a useful lightweight in the years after the war when that division was in the doldrums. He held the Australian title for a short time and lost it to someone whose name I forget. It doesn't matter because Jack Hassen came along soon after and cleaned them all up. Sammy kept enough of his dough to get a long lease on the gym. He kept the equipment in reasonable shape and he'd trained a few boys who did alright without ever making headlines.

He came shuffling towards us as we came through the door into the gym. He was wearing shoes, old grey trousers and a V-necked sweater the same colour. The top of a mat of grizzled chest hair showed over the V. Below that the sweater ballooned out like a yacht's spinnaker in a high wind. Sammy was hog-fat, as the old-time fight writers used to say. He looked nearly twenty stone, double his old fighting weight. But then it had been a quarter of a century since Sammy had been in the ring and since then he'd spent more time with the bottle than the heavy bag.

"Harry—Cliff boy," he wheezed. "Good to see youse. Come to look over the new Dave Sands."

I shook his hand. "I guess so. I saw the last three."

Sammy's wheezing changed to a note that suggested he might be laughing. He thumped Tickener on the arm. "No way to talk is it, Harry? This boy's the goods, eh?"

"Could be, Sammy, could be. I hope so anyway, the fight game's in the shits at the moment."

"You never said a truer word," Trueman said sadly. He didn't add that it was mis-match merchants and dive-dealers like him who'd helped it to get that way.

"It's wet enough outside, Sammy," I grunted. "Don't get your sawdust damp. Let's have a look at your boy."

"You're a hard man, Cliff, but OK, stick around, you'll really see something." He turned around ponderously and waddled off to the changing room. A tall thin young man came out of the door before he got there and Trueman grabbed his arm.

11

"Get your gear on, Sandy," Trueman spluttered, "you're going there with Jacko."

The youth nodded but darted a few looks around him as if he was looking for a place to hide. He walked across to a locker, pulled out tape, gloves and protective devices for above and below the belt, and went through the door after Trueman.

Tickener and I walked across and sat down in canvas chairs with steel frames in a row of ten lined up beside the ring. As we did so two men came into the gym. They were both dark, Mediterranean-looking, with the same cut to their clothes. They shook water off their hats, peeled off their coats and sat down in the chairs at the other end of the row. One of them, more burly and swarthy than the other, shot six inches of gleaming white shirt cuff and looked at his watch. Tickener pulled out his Camels and started one without offering the pack to me—he knew what I thought of them.

"Fuckin' depressing place," he said.

"Always was. Think this boy'll make a difference?"

"He just might. Here he comes, take a look."

Trueman came out along with a young Aborigine who had to lean down from his six feet to hear what the fat trainer was saying. He was wearing old boxing boots, baggy shorts and a torn singlet—not a gymnasium cowboy then. Trueman broke off when he noticed the Latins in the chairs. He gave them a quick nod and muttered something to his fighter. The boy put his sparring helmet on over a thick crop of bushy hair. With the hair covered he looked a bit like Dave Sands whom I'd seen once—the night he'd knocked Chubb Keith out cold in the fourteenth round. Four months later Sands was dead, his chest crushed in a truck smash. This kid had the same neat, handsome head, massive shoulders and those spindly Aboriginal legs that never seem to give out. Trueman led him across to where Tickener and I were sitting.

"Jacko Moody," he belched through the words. "Scuse me. Jacko, this is Cliff Hardy and Harry Tickener."

"Gidday," he said, "pleased to meet you." His voice was young but gruff. He looked about seventeen or eighteen, a hundred and sixty pounds or so and as tough as teak. We shook hands. Moody did a little jig. He was raring to go and made me conscious of my beery breath, tobacco-stained fingers and short wind. Still, I didn't have to be that fit. Taking and handing out beatings was only incidental to my work.

The thin lad called Sandy had togged up and was standing about lackadaisically in the ring. Moody climbed through the ropes and leaned back against one of the supports while Trueman taped and gloved his hands. The trainer squeezed a dirty towel out in a bucket of grimy water and hung it over the lower strand of rope near Moody's corner. No one was was attending Sandy but he was probably better off.

"Orright, Jacko, Sandy, let's see what youse can do. I want a lot of punches, not too much steam in 'em, but mix it a bit if you feels like it. Bit of a show for the gentlemen, eh?"

Trueman hit the gong mounted at the base of the ring support and the boys moved forward towards the centre of the canvas square. I knew Moody was something special when I missed seeing his first punch. He put a hard straight left into Sandy's face and a right rib into his ribs before the white boy got set, and that was the pattern of the round. Sandy wasn't unskilled and he wasn't slow, Moody was just immeasurably better in all departments and he hit clean and often and tied Sandy up in knots. They broke out of a clinch of Sandy's making at the end of the round; Sandy's chest was heaving but the Aborigine hadn't raised a sweat.

It was much the same in the second session except that Moody stepped up the pace a little and made Sandy look worse. But he still hadn't thrown or taken a really hard punch and if they can't do that they can't do anything. The fighters took their rest, shaped up again and Trueman

13

suddenly yelled at Sandy to have a go. He bullocked forward and got a good short right up under the Aborigine's guard onto his chin. Moody moved his head back a fraction to take some of the force out of it and to bring Sandy in, then he stopped him short with a straight left and brought over a right hook. The fair boy's arms flopped to his sides, his knees buckled and he went down, disintegrating like a demolished chimney tower. Moody stepped back, instinctively seeking the neutral corner then he moved toward Sandy.

"Leave him, Jacko," Trueman roared. "Don't spoil a good punch. Go and have a shower."

Moody nodded, banged his gloves together and took off his helmet. He vaulted over the ropes and danced off to the dressing room. Sandy sat up groggily and Trueman wiped his face with the dirty towel; the boy swore and pushed it aside.

"You're orright, Sandy, you had a go, done your best. I'll fix you up later." Trueman thumped the sitting boxer on the back and got out of the ring. Blood suffused his face from the effort of bending and it was a full minute before he got together enough asthmatic wind to speak.

"Great, eh? What did I tell youse? Bit of work on the killer instinct and he'll be ready."

"Is that why you wouldn't let him help the other boy?" Tickener asked.

"Yeah. He's got to get tougher, enjoy seeing 'em down."

"Bullshit," I said.

Trueman was about to reply when a noise over by the door stopped him. The big pink man who'd been pounding the bag the whole time was barring the way to a man trying to get into the room.

"Let me in, get out of my way." His voice was high and thin. "I don't want to make trouble, I just want to see Ricky." He struggled against the immovable flab and muscle in front of him, then he yelped when he caught a smack in the mouth delivered at about one tenth of the

14

bruiser's force. I got up as the big man was manoeuvring the intruder into a position where he could get a good swing at him.

"Sick of you," Pinky grunted.

"Sling him out, Tiny," Trueman yelled.

I grabbed the big, fair arm and pulled it down.

"Better not, Tiny Pinky," I said. "You could go for assault." I tightened my grip but he could still have broken it easily. Confusion spread across his flat, piggy face and he looked across at Trueman.

"Fuck off," the trainer said to the intruder. "I'm sick of people coming around looking for that bum. Fuck off, Ricky's not here. You're upsetting my boys."

Tiny let go of him and the man straightened his clothes. He was on the small side with brown hair, regular features and a rather glossy, artificial look to him. His voice was stagey, clearer than necessary.

"Just tell me where he lives then, and I won't bother you."

"Dunno," Trueman growled. "Piss off. Tiny, get back to the bag."

The gorilla moved away and the newcomer turned to go.

"Just a minute," I said. I went over and put my foot down on Trueman's instep. "Where's Ricky live?"

"I said I dunno," he gasped.

I bore down a little harder. "Where, Sammy?"

Pain screwed up his eyes and cut his voice down to a reedy whisper. "Albemarle Street, Redfern, 145." I lifted my foot. "Shit, Cliff, what's it to you. Look, what do you think of my boy? Good?"

I beckoned to Tickener who got up and moved to the door with me.

"He's great, Sammy. I hope he's got some brains left when you're finished with him. He won't have anything else."

Trueman staggered to a chair, sat down and started

massaging his foot. Tiny sank his fist into the heavy bag. The boy with the withered leg tapped the light bag. Sandy sat on the canvas rubbing his chin. The Latin gentlemen hadn't moved. We went out.

3

He was leaning against a wall lighting a cigarette when Harry and I came out of the gym. Again, there was something exaggerated about the way he did it, the way he cupped his hands and flipped the spent match down the stairs. He was good-looking in an old-fashioned, Leslie Howard sort of way, and he turned a boyish smile on us.

"Thanks very much. That ape could've hurt me." He put his hand to his face to make sure it was all there just the way he'd left it.

"Forget it," I said. "Gymnasiums aren't places to barge into shouting names. You're Saul James, right?"

He looked pleased and trotted along abreast of me as I started down the stairs after Harry.

"That's right. You've seen me on TV?"

"No, I only watch TV when I'm sick. Big Ted Tarelton told me about you."

It deflated him. He said nothing more while we went down the stairs and he seemed to take a great interest in the end of his cigarette when we stopped in the doorway.

"I know about Noni." I said. "We better have a talk about it. Drink?"

He nodded. Tickener wanted to talk about Moody and so did I but it looked like work would come first. He tagged along when I suggested the pub across the road. We made the dash through the rain again.

"Let me get them," James said. Harry and I didn't kick. We sat down at an ancient table; I rolled a cigarette and Tickener got a Camel going. We watched cynically while James got served. He was slim and he wore a waisted suede coat to accentuate the fact. They'd eat him alive in Redfern. He couldn't even get himself served in a Newtown pub. He tried waving his money and clearing his throat and the barman ignored him until he was good and ready. James was red in the face when he got back to us, but we watched with polite interest as he lowered three double Scotches onto the scarred beer-ringed boards. He sat down.

"Cheers."

We drank a bit. I studied his face. It was mostly full of conceit to my eyes but there were some signs of something else. Maybe it was character, maybe worry. He had tried to get into Trueman's after all.

I introduced Tickener and told James that he was a reporter. The actor looked interested and asked what branch of reporting Harry was in. When he was told he lost interest. He transferred his attention to me.

"And what do you do?"

I told him. "I would have had to see you soon anyway," I said, "I take it you'll co-operate with me?"

He nodded.

"Give me the story."

He told me that he'd met the girl two years before when she had a small part in a play he was in. They set up house with an understanding that there were no ties. The girl went off for a week once a month and she claimed to spend this time with her father. James said he didn't check.

"That seems odd," I said.

He shrugged and drank some of his Scotch. "That was the deal."

"Did you go off, too?"

He looked smug. "Occasionally."

17

I was liking him less by the minute and wanted to get the interview over. Tickener looked bored. He finished his drink.

"Look, Cliff, I've got to go. What did you think of Moody?"

"He's good, give him a bit of time."

"Yeah. He's fighting soon, I'll get you a ticket."

I thanked him. The reporter nodded to James and thanked him for the drink. He wrapped his big tweed overcoat around him and bustled out of the pub. For no good reason it crossed my mind that I knew nothing about Harry's sex life.

"Can you remember that address?" I asked James.

"Yes." He recited it back.

"What do you know about this Ricky?"

"Almost nothing. He's an Aborigine, but not dark I gather." He said it quickly as if it made a difference. "Noni met him when she was doing a TV film, he was an extra."

"How old is he?"

"Young." He hated saying it. "About eighteen."

"Why do you bring his name up?"

He shrugged. "I don't know. She's disappeared, I just thought . . ."

I got it. It was like that, never far below the surface silvertails like him. I pulled out the street photo of the girl and showed it to him. He confirmed that it was a good likeness. I grilled him a bit on other contacts the girl might have had but he had the idea of the black stuck in his mind and had nothing else to suggest. He offered to buy another drink but I refused. I didn't want to be obligated to him.

"Has Mr. Tarelton hired you?"

I said he had.

"That means I can't?"

"That's right."

"I would if I could. I want her back."

I believed him. It was the only plus about him I could see.

"I'll keep in touch with you. Where do I reach you?"

"The Capitol theatre, I'm rehearsing a new play. I'll be practically living there for the next few weeks."

"Carrying on, eh?"

He looked at me sharply. "I have to, work's scarce, even for me."

The Scotch he'd bought me suddenly tasted thin and sour. I put the glass down and reached for my tobacco packet. He offered me a filtertip.

"No thanks. What do you know about the girl, her background and friends?"

"Not much." He lit up himself and held the match for me. Nice manners, but my foot itched. "You've met the ther, I haven't. I know her mother died some years back. e went to a private school on the north shore . . . I'd remember the name if I heard it. Friends? None that I know of, she doesn't make friends easily. She used . . ."

"What? What were you going to say?"

He took a deep draw on the cigarette. "I was going to say she used my friends. Funny expression but I suppose that's what I meant."

She was sounding more and more like someone who uld stay lost. It's often like that. Nice poor people get t and nobody gives a damn. Someone rich and nasty goes issing and there's a stampede. But I had to know a little more about her than I did.

"Did she have any money?"

"No, only what she earned, which wasn't much. Her father paid some bills when she got stuck but he didn't give her money. She was very bitter about that."

"Ted looked like a soft touch as far as she was concerned, why didn't he see her right?"

"A stepmother, I believe?"

"Right. That fits. And you're surprised to find that she had connections down here?"

He raised a theatrical eyebrow and spoke through tobacco smoke.

19

"Very."

I couldn't take any more. I got up, put out my cigarette and tossed off the drink. He did the same then stood looking helpless. I gave him a nod and walked out of the pub.

My car was parked a block away; I ran through the rain, risking instant paraplegia on the wet pavement. I pulled the Falcon's door open and sat down in a pool of water that had come in through the gap between the window and the frame. I swore and turned the key viciously. The answer was a choked whirring noise that indicated water where water didn't ought to be. I leaned my head forward on the steering wheel and sighed. It was a bad start to a job and I felt like giving it up and getting a taxi over to Ailsa's place and having a few drinks and getting into bed with her for twenty-four hours or till the rain stopped. But Ailsa was on a Pacific tour, looking in on her investments. I'd refused a free ride and had to stick with what I had.

I got out of the car and stood proudly in the rain until a taxi condescended to stop for me.

4

Redfern is like an untidily shaped ink blot to the east of downtown Sydney. It's one of those places that look worst around the edges where it's bordered by factories with stained, peeling walls and rows of old terraces with rusting wrought-iron and gap-toothed skew-whiff paling fences. A couple of high-rise monsters in the middle help to make Redfern's population density one of the highest in Australia. The taxi took me past tiny houses with flapping galvanised iron roofs, shops presenting blank, defeated faces to the streets and pubs full of Aborigines and Islanders drinking their dole money, improving their snooker and resenting Whitey like hell.

The house in Albermarle Street was a big sandstock terrace that had once been a prosperous townhouse but was now given over to flatettes and single rooms. I held the taxi outside for a minute while I tucked Tarelton's fifties down under my sole inside the sock. I paid off the driver, scooted through the rain, pushed open the gate and went up the steps to the door. There was no bell and the knocker had rusted solid and immovable on its hinge. Heavy metal music was blaring inside and I waited for a break in the monotonous riffs before knocking. I knocked and the music went down from ear damage level to loud. I heard feet in the passage and the door was opened by a black giant. He was wearing flared jeans and an open weave singlet; his shoulders blotted out all the light behind him and the fist he had wrapped around the door handle could have done sleight of hand tricks with a football.

"Yup?" He left his mouth open to show fifty or so pearly white tombstones inside his pink cavern of a mouth.

"Ricky Simmonds live here?"

"Who wants to know?"

"My name's Tickener, I'm a sports writer for *1.   vs*. I want to talk to Ricky about boxing; I hear he's a mate of Jacko Moody?"

His laugh sounded like a chain saw going through knotty yellow box.

"You've got it arse-up, mate, I'm the one who knows Jacko, comes from Burnt Bridge, same as me."

"Where Dave Sands came from?"

"S'right, we're all related. Look, come in outa the rain if you wanna talk about it."

I did. we walked down the narrow passageway through to a small living room. The giant stuck his hand out.

"Ted Williams," he said. "How you goin'. Beer?"

His hand was hard but he didn't put any muscle into the handshake. Closer up and in the light he looked well under seven feet and probably didn't weigh more than seventeen stone. He was a bit soft in the middle, not much, just a friendly amount. He was one of those big men who never have to get to their feet in anger in their lives. There were no fighting marks on him. I said yes to the beer and sat down in an armchair between the TV set and the stereo equipment. Williams had turned the volume right down and the record was spinning around on the turntable making angry, soft scratching noises as if the musicians were furiously struggling to be heard. A refrigerator opened and closed in the kitchen, there were two popping noises and Williams ambled back with two king-size cans of Tooheys Draught in his left hand. I took one and he dropped down into a chair opposite. He took a long pull on the can and then leaned forward, stretched out a hand and plucked the arm of the stereo player off the disc with the delicacy of a scientist extracting snake venom. I said "Cheers" and drank some beer.

"Yeah. Now, what d'you want to know about Jacko?"

"How old is he?"

"Eighteen."

"How many fights has he had?"

"Ten or eleven, prelims, won 'em all."

"Knockouts?"

"Mostly. Look, Sammy Trueman coulda told you all this."

"Yeah, I don't like Trueman, that's why I want to see Ricky."

"I don't get you."

"He trains there doesn't he?"

"Sort of. Ricky had two fights and lost 'em both."

"What's wrong with him?"

The laugh ripped out again. "Nothing, mate, just this," he held up the beer can, "and this." He made a ring with his left thumb and forefinger and stuck the little finger of his other hand through it. He didn't let go of the can. I laughed.

"I see. Well, he's probably better off sticking to that. I wanted to have a word with him about Trueman, whether he's right for Jacko, you know. He might be too good for Trueman. Do you know where I can find him right now?"

He lost interest a bit and took a minute before answering me. He used the time to suck the rest of the beer in the can out in one long gurgle and crush the aluminum tube as if it was cardboard. He flipped it across the room at a beer carton. He missed.

"Anything in it for me?" His black pupils were stark against the cloudy whites, his lids fluttered down a bit and I was conscious that it hadn't been his first beer of the afternoon.

"Tickets to Jacko's next fight?"

He sparked up. "That'll do me. How do I get 'em?"

"I'll leave them for you the day before at the front desk in at the paper, King Street, know it?"

"Yeah, good. OK, I'm not exactly sure where Ricky is but I know he went down to La Perouse. You'll find him down there if you ask around. Can't miss the car—a black Chevie, a Biscayne with white stripes on the sho."

I asked him whether Ricky had gone down there on his own and when he went.

"What's today, Monday? He went early last week. Monday or Tuesday. Not on his own, he had that white chick Noni with him."

He seemed to be about to speak again and I finished my beer and let him have the silence.

"Funny thing, Ricky's a popular boy just now, you're the second bloke been asking for him."

"Who else?"

"Don't know, didn't see him. Freddy, he lives here too, he saw him and told me."

"Oh yeah. White man was he?"

"Yeah, old guy, real pale."

I nodded and stood up. I held the beer can in my hand and Williams pointed to the carton. I tossed the can in and thanked him. When I left the room he was putting the arm back on the record; an ear-splitting guitar chord, distorted by the wah-wah pedal, tore into me as I reached the front door. I put the wood between me and the sound and went down the steps to the street.

The rain had stopped and the grey sky had thin, pale blue rents in it. I stood outside the house and a young Aborigine in a faded green track-suit came jogging down the street sticking out his hands in jabs and hooks. He went through the gate and bounded up the steps. I walked down the street toward a phone booth. A green Fiat pulled out from the kerb on the opposite side of the road and took off up the hill in a smooth, effortless glide. The driver looked vaguely familiar in the quick glance I got at him but I dismissed the possibility. The only person I knew who could afford that car was Ailsa and she drove other things. I called the NRMA, gave them the location of my car and took a taxi back there. In the cab I pried Tarelton's money out of my sock. Some of it was mine already.

The blue van was pulled up beside the Falcon and the guy in overalls had his head under the bonnet when I arrived the cab. I waited while he did what I could have done except that for fifteen bucks a year I reckon I should keep my hands clean. He pulled himself out, took a look at my membership tag and told me to start the car. It kicked first time, he slammed the bonnet down and waved. I gave him a thumbs-up and crept out into the five o'clock rush.

To get to La Perouse you stay on Anzac Avenue all the way passing through the suburbs that blossomed there after the first war. The old permanent building societies and friendly societies lent the money to fill up this part of Sydney and its red brick uniformity is their monument. The streams of cars moved sluggishly along the wet road between the traffic lights in congested fits and starts. I battled along in the middle lane letting the wild men barrel

this Noni, report back to her old man and pocket a few bucks. I'm not looking for trouble."

"No trouble for Ricky?"

"None, why?"

His mouth split open in a wide grin that showed white teeth stained around the edges by tobacco and a fine network of white scars around his eyes. I realised suddenly that he wasn't young at all, he was closer to forty than twenty.

"Nothing. We're related, and trouble follows Ricky. Who told you he was down here?"

"Ted Williams." I explained the way of it, he listened, not very interested except when I said I'd seen Moody spar.

"What'd you think of him?"

"Terrific. Too good for Sammy Trueman."

"That's what I reckon." He grinned again and the scars showed like badges of rank on the dark face. "He's a bastard, Sammy. Rooked me rotten. You interested in fighters?"

I said I was.

"Maybe you seen me. Jimmy Sunday."

"Jimmy Sunday. Yes I did. You had a great go against Booni Jack. Draw wasn't it?"

"Yeah. I fought two draws with Booni, Melbourne and Brisbane. Bloody hard man Booni."

"You weren't bad yourself."

He sucked on the last inch of his cigarette and flicked the stub away. He expelled the smoke with his wheezy fighter's breath and did another little shuffle on the spot. He was wearing only a thin football sweater over a singlet and the wind coming off the water was sharp. I shivered inside my layers of cloth.

"Why don't we go and have a drink," I suggested, "while you make up your mind whether you're going to talk to me."

He slapped the boomerang in his palm. "Orright." He lifted his arm and sent the boomerang off again. I moved away and watched it swing up into the pallid, darkening sky. It came back about knee high and he jumped neatly over it and let it land a few feet behind him.

"Nice one." I picked it up. "You're good. Where'd you learn, Burnt Bridge?"

"How'd you know?"

"A guess. Fighter country." I tossed the boomerang over to him and we walked towards the path up the low cliff. He asked my name and I told him. He nodded. We reached the car and I got in.

"Bit of a bomb," he said as I turned the key a few times till the motor caught.

"Yeah. I hear Rickey's got a Chev."

He grunted. He disapproved of the Chev.

"Where to?" I asked as the engine was ticking over.

He named a pub and directed me through the streets. We went through a smart section on into the low-grade housing with the overgrown privet hedges and the bungalows wearing defeated looks like the faces of old men in a dole queue. I parked outside a pub that looked nearly old enough for La Perouse to have had a few *vins* in. Like all the best pubs it occupied a corner block and had a balcony running around two sides above the street. The timbers were lifting on its walls and the wrought iron was pitted and blasted by the salt air. It was dark now and the rain had started again. The light flooding out through the windows of the public bar had a soft, amber glow like the beer itself.

Jimmy Sunday pushed open the door which had "Public Bar" etched into the frosted glass. The room was quiet, the after-work drinkers had gone and the evening regulars hadn't come in yet. Two old Aborigines were sitting over their middies and a game of cards in one corner and in the narrow space between the short section of the L-shaped bar, an intense quiet game of darts was in progress. One of the players was dark, the other two were young white men with the long greasy hair and leather jackets of bikies. The painted circle, flanked by ancient, cracked black boards, was flooded with light from a naked bulb mounted above it.

We moved up to the bar. Spilt beer had lifted strips from its rubberised surface and the draining trays were rusted around the edges. We both put one foot on the rail and an elbow on the streaked surface in a ritual that means absolutely nothing. The barman looked like a football player gone to seed. Flesh hung off his face and shirtsleeved arms and his belly kept him well back from his work.

"Two middies," I told him. "Old?"

Sunday nodded. The barman pulled them, his thick fingers were puffy and mottled like supermarket sausages but they did the job neatly. I slid five dollars across to him, he made the change and I left it on the bar. We drank some beer. I asked Sunday if this was his local. He said it was and borrowed the makings from me. He rolled a cigarette, lit it and expelled the smoke in a thin stream through the next mouthful of beer.

"Made up your mind yet?"

"Not yet," he grunted. He looked at the money on the bar, reached into his pocket and pulled out some change. He signalled to the barman and spread the money out on the bar. The fullback pulled two more, the sausage fingers flicked out the right money with the delicacy of a croupier. I looked around the room. The greasy cards flipped over noiselessly, the darts bit into the pig bristle with soft pops like reports from a silenced pistol.

I finished my drink and pulled the second one across. "Thanks." I lifted the glass and drank. Sunday did the same.

"You'll do," he said. "At least you're not a bloody sociologist. They come down here with some weird fuckin' stories."

"How do you know I'm not?"

He grinned. "They never let a man buy them a drink. This the dinkum story, about Ricky and the girl?"

"Yes, any reason why it shouldn't be?"

"Two. Ricky's had trouble with the pigs before, I wouldn't want to put him in the shit."

"And . . . ?"

"Someone else's been asking."

"Little white guy, oldish?"

"That's right, who is he?"

"I don't know. I heard of him up in town. He could mean trouble but I'm not part of it. I just want to find the girl, she's a free agent as far as I'm concerned."

"Fair enough. I reckon Ricky'd be at his auntie's. If he's not she'll know where he is. He moves around a bit, could have gone up to Macleay even. Anyway, try his auntie, Mrs. Sharkey, she's on the corner opposite the bakery. You go left up beside the pub and it's one street along on the other side. Want me to come?"

"No, I'll be all right. Thanks, see you around."

"Yeah, right." We each scooped our change off the bar. He picked up his beer and wandered over to sit with the old card players. They gave him a nod and took sips from their glasses, acknowledging his presence in the ritualised way of drinkers everywhere, but the sips were small because those beers had to last.

I walked out of the pub, crossed the road and used the public toilet. The hum of an aeroplane landing at Mascot filled the night air, which was moist, with a faint chemical tang. The area is ringed about with industrial plants of different kinds; tongues of fire shoot out from them like ignited gases from the escape valves of Hell. I walked over to my car, opened the door and dropped into the seat. I knew at once that something was wrong. There was something missing and something was there that shouldn't have been. I put the key in the ignition in a reflex action and then jet engines roared in my ears and an oil refinery exploded in my skull. Cascades of sparks and glowing concentric circles flared and died.

30

5

The hand shaking my shoulder seemed to be rattling the vertebrae like dice. I lifted my head off the stem of the steering column and blood dripped down into my eyes. As I came up out of the gloom I remembered what had been wrong—Sunday's boomerang wasn't on the seat where he'd left it.

"You all right mate?" Sunday was trying to steady me and get a look at the back of my head as I swayed about in the seat. I put both hands on the wheel.

"Think so." My voice was a squeak, the beer rose from my belly and burnt my throat. I choked it down. "Did you see anyone? How long have I been out?"

"Dunno. I had another drink then I remembered I'd left me boomerang in your car. Thought I'd catch you up at Sharkey's. Came out and saw the car was still here. Didn't see no one though."

I put my hand up and felt the back of my head; the hair was clammy and matted. I pressed down and located the cut, it didn't quite run from my forehead to the nape of my neck and it wasn't six inches wide, but it'd do. Sunday eased me back against the seat and fumbled around in the car. He straightened up and leaned resignedly against the open door.

"Fuckin' gone. Best one I had."

"Don't worry, he probably threw it away—it'll come back."

He groaned. "Jokes. I should leave you here."

"Why don't you?"

"Couldn't have you on me conscience. If you can't have two beers and get into your car without getting done there's no hope for you. Come round to Sharkey's and get cleaned up."

I remembered that that was where I had been going and there seemed no good reason not to go now. I nodded and every hair on my head turned to a needle and dug in. I eased myself across and Sunday got in behind the wheel, started the car and drove up past the pub. We stopped in front of a house on a corner block. The street light lit up a rusty gate. The fence pickets started a few feet off from the gate on one side and marched off irregularly with many missing from the ranks. The house was a wide, double-fronted weatherboard. A wooden porch ran across the front of it behind two beds of healthy, waist-high weeds.

I pushed the car door open and swung my feet out onto the ground. Sunday came around and helped me through the gate and up the path. He lowered me onto the arm of a derelict sofa standing beside the front door and rapped his knuckles on the weatherboard.

I looked up and light flared painfully into my eyes from the glass pane above the door. The door opened and a girl stood there holding open the tattered fly wire screen door. She looked about seventeen, she was tall, slim and flat-breasted, in jeans and a tight, high-waisted sweater. Tears were making silver streaks down her coffee-coloured face. My brain was still reacting to the blow and for a crazy second I was convinced that she was crying for me. But she wasn't; she couldn't see me. She pushed the screen door wide open and lurched forward onto Sunday's chest. He caught her, put his arms around her tentatively and tried to keep his head clear of hers.

"What's the matter, Penny?" He jerked his head out of the way of her thrashing frizzy mop and looked down at me, puzzled. The girl sobbed and couldn't make it on her first attempt to speak. Then she got it out.

"It's Ricky," she wailed. "He's dead."

Sunday took her full weight and let her head fall on his shoulder. Her voice came through muffled and incoherent but I thought I caught the word "Noni." The rough horsehair springing through the ripped fabric stuck into me through my clothes and I wriggled. The girl caught the noise and movement. She jerked free of Sunday.

"Who's that?" she hissed.

"Take it easy, Penny, it's just a bloke been in a fight. I brought him here to tidy up. Let's go inside. Jesus . . . Ricky. He wasn't twenty."

He pushed the girl in ahead of him and I followed them through. We went down a short passage and into a small living room, part of which had been partitioned off to make another bedroom. An enormously fat black woman was sitting in an armchair. Her breasts rested comfortably in her lap and grief had twisted her face out of shape. She looked like a perpetual smile and the lamentation had forced an unaccustomed arrangement of her features. A thin man with a grooved, teak-coloured face was sitting at the table cutting his fingernails with a penknife. The sight of the thin, sharp blade slicing into the pink cartilage curdled my blood. His face was an older male version of the girl's—thin with high cheekbones and a perfect symmetry between the thick lips and the flared nostrils. But his hair was an iron-grey crop whereas the girl's was brushed out into an Afro frizz.

Sunday went over to the woman and put his arm around her. He spoke softly to her. She rocked slowly back and forth and I realised she was chanting the Lord's prayer. I stood feeling useless, like something inedible cast up on an island of starving men. Sunday detached himself from the woman and beckoned me across the room. I went and stood near him across the table from the man. The girl threw herself down in a chair and sobbed quietly.

"Where is everybody, Rupe?" Sunday asked. "Thing like this, people should be around."

The man sliced a thin, curling paring from his nail and didn't answer.

"Uncle Rupe," Sunday said urgently, "snap out of it and tell us what happened."

The man looked up. His eyes traveled across Sunday's face and came to rest on mine.

"Who the fuck's this?" he said softly.

I was conscious of my appearance and irrelevance. I put my hand on Sunday's arm. "It's a bad time for me to be here. I'll push off."

Sunday snaked out his hand and hooked me back. "No, hang around, Hardy, we might need some help here." He tapped his pockets and then held out a hand for the makings. I handed them over and he dropped the packet on the table.

"He's a mate, see Rupe? Have a smoke and let's hear about it."

Rupe drew a deep breath and reached for the packet. He teased some tobacco and rubbed it on his palm.

"OK, Jim. Bit of a shock." His voice was slow and harsh like a file on metal. He gave me another look, pulled out a cigarette paper and rolled his smoke.

"Not much to tell, Jim. Copper come around here about an hour ago and said they'd found his body on the rocks at Bare Island. He was a bit of a mess but they reckoned it was Ricky from the clothes. Young Clivie went with them . . ."

"Them?" Sunday interjected.

"Noni was with the copper."

"Where is she now?" I blurted out the words unintentionally, knowing it was a mistake as I did so. They distanced me from the people in the room, cancelling out the spark of good will and arousing suspicion. I was asking about my own when one of theirs was hardly cold.

Rupe stared at Jimmy before deliberately crushing out his half-smoked cigarette. "Who is this bugger, Jim? I'm not sure I want him around."

Sunday glared at me. I felt his approval dropping in

notches like a mechanical jack. There was no warmth in his voice when he spoke.

"Yeah, well, he's looking for Noni. Her father hired him."

Rupe looked at me as if deciding whether to spit. After a time he shrugged and reached for more tobacco.

"Keep lookin' then. She pissed off, don't know where."

"What were Noni and Ricky doing down here?"

"Hanging around, same as usual."

"Anything unusual happen today, Mr. Sharkey?"

The courtesy didn't noticeably soften him. Maybe he just felt better dealing directly with questions relating to Ricky's death.

"Yes—Ricky seemed excited today, but I don't know why."

"A letter, telegram?"

He looked across at the woman who stopped praying and was taking an interest. She shook her head.

"No."

"Was the girl excited too?"

"Hard to tell with her, she just tagged along with Ricky. She didn't seem no different today."

"I'm sorry for all the questions. Just one more. What did Ricky and Noni do down here, really?"

"They talked to people."

"What about?"

He shook his head and relit the cigarette which had gone out while we were talking. I'd run out of questions and answers.

"I'm sorry about Ricky," I said to the room in general.

"Yeah," Sunday grunted. "Maybe."

The girl had stopped sobbing and was looking at me with an expression I couldn't fathom. I was conscious again of the mess I looked, but that wasn't what was on her mind.

"You came down here looking for Ricky did you?" she said.

I turned to her. "In a way . . ."

"Is that a gun you're wearing?"

My coat was open and the shoulder strap was showing. I adjusted it.

"Yes."

"You were too late, gubb, someone else got him first."

"What's that?" Sunday snapped at her.

"Ricky was shot." Her voice started to break then she gathered it up again and went on hard and cold. "By a shotgun, in the face and chest, close up."

Sunday swore and the woman started praying again. Sunday led me off to the kitchen. I started to apologise for the tactless remark but he brushed the words aside. He ripped a piece from a greyish sheet hanging over a chair and handed it to me. I ran some water in the sink, wet the cloth and mopped at the back of my head. The cloth reddened up and got sticky. I wrung it out and mopped a bit more. I washed my hands and flicked the water off into the sink. I put the cloth in the kitchen tidy. Sunday watched, saying nothing. Up on the wall behind him was a photograph of Dave Sands, a newspaper shot of him wearing a championship belt, blown up to poster size. His dark, handsome face looked angry, as if he was thinking that being the champion didn't mean a damn thing.

"Sorry I upset your uncle," I said.

"S'all right, you've got a job to do."

"Is he Ricky's father or what?"

"Uncle, real close, his mother's brother. What are you going to do now?"

"See the cops, see the body."

We shook hands. We had some sort of understanding but it was pretty fragile. I walked out through the sitting room. Rupe was sitting at the table smoking, the woman was sitting like stone in her chair. The girl had gone. They ignored me and I went down the passage and out the front door.

I was more cautious about getting into the car than before but the girl sitting in it wasn't trying to hide. She was

36

huddled against the window on the passenger side. I got in and settled down beside her about three feet away. White men have to be careful about sitting in cars with black girls in this part of the city and one gun under my coat and another under the dash didn't make me feel any safer.

She asked me my name and I told her.

"I knew that white bitch would get him into trouble." Her voice was thin and bitter.

"What did they talk to people about down here, Ricky and Noni?"

She looked at me. In the dim street light her eyes gleamed dark and cold.

"Are you going to look for whoever killed him?"

"It might turn out that way."

"Let me know when it does, I might help you."

I started to say something but she raged at me.

"Look, they fucked, got off, got pissed. She liked gang bangs, Ricky said. He was teasing me. Jesus."

She started to cry again; her thin shoulders shook and her breath shuddered in and out with a thin, reedy sound like papers being shuffled. I wanted to reach over and comfort her but it was the wrong move at the wrong time. I felt for my tobacco and remembered that I'd left it inside the house.

"What was Ricky to you, Penny?"

"Nothing, worse luck." The childish expression seemed to stop the crying. "He was wrapped in Noni. She came down here from Paddo or wherever the fuck she lives and I wouldn't see him . . ." She pulled herself up in the seat until her back was ramrod straight. In that position there was just a suggestion of swellings under her sweater. In profile there was a slight heaviness to her face that suggested strength and stubbornness. She swung her head around, the heaviness disappeared but the strength was still there.

"Take me to Bare Island, I want to see Ricky."

Her voice was steady with no note of hysteria in it and I couldn't think of any reason not to do as she said. She didn't look like someone who had to ask permission to go out at night. I started the car and drove off. I took a quick look at her. She was staring out the window as the familiar places whipped past in the dark but the look on her face made me think that she was about ready to leave La Perouse.

6

Bare Island is connected to the rest of Australia by a hundred yards of old wooden causeway over a rocky deep water channel. A wind off the ice cap was blowing in all directions at once and whipping up the spray from the water and blending it with the drizzle when I drove down to the foreshore. I rummaged in the back of the car and found a yellow plastic slicker for me and an ancient, mouldering duffel coat which I gave to Penny. We coated up and ran to the police truck parked near the beginning of the causeway. Two cops were sitting in the truck and I pounded on the glass of the driver's window as we flattened ourselves against the side trying to get some shelter. The window came down and the occupant swore as some rain whipped into his face.

"What the bloody hell do you want?"

I'd seen his face down at police headquarters on one of my not infrequent and ill-starred trips down there. I dug deep for the name that went with it.

"Evening, Mr. Courtenay," I said. "Nice night?"

"Yeah, great, who're you?"

"Hardy, private enquiries, I've seen you down at Brisbane Street."

"Yeah? Who do you know there?"

"Grant Evans."

It wasn't a bad name to throw around just then. Grant had recently got a promotion and men on the way up sometimes take others up with them. Courtenay wasn't unimpressed, as the writers say. I thought I'd better move in on him quickly.

"This is Penny Sharkey," I said, guessing. "She's a relative of the dead boy."

The other cop leaned across and looked out. "I can see that."

"Shut up, Balt," Courtenay snapped.

I looked at Balt. The collar on his gabardine overcoat was turned up and some wisps of straw-coloured hair stuck out from under his hat. His head was long and his eyes were as pale as an arctic night. When the migrant rush from Europe got going after the war we called them all "Balts" wherever they came from, but this one looked like the genuine article.

"What's your interest, Hardy?" Courtenay asked.

"I'm on a missing persons case—girl. She was last seen with Simmonds. I hear she was on the spot but isn't around now. Thought I'd come and have a look and ask you about the girl."

"Did you now?" Balt rasped. "What about *her*?" He jerked a thumb at Penny. His hostility was undisguised and probably stemmed from trouble he'd had himself as a migrant. Race prejudice has a pecking order and the Aborigines get no one to peck. Balt seemed to be the wrong man on the wrong job, or perhaps the cops thought he was just right for it.

"I thought she might be able to help," I said mildly. "She saw Simmonds this afternoon, might spot something important now."

It was lame, I knew it, Courtenay knew it, Balt didn't even listen.

"Who's your client?" he rapped out. "Who're you looking for?"

"Ease up, Balt," Courtenay soothed him. He looked

down at the girl who was huddled inside the duffel coat. The talk had washed over her like a wave of nothing. The water drops in her hair glistened in the light from the inside of the truck. She looked stoical and immovable, able to outlast us all.

"I heard he was on the rocks. Still there?"

Courtenay nodded. "Down on the rocks outside the wall The place is a fort. You know it?"

"No."

"Well, it's a fort like I say, with these high walls around it. Built to fight off the Japs."

"Russians," Penny said suddenly.

"Alright, Russians. Anyway Simmonds was shot somewhere up on the island and fell down to the rocks. Ended up in a sitting position. He's still there. We need some pictures."

"Who found him?"

"Girl. She called us, went around to the house. Then she shot through. She your missing person?"

"Yes. Can we take a look out there?"

"If you like. He's not pretty. No face to speak of."

Penny turned away, her nails scratched the smooth surface of the truck as she reached for support. I moved closer and put my arm around her. Balt's sneer was a hiss of stinking gas in the dark.

"Let's go," she said.

"Who's out there?" I asked Courtenay.

"Foster, forensic guy, photographer, stretcher boys on the way. Tell Foster I OK'd you."

"Right." We crouched ready to move off into the rain which seemed to be easing a little.

"You might remember the co-operation when you see Evans," Courtenay muttered, trying to keep the sound from traveling to Balt.

Penny sprinted off into the drizzle. We dodged the posts that prevented vehicles driving onto the causeway and started across. The visibility was poor and we had to watch our footing; the wooden handrail and the planking were twisted as though the island had tried to wrench itself free of the continent. There was an oasis of light down under where the causeway ended at a gate that stood up like a stand of spears. We struggled down some steps to where two men stood in stiff formation near a dark shape on the ground. A roughly rigged-up floodlight on a six-foot-high stand threw shadows around and caught flecks of spray and drizzle in the air. One of the men was wearing a white boiler suit and heavy rubber gloves, the other was fiddling with one of the cameras slung around his neck. The dark crumpled heap against the pitted cement wall looked like something that had been screwed up and thrown away. One of his legs stuck straight out and the other was tucked up under him at a crazy angle. His face was a sagging collapsed hole. He was wearing a light khaki jacket and denims. The left side of the jacket was an oozing dark stain. Penny looked down at him, a shiver ran through her and I could feel her trembling across the distance between us. Then she turned away and leaned her back against the wall. She stared straight ahead of her, across the water to La Perouse and beyond.

"How do you read it?" I asked Foster.

He pointed up. "He got it up there and fell down. Got the head shot, I mean."

"And then?"

"Can't be sure, but I think he was propped up and shot in the chest."

"To finish him off?"

He shrugged. "Could be."

"When was this?"

"Sometime this afternoon. Look, who're you?" I'd wondered when he was going to ask. I told him that Courtenay had given me the nod. He looked happier, as if he'd done his duty as a policeman. The cameraman suddenly let off a flash. We all jumped.

"Sorry," he said sheepishly.

I asked Foster what was on the body and he told me

"nothing remarkable." I bent down to get a closer look at the corpse. The belt was fastened about two holes too loose and one of the laces on the canvas sneakers was untied. This could have been the result of the body being searched and I was going to ask Foster about it when the stretcher bearers arrived. They came down the steps and we all stood aside. They lifted the body onto the stretcher, covered it with a dark blanket and secured the load with broad straps. The procedure finished off the process of the elimination of a person that had begun with the first shotgun shell.

The drizzle had stopped. We watched the men in their pale blue uniforms carry the stretcher up the steps and back along the causeway. On the bridge, with the long, flat burden between them, they looked like a strange monster, low backed, with a high, pale rump and head.

The cameraman assembled his gear and unhinged the stand. I thanked Foster for his co-operation, then the girl and I started back to the land—where this had all started and where the reasons for it lay. Her high-heeled boots thudded on the wooden planking and I glanced down at them; they gave her an extra three inches; without them she would only have been medium tall. Lost in the duffel coat, she looked small and young, and I wondered about what having your dream man shot to death when you were seventeen did to you. It couldn't be good.

Courtenay and Balt and the ambulance had gone. The car for the photographer and forensic man was parked a little further on and it made me think of Ricky's Biscayne, the car you couldn't miss. Where it was and how it had got there would be important. I'd have to get Grant Evans's help on that. We got back into my car and she huddled in the corner again.

"Home?"

She snorted. "If you can call it that."

"They your parents?"

"No."

"Is your name Sharkey?"

"Is now."

I started the car and drove back through the wet, empty streets. The pubs were still open, letting out a fitful light and a trickle of people. I pulled up in front of the house. The girl shrugged out of the duffel coat and folded it before putting it on the back seat. She opened the door.

"Just a minute," I said. "You can help me."

She raised her eyebrows, theatrically bored and sceptical. "How?"

"What did Ricky and Noni talk about down here, what did they do?"

"Why should I tell you?"

"You want Ricky's killer caught."

"I know who killed him."

"The girl, you mean?"

"Yes."

"I doubt it."

"You would. What would you do if it turned out to be true?"

"I'd let it be that way."

She sneered. "Why?"

I was getting tired of the conversation and let some impatience come into my voice. "I'm not a crusader and I've cooked the books in my time, but I let the facts alone unless there's very good reason not to. I can't think of any reason to do differently in this case."

She turned her head and studied me through the gloom. The inside of the car smelled damp and old; it didn't reek of high-priced corruption or the sweet smell of success.

"All right, Mr. Cliff Hardy," she said slowly. "Maybe you're telling the truth. I can't tell you much anyway. All I know is that Ricky's father was a crim and he dropped out of sight about twelve years ago. No one knows what happened to him. For the last couple of years Ricky has been driving people mad around here with questions about his father. I don't know what he's found out." She let the sentence hang there.

"That's interesting, but not much help. There's something else you can tell me?"

"Yes. It's just a feeling. I went around with Ricky a bit and saw him talking to people. I got the feeling he wasn't the only one interested in his father. He seemed to be almost looking for someone else as well."

"Can you make it clearer?"

"Not really, it was just a feeling. He seemed to stare at people, men, who couldn't have known his father because they were too young. Men his own age, you know?"

I nodded and stored the information away. It could mean something but I felt tired, my head hurt and I remembered that I hadn't had a drink for too many hours.

"Thanks, I'll think about it. Tell me about the girl."

"Noni?"

"Yes. What's she like?"

She clenched her hands in her lap to stop them from flying about like angry birds. When she spoke her voice was full of malice with a note of fear. Maybe she believed Noni really had killed the boy.

"She's a blonde, thin, a bitch and a bloodsucker. She acts freaked-out, you know? But she's really ice-cool. Know what we call her down here?"

I shook my head.

"White meat," she hissed. She opened the door and started to get out of the car.

"See you, Penny," I said.

"Not here you won't."

She slammed the door and moved off. I watched her go through the collapsed gate and up the overgrown path. She was an elegant parcel of brains, bone and muscle wrapped up in hate. Seventeen. I drove away.

I had two fast Scotches in a pub in Kensington and bought a half bottle for company, so I was feeling better when I parked in the lane beside the Capitol theatre. The Capitol is a grimy old matron on the outside; it hasn't had a face-lift for a good many years and the layers of old posters splattered over its walls seemed to mark its age like the rings in tree trunks. The posters for Saul James's musical were up now covering over last year's spectacular and greatest shows on earth long forgotten.

A chink of light showed through the door at the side of the building. I pushed the door open and went up a flight of stairs that ascended nearly as steeply as a ladder. I moved slowly, smelling unfamiliar odours, not the usual urine and garbage smells you get on dimly lit stairwells, but something richer, more exotic. The stairs ended at a corridor that had rooms going off it on both sides. One of the rooms had a light and I could hear soft voices. I paused outside and placed the odour, a combination of perfume and the sweet herbal smell of marijuana smoke. The door at the end of the passage opened out onto a backstage area behind a massive green velvet curtain. A few props, a coffee table, some chairs, a bookcase, and a wheelchair, were scattered around. Against the wall, on the floor, was a big tape deck flanked by two king-size speakers and connected by a heavy cable to a power point that bristled with double adaptors. I could hear voices through the curtain and I stepped forward to where its two sections met.

"It has to go in there," I heard a woman's voice say. "If you move it it'll be out of place and you'll cut it later. I know you bastards."

"We won't, Liz." A high voice, wheedling. "I swear to you, darling, that the song stays in, whatever happens."

"What do you mean?" Her voice rose to a near-shriek and I took a peek through the curtains. She was wearing body paint and a spangled G-string; her nipples, showing through the paint and tinsel, looked naked and obscene. She was lean and sinewy like a stockwhip and she was stalking up and down in nervous, gliding strides. Saul James, wearing jeans and a striped, matelot-style T-shirt, was sitting on a turned-around chair. Another man squatted on stage. His fat thighs bulged in brown corduroy and his body was heavy and gross inside a flowered Hawaiian shirt.

"It's an essential song, Liz," James said quietly. "It won't be cut, it can't be. You do it superbly."

The woman stopped prancing. James's mild tone seemed to calm her down and I was interested to see that he had some authority when operating professionally. She moved smoothly up to the actor and stood in front of him, her breasts almost touching his chest.

"Alright, Saul," she purred. "I'll take your word for it, and if the song doesn't stay in, I'll hold *him* responsible." She pointed to fatty who got creakingly to his feet. The stage lights were dim but I could see the flesh shaking on his red face.

"Now that's not fair sweetie, I . . ."

"Don't call me sweetie, you slob," she snapped. "Half of those fancy boys of yours can't sing for shit and you know it."

She turned and marched off the stage to the right as if she'd just delivered the last line in the first act. The fat man pulled out a flowered handkerchief and wiped his face.

"Nerves," he said. "Jitters, highly strung. It'll be alright."

James nodded. He seemed to have lost interest in the

scene and its implications very quickly. I opened the curtains and walked forward. The fat man stared at me.

"More trouble," he said.

"Why do you say that?" I asked.

"Your face, your eyes. You want money. You're going to threaten me."

"You need to watch your guilty conscience, sport. I don't care if you're the Woolloomooloo flasher and keep an unlicensed dog. I want to talk to Mr. James here."

James looked at me. His face was pale and more Leslie Howard-like than ever; he looked as if Scarlett O'Hara had just given him the latest piece of bad news.

"Have you found her?"

"No. But I've been close. We have to talk some more. Here?"

James glanced across at the fat man who was looking on with interest. He seemed to be enjoying James's distress.

"Lost her again have you, Jamie?" he said maliciously. "I do hope you find her. This gentleman looks . . . capable."

"Just shut up, Clyde, or I might sic him on to you."

"Charmed, I'm sure."

I didn't like being their verbal plaything and said more roughly than I needed: "The talk, James. Where?"

He swung off the chair and walked through the curtains without giving Clyde a glance. I followed him down the passage and into one of the rooms on the right. He turned on the light which showed the room to be pretty bare apart from a cupboard, a make-up table in front of a mirror, and coffee-making things on a card table. There was a chair in front of the make-up table and I hooked it out and sat down. James looked at me, then went out of the room and came back with another chair. I rolled a cigarette and lit it. James tried to let go one of his boyish smiles but it came out thin and strained as if only half the required voltage was available. He got up and shook the jug, it responded and he plugged it in.

"Coffee?"

I shook my head. I was wondering how to play him. I needed more information on the girl. Maybe he had it, maybe he didn't. I didn't want to tell him too much, possibly out of sheer habit, but I must have looked worse than I felt.

"What happened to you?" He spooned instant coffee into a mug and added boiling water. He held up the other mug. "Sure?"

"I'm sure."

He shrugged elaborately and anger flared in me.

"Listen, I've been bashed and seen a man dead on the seashore while you've been pouncing about on the stage. I'm not in the mood for games."

His eyes looked moist and he spoke softly. "Sorry."

He was a deal too sensitive and raw in the nerve endings for my comfort. He wasn't a kid. Late twenties probably. I remembered how well he'd handled the scene on the stage and wondered whether his personality was completely professional. His private role looked to be a bit beyond him and he seemed to need to set up a particular emotional atmosphere in order to operate. I didn't want to play along and he wasn't employing me, but somehow I'd begun to feel responsible for him and the feeling irritated me.

He sipped his coffee and tried again. "You said you'd come close to Noni. What did you mean?"

I gave him a version of the events of the past couple of hours. He looked concerned when I mentioned the strip off my scalp and he flinched when I gave him a watered-down version of Penny's remarks about his girlfriend. He looked concerned again when I told him that I'd turned up at a murder scene and couldn't avoid telling the cops exactly why sooner or later. I'd protect Ted Tarelton's private affairs as long as I could but the pressure was on me now to find the girl quickly. I needed to know everything about her, particularly where she might have gone.

He caressed his coffee mug and took a long time in answering.

"Well, one thing. Noni has a drug habit."

"Hard drugs?"

"Yes. She handles it pretty well most of the time, not always."

"That's great." I suddenly felt old and weary, running up again against that problem which symbolised the generation gap for me. He misinterpreted my action.

"You aren't going to give up, are you?"

"No, I'm not going to give up but it's not going to be easy. I must know where she's likely to run when she's in trouble. That fat queen out there implied she'd taken off before. Where to?"

James was shaking his head and opening his mouth to speak when the door flew open.

"I resent that," Clyde squeaked. "I belong to a noble brotherhood which roughnecks like you wouldn't begin to understand." His plump face creased into a plummy smile. "But I understand all about little Noni. Jamie here barely knows her name."

"Shut up, Clyde," said James. "You don't know a thing about her."

"Oh, yes I do." Clyde sang the words in a near falsetto. "Are you a policeman?"

I told him who I was and what I was doing. James protested but Clyde hushed him and I didn't back him. Clyde rested his chin in the palm of his left hand and sat that elbow in the other hand.

"Little Noni now, she's a *naughty* girl. You wouldn't believe the things she does and the people she does them with."

"Maybe I would," I growled. "I'm just back from her hang-out in La Perouse."

"Ooh yes, loves the *noiros* does our Noni, the blacker the better."

I shot a look at James. He was nursing his empty coffee mug, just taking it. Clyde was enjoying himself immensely.

"Why do you take it, Jamie? What do you want now?"

"I want her back with me."

Clyde cackled. James sounded defeated, beaten hollow by something he couldn't understand. I understood it in part. My ex-wife Cyn had affected me the same way. I kept crawling back, signing cheques, waiting up till dawn and hoping everything would come right. It never did and I felt sure it wouldn't for James. But no one else can tell you that, and you can only see the end when you get there on your own. Still, I didn't want any part of Clyde's baiting game. I stood up with my coat open and let him see the gun.

"Cut out the crap. Tell me something useful or piss off."

He recoiled and his jowls shook. The plummy malicious smile dropped away.

"Newcastle," he muttered. "She lived in Newcastle and she knows the heroin scene there."

"This true?" I asked James.

He shrugged.

"It is, it is!" Clyde squealed, "and she has an uncle there named . . . Ted or something."

"Bert," James said wearily. "Bert, and he's in Macleay not Newcastle. I remember now, she lived up there when she was young."

Clyde looked deflated at James's knowledge. He changed posture and waved his hands about as if he was trying to think of an exit line. He didn't find one and I jerked my chin at him. He went out and left the door open. I closed it and noticed for the first time a photograph pinned to the back of the door. It was a glossy postcard-size print with the Capitol theatre showing behind a woman. She was wearing denim shorts that looked like cut-down jeans with enough material whittled away to show the beginnings of the cheeks of her buttocks. She had on a blouse rucked up and tied under her breasts, striped socks pulled up calf-high and high-heeled sandals. In the black and white picture her hair looked as fair as a wheatfield and the set of her body dared you to touch her. Anyone with the juices still running would want to.

I put my hand on the door knob and pulled the door open. James started in his chair.

"Where are you going?"

"Newcastle, first off."

"Now?"

I had no one waiting up for me and the paper boy stayed his arm if he saw one uncollected on my doorstep.

"Why not?" I said.

8

A private detective leads a throw-away life for much of the time. Some men in the game overplay this by sleeping on couches in their offices and never changing their underwear. I don't go so far; I've got a house in Glebe with reasonably civilised fittings and I sleep in a bed more nights than not. But some cases don't let you go to bed on them and this was looking like just such a one. The Tarelton girl was running from one piece of trouble to another and there was no time for packing the matching pigskin luggage. I didn't have too much to go on except that she and the car would stand out in Macleay like Gunsynd in the Black Stump Cup. She could become detached from the car but it would take a lot of work to tone down her eye-turning image and she was probably too vain to do so. Half the people I'd met that day seemed to come from Macleay or thereabouts and the place was fixing itself in my mind as a destination, a source and an answer.

I made two calls from a box outside the theatre. The first got me a sleepy-sounding Madeline Tarelton who said nothing while I gave her a sketch of events. She refused to wake Ted and wouldn't or couldn't confirm that Noni had an uncle up north. Just on spec I asked her what name the girl went by.

"Rouble, Noni Rouble."

"Professional name?"

"No, her mother's. She took it back when she broke up with Ted."

"When was all this?"

"Years ago. Look Mr. Hardy, this is scarcely the time . . . you should have got all this information from Ted this morning. Do you know your job or don't you?"

"Sometimes I wonder," I said. "I agree with you. Just an outline will do. Noni didn't live with your husband for how long?"

"Oh, most of her childhood."

"Where did she live?"

"Somewhere north. Really Mr. Hardy . . ."

I apologised again, told her I was going north and called off.

The second call was to police headquarters in the hope that Grant Evans was on duty. He was and not too happy about it. He wasn't working on the Simmonds killing but had heard the talk about it; so far the cops had nothing but questions.

"Like what?" I asked.

"Like who was the blonde and what was that snooper Hardy doing on the scene?"

"And like, where's the kid's car?"

"Yeah. Can you help a little on some of these points? Hate to press you."

"Quite all right. Maybe soon. Thanks, Grant." I hung up in the middle of a curse from him and it occurred to me that

52

most of our telephone conversations ended like that. Lucky we were friends.

I drove through the city and over the Harbour bridge. Theatre-goers clogged the roads and the drizzle had started in again making for slides, swearing, and crumpled mudguards. I crawled along like a link in a slowly moving chain and failed in every attempt to jump a light and get a run. On the north side the traffic moved faster and I could have got into top gear. Instead I pulled into a garage for petrol and a check on the oil and water. I used the lavatory and the smell of the greasy food in the place's snack bar reminded me that I hadn't eaten for ten hours. I bought a hamburger and a carton of chips and ate them as I drove. The Falcon groaned a bit under the unaccustomed load of the full tank, but nothing dropped off and when I'd made it to the beginning of the tollway, I felt confident that she'd go the distance.

Since they put the tollway in, the drive to Newcastle is easy. The only danger in driving it at night is falling asleep at the wheel. I warded this off by taking quiet slugs from the Scotch bottle, letting the liquor jolt me but not taking enough to get me drunk. My head was aching and the whisky was good for that, too. I should have been asleep in bed. Instead I was driving a tollway at night and drinking whisky. Mother wouldn't approve. Father wouldn't approve. But then Father never did approve. Funny thoughts. Maybe I was drunk. A few cars passed me but neither the Falcon nor I was feeling competitive and we couldn't have done much about it anyway. The road was slippery and I swayed about a bit and got bored by the dark, indeterminate shapes whipping by. I wished I had a radio. I wished I had new tyres, but I stayed loyal—I didn't wish I had a new car.

Like all big cities, Newcastle emits a glow which you pick up a few miles out. It's composed of neon glare, factory smoke and the small glimmers of a hundred thousand light globes and television screens. There's a good measure of the day's wastes drifting about as well; Newcastle is like Sydney, you can taste it about as soon as you can see it. I felt the grittiness of the air and its load of rubber and gas between my teeth as I began the descent from the hills toward the city.

Newcastle sprawls about like a drunken whore: it trickles off toward the coalfields in one direction, climbs up into the hill country in another and slides down to the sea on the east. The beach is a surprise; a fair-sized slice of white sand in front of a reasonable stretch of water for humans to swim in. It's like a reward to the city's inhabitants for putting up with so much else that is appalling. I hadn't been there for five years but the bird's-eye view I got of it from the highway suggested that it was much the same, only worse. The long flat approach from the south is a ribbon of used car yards, take-away food stands and decaying wooden houses. A string of motels five miles out from town invite you to stop over, miss the city and push on to the clean country up ahead. I pulled into one of them, the Sundowner, which had a "Vacancy" sign with the second "a" flickering fitfully on and off.

A middle-aged blonde woman with big bouncing breasts under a black polo neck sweater was behind the desk in the office. She ran an experienced eye over my clothes and wasn't too happy. Also I wasn't carrying luggage and they never like that. She sneaked a look past me at the Falcon and wasn't impressed by that, either. Luckily I wasn't planning to stay. She probably would have made me pay in advance and leave a deposit. I reached into my pocket for the photograph of Noni and laid it on the desk in front of her impressive mammaries. I opened my wallet, letting her see the fifties in it and took out my operator's license which I put down next to the picture.

"Ever see her?" I asked.

She looked at it for a hundredth of a second. "Sure."

I was so surprised I had to ask her again. It isn't usually that easy. My puritanical soul told me it *shouldn't* be that easy. But I'd heard her right.

"Anyone along here'd know her." There was a tone in

her voice that was hard to interpret, maybe amusement. I looked at her and noticed her colossal double chin. She smiled and the chin tensed up a bit. "That's Noni Rouble. Haven't seen her for years."

"How is it you know her then?"

She asked me what I was asking and I told her some lies. She looked closely at the photograph of me on the license, the one taken three years back and in a good light. She wasn't too happy about it so I eased a five dollar note out of the wallet and let it sit on top to get some air.

"I suppose it's alright," she said, eyeing the money. "Noni was an R and R girl around here—oh, seven or eight years back."

"R and R girl?"

"Right. Not to put too fine a point on it, she slept around with the American soldiers. You know, the ones on leave from Vietnam. She stayed here a couple of times. She stayed all up and down this strip." She waved her hand at the road.

"Somebody had to do it, I suppose," I said.

"Yes." She shrugged and her heavy bosom lifted and subsided like a swell on the sea. "Nothing to do with me."

The thought crossed my mind that she was just the right age to have done the same thing when the Yanks were here in World War II and to resent the passage of time.

"You didn't like her?"

"No."

"Why not?"

"Too flash, she made you feel she was doing you a favour shacking up in your place."

"I see. Well my information is she's headed this way. You wouldn't know where she'd go?"

She sighed, the way hotel keepers do when the beds aren't full and the overheads are going up all the time. She reached out a meaty hand, knocked about from cleaning rooms and wrinkled about the three rings on her fingers. The fingers closed over the money.

55

"I haven't seen her, but if Noni's back in Newcastle she's at one of two places."

I waited.

"If she's flush she'll be at the Regal in the city."

I thought about it. "I don't think she's flush but I'll check it out anyway. What if she's not?"

"She'll be at Lorraine's boarding house, Fourth Street. It's a brothel."

"Literally?"

She looked puzzled.

"I mean is it really a brothel?"

"Oh no, not strictly speaking, not any more. Probably was once. I mean it's a dump, you can flop there for a dollar a night, single or double."

"Sounds choice."

She chuckled. "Right. Lorraine's got one rule."

"What's that?"

"No blacks."

I grunted and asked to use her phone. She pushed it across the desk to me and I reached into my jacket pocket, took out a pen knife and sawed through the cable.

"Hey!" she yelped and banged one of her big red hands down on the desk.

"You can splice it," I said. "Give you something to do in the wee small hours."

"You bastard. I could go out and phone."

"You won't. You don't care that much."

She grinned and picked up the cut ends of the cord. "You're right. Give Noni a belting for me." She rubbed the ends together. "Hey, there's no electricity in this is there?" I told her there wasn't.

Outside the Falcon was clicking and squeaking as it cooled down after the long drive. It started under protest and I had to coax it out onto the road. I joined in the thin stream of traffic, mostly trucks, heading for the city. The drizzle had stopped and the clouds had peeled back leaving Newcastle squatting sullenly in a pool of moonlight. It opened its mouth and sucked me in.

9

The Regal Hotel is in the middle of the city and it dominates the scene on the skyline and at ground level. The building is a tower with black and white facades alternating each story so that it looks like a giant pile of draughts. I parked outside and made my usual mistake of trying to push open the self-opening doors. This leaves you with a hand held out impotently in front of you and gives the desk staff an initial advantage. Under the lobby lights my boots looked more scuffed and my denims more wrinkled than they did normally. The girl behind the desk was lacquered and painted like a Barbie doll; her fingernails were purple talons and her mouth was a moist, ripe plum. I marched up to the desk and looked straight and hard into her eyes. She blinked and lost a fraction of the sartorial advantage. Her greeting was an incline of the head. No "yes, sir." That would have been a total defeat. I took out my license and the photograph of Noni and held them at her eye level, one in each hand.

"I'm a private detective on a missing persons case. Nothing sordid. I want to know if this woman is registered here."

Her eyes moved lazily across my offerings. She might have been short of sleep or her lids might have been tired from heaving the enormous false lashes up and down. Her lips parted and tiny fissures appeared in the make-up beside her mouth. She was got-up to be looked at, not to talk.

"I can't disclose any information about our guests." She

spoke as if she was reading the words off an idiot card pasted to my forehead.

"I'm not asking for any information. Just yes or no. If you say yes I'll ask the manager and go through all the proper channels. If you say no I'll be on my way."

The impossible lashes fluttered up and she looked at the picture.

"No, then."

"Thanks." I put the card and the photograph away. Her face fell back into its fixed repose as if I had never caused it to move. I bounced away across the carpet and remembered not to try to open the door. Along to the left of the entrance a concrete ramp sloped down under the building. I went down into a dimly lit half-acre car park; there were a few score cars parked in rows. I walked quickly up and down the aisles between the cars—no Chev Biscayne.

I had a map of Newcastle in the car and checked it for Fourth Street. It runs through a housing estate near the northern edges of the suburbs up into the coastal ranges. It was a thirty-minute drive from the Regal to Lorraine's boarding house but in terms of class and cash they were a million miles apart. The boarding house was a two-story wooden job with peeling paint and a collapsed front balcony on the top level. There was about two acres of land around it and, as far as I could judge in the moonlight, what wasn't covered by blackberries and bracken was serving as a motor car cemetery. A driveway at the side of the house was a shadowless black hole. The road ran steeply past the building and there were empty paddocks opposite it. Lorraine's was flanked by cheap brick bungalows on either side, but there were vacant lots up and down the street as if parts of it had been blighted and made unfit for human habitation.

I cruised up the street and parked at the top of the hill about fifty yards beyond the house. The steel works was belching out white smoke and laying down a background hum a couple of miles away toward the water. A few headlights flicked along the roads below but Fourth Street was empty and silent. I checked the Smith & Wesson. The drizzle started again as I eased open the passenger side door and slipped out onto the road.

The gravel road was slushy under my feet as I moved up to the black tunnel beside the house. Bushes overgrew the driveway, their straggling ends whipped clean by cars brushing past them. The ground's surface changed abruptly and I bent down to examine it. Deep fresh ruts were etched into the earth in an arc that curved around to a clear patch in front of the house. The ruts ended in a shallow ditch where the wheels of a vehicle had spun before getting a grip on the damp ground. Someone had left here in a hurry not so long ago. I moved up into the tunnel; blackness closed around me like a cloak and I bumped into the rear end of a car when I was about half way along the side of the house. I ran my hand across its boot which seemed to be about as wide as a bus. I put out a hand for the tail fin and the cold chrome rose up just where it should—a Chev Biscayne if ever I felt one.

I unshipped the pistol and held it stiffly in front of me like a divining rod. I skirted the car and felt my way along the weatherboards to the back of the house. A dim yellow light seeped out through a window and another thin block of it outlined a partly opened door. I kept my back pressed against the rippled wooden walls and scraped along to the door. I couldn't hear anything except the droning of the steelworks and the tight hiss of my own breathing. A fly wire screen that looked as if a large dog had gone through it flapped open. I eased it away with the toe of my boot and pushed the door in. It swung easily, creaking a little, and gave me a view of several square feet of greasy green lino. I stepped into the room and my foot skidded in a dark patch just inside the doorway.

A woman was sitting on the floor with her back against a set of built-in cupboards. Her head lolled crazily to one side and a dark trickle of blood had seeped down from her mouth over her chin and onto the bodice of her cheap chain store dress. She was a thin, yellow woman with lank black hair and a scraggy neck with dirt in the creases. A vein in her forehead was throbbing and her flat chest was rising and falling in millimetres. I opened a door which let on to a long passage running toward the front of the house. The light barely penetrated six feet of its length but it seemed to be empty. I closed the door and bent over the woman. Her breath, what there was of it, was coming out in little erratic gasps and each one smelled more of stale gin than the last. I looked around the room. The bench tops were littered with bottles of sauce, food-encrusted plates and empty beer bottles. An electric toaster had one of its sides down like a drawbridge; crumbs were scattered around it and a fly was trapped in a smear of butter across its top. The mess—jars of jam, brimful ashtrays and slimy cutlery—flowed across the benches and into the sink. The detritus leaped across to the laminex kitchen table which carried a number of grimy glasses, pools of liquid and a two-thirds empty bottle of Gilbey's gin.

I put the gun on the table and hooked my hands under the woman's shoulders. She was a dead weight like a sack of grain. I dragged her across the room, kicked one of the chairs out from under the table and dumped her into it. She didn't move except that her head slumped across the other side. I pushed her hair aside. There was a long jagged tear near her ear and a deep oozing cut on her mouth, the sort of wound the foresight and backsight of a pistol make across a face. There was a lot of blood on her face and on the floor but there didn't seem to be any other injury to her and this one wasn't fatal. The dishtowel on the sink gave off a stomach-turning smell but I ran water on it, screwed it out and dabbed at the blood. She flinched as the water went into the cuts and her eyes flickered open. I pressed the wet cloth against her forehead. Her head tried to slide away to the right but I held it steady. Her eyes opened into dark slits and stared fixedly at the bottle on the table.

"Are you Lorraine?" I asked.

She nodded. The action must have sent waves of pain through her because she shuddered and slid lower on the chair. I hoisted her up.

"Water?"

She made a sound that could have meant yes, so I rinsed one of the dirty glasses, half filled it and held it to her lips. She sipped a thimbleful then shook her head. On a close look her Chinese ancestry was apparent. Her eyes were jet black and sloped a bit and although there was practically no flesh on her face the bone structure was broad and oriental. She picked up the damp dishcloth from where I'd dropped it in her lap and mopped at the slash beside her mouth.

"Did Noni do this to you?"

Her mouth twisted into a grin, the movement brought fresh blood out of the cut and she checked it.

"Not likely," she croaked. "I can handle Noni any day."

"Who then?"

"Guy with her. Dunno his name."

"What happened?"

"They got here late this afternoon—no, a bit later. Noni said she wanted to stay the night, her and him. I said alright and gave them the room. Then they went out for a while, came back with the booze."

She nodded at the bottle on the table and immediately regretted it. I gave her another sip of water. She held on to the glass and some colour came back into her face making it grey like old, stained china. I waited.

"I made them something to eat, we had a few drinks, friendly like. Then the bloke started to talk about him and me swapping cars. I've got a Holden ute—bomb, but it goes. I said alright. I thought he was joking. I asked him to throw in the rest of the gin. He said OK and to give him the keys. I thought he was joking. When I wouldn't he smashed me."

"With a pistol."

"Yeah. Big bastard."

"The man?"

"No, the gun."

"What did he look like? What did the girl call him?"

She handed me the glass. "Get me a drink and a smoke and tell me who the hell you are and I might say some more."

I tipped the rest of the water in the glass into the sink and poured in a slug of gin. I looked around for something to put in it but she snapped her fingers and held out her hand.

"Put that much in again and give it here."

I did and rolled her a cigarette. I lit it and she drew it down half an inch and pulled the smoke deep into her lungs.

"Thanks, that's better. Now, who're you?"

I told her the story quickly, suggesting that the man traveling with Noni had probably killed Ricky Simmonds.

"Jesus," she said when I'd finished, "I was lucky; he might've done me."

"That's right. Will you answer my questions?"

"Yeah, what were they?"

I repeated them and she drank some gin and smoked while she thought it over.

"I can't remember that she called him anything," she said at last. "They weren't getting on too well seemed to me. You know Noni?"

I shook my head and produced the photograph.

"That's her, the slut. Well, the bloke's not big, about five foot six or seven, not more. He's thin but sort of flabby thin, you know?"

I said I didn't know.

"Well, there's not much meat on him but what there is looks sort of soft. His chest's sort of slid down to his gut. Can't make it no clearer. Gimme another smoke."

I got out the makings and started to roll one but she reached over impatiently and took the packet away. Her fingernails were black-rimmed and the thin skin on her hands was stretched tight like the fabric on a model plane. She made a fat cigarette and twisted the end.

"Anything else about him?"

"You mean clothes and that?"

"Anything."

"He had an old suit on, blue with a sort of checked shirt under it, like tartan. Looked a bit funny with the suit. He was real pale, like he's been in hospital. Oh, and his ears stuck out, like this." She fanned her ears out from under her lank, greasy hair.

"What did they talk about? Did they say where they were going?"

"Let's think." She put a black fingernail through the black hair and scratched. "He didn't say much but Noni blabbed a bit. She was pissed and I reckon she was taking something else as well. You know?"

"I know. What did she say?"

"Well, I went out to do somethin' and I heard her say, when I was coming back, that it was a long time ago and he should forget it and it was only money."

"What did he say?"

"Told her to shut up. Then she said something about Macleay and he told her to shut up again. Listen, did they take the car?"

"Was it parked out front?"

"Yes."

"They took it."

"Fuck 'em. They leave the big one?"

"The Chev? Yes."

Her thin, ratty eyebrows went up. "Is that a fact? Reckon I can keep it?"

I thought of Ricky Simmonds, slumped down dead in a ditch around a fort built to repel invaders of an already invaded land. Crouched over like an Aboriginal warrior buried with all ceremony as in the time before horses and guns and arsenic and venereal disease. His car had been his shield and his weapon and now it was discarded beside a house where black men were banned by a yellow woman. Australia.

A man in a dressing gown and three days of stubble came

63

through the passage door before I could answer about the car. He shuffled into the kitchen and stopped short when he saw the gin.

"Piss off, Darby," Lorraine said sharply.

The man looked at her with bleary eyes that sagged down into deep pouches about his cheekbones. With the eyes and the stubble and the grizzled grey hair poking through the top of the dressing gown, he looked like a tired old owl who'd lost his way.

"Go on, Lorraine," he whined. "Just a small one."

She shrugged and nodded at me. I poured some gin and handed him the glass; he didn't seem to notice me, just lifted his hand and let the liquor slide down his throat. His neck convulsed once and he set the glass down carefully on the table. He let it sit for a few seconds, then tilted it again and got a few drops on his tongue.

"Right, piss off," Lorraine snapped.

He pulled the dressing gown around him and dragged himself out of the room. I looked at the woman.

"A bum," she said. "Probably came out to piss in the sink. Now, about that car?"

"Not up to me. Give me the details on the ute."

She did, the number and colour and a description of the frame mounted over the tray. I picked up my gun from the bench and tucked it away. I nodded to her and headed for the door. She ignored me, her hand snaked out for the gin bottle and she wasn't worried about her glass.

Outside the drizzle was steady and the ground was slippery underfoot. I walked slowly along the side of the house and pulled open the driver's side of the Chevy. The interior light came on. A profusion of wires and fuses spilled out over the floor like a heap of multi-coloured guts.

10

I was tired and Macleay was three hours away by road if I didn't kill myself by falling asleep at the wheel. It was three a.m. and I needed some sleep badly. I drove to Newcastle airport and bought a seat on the flight leaving for Macleay, Coffs Harbour and points north at six a.m. I parked my car in the airport lot and locked it after taking out the duffel coat and the whisky. I wrapped the .38 in a scarf and stuffed it into the coat pocket. The bottle went into the other pocket. I found the dimmest corner of the passenger lounge, stretched out on the seat and took a long pull at the whisky. It hit hard and started to close down some departments in my mind. I pulled the coat over my legs and went to sleep.

Three hours later I was awake with stiff joints, a headache and a vile taste in my mouth. The lounge canteen wasn't open this early so I went into the toilet and swilled water around in my mouth and lapped it into my face. The black-bristled mug that looked back at me from the mirror was red-eyed and pale-skinned.

"You look terrible," I said to it and it insulted me right back.

There were a few people standing around in the drafty lounge. There was a sleek guy in a suit carrying a steel-rimmed briefcase, and a girl in overalls and a fringed shawl straddling a big New Guinea-style string bag who looked aggressively at me when I glanced at her. A clutch of kids swarmed around a woman in black who had the longsuffer-ing, my-reward-is-not-of-this-world look of an Italian matron. A young man with a thin, aquiline face like a Spanish gypsy was reading a paper and seemed to be taking some trouble to ignore me as I walked through to the seat allocation desk. The clerk ripped leaves out of the ticket and when I looked around again the gypsy had gone and left his paper behind. I went over and picked it up. It was the *Newcastle Herald* of three days before.

More people turned up and about twenty of us got on the plane. We took off dead on time and ran straight into a headwind which we battled for the whole trip. The dark widow fed sweets to the children like a conveyor belt. The executive type took papers out of his briefcase and worked on them with a gold ballpoint pen. The girl in the overalls dug a paperback copy of *The Golden Notebook* out of her bag and didn't lift her head from it the whole way. I looked down across the wing of the plane as the central coast of New South Wales slipped past beneath us. The mountains and valleys were wrapped in swirling blue mist and the ground, when it showed through, was a patchwork of brown and green and white like camouflage. I rubbed my hand across my face and promised myself a shave and some breakfast in Macleay. The eight-hour sleep in a soft bed would have to wait.

The plane bucked about on the descent but the weather up here, a few degrees north of Sydney, was clear and the moist wind blowing across the little runway was warm. The terminal was a fibro-cement affair with a galvanised iron roof, the whole structure sitting up on yard-high brick piers. We trooped across the tarmac, went up some rickety wooden steps and into the arrivals lounge which was also the departure lounge and the cargo despatch. I had all my luggage in my pockets so I went through the building and out into the real world before anyone else. The executive was hot on my tail but I caught the first taxi going. The driver seemed half asleep when I got into the cab and he stayed that way. We ran out of the airport standing area and along a road that was only wide enough for one car to drive on the metal; the gravel beside the road was washed thin and runnels threatened to undermine the surfaced section. I sat in the back seat and rolled a cigarette for want of anything else to do. The rainforest grew close to the road on either side and screened out everything else, only the occasional track running in, showing deep caterpillar treads, betrayed the logging going on inside that would eventually thin the forest away to nothing.

After a few miles the straggling houses and half-hearted fences that mark the outskirts of all Australian country towns appeared and then we crossed a bridge over a river and houses stood side by side and we were in the main street of Macleay. The shopkeepers were out, splashing water over the dusty footpaths and sweeping the night's rubbish into the gutters. On both sides of the street most of the shops had iron awnings which covered the whole depth of the footpath. A couple of gnarled old jacaranda trees buckled the bitumen and the streetscape was dominated by two pubs on either side of the road. Rusted tin signs on their sides advertised brands of beer long since defunct and both buildings boasted acres of trellis work, painted white, around the balconies which ran across the front and along one side. The Commercial Hotel had a sign out front promising breakfast for non-residents. I paid the cab fare and went in.

I wolfed down the mediocre breakfast of chops and eggs and put a little character in the thin instant coffee by adding some whisky. An old biddy eating crumpets at another table and dabbing at her thin, bloodless lips with a lace handkerchief caught me at it. I stared defiantly at her and was surprised when she gave me a tolerant smile. When I crossed the room to pay the bill I noticed the patchwork of blue veins under the powder on her nose. I'd made her day. She probably didn't start till ten.

Barber shops are getting thin on the ground everywhere, but they're hanging on better in Macleay than most places. There were three in the main street. I chose the cleanest and sat down to think while the artist went to work. The coolness of the lather on my face was nice and the razorman's total silence was soothing but they didn't change anything. I was still just chasing people, following thin leads and not understanding the pattern of things. I tried to tell myself this was flexible, open thinking, but I wasn't convinced. I refused a hair trim, gave a good-sized tip and got the address of Bert's garage. He said I could walk it from there so I walked.

The garage was set on a narrow block with the pumps right on the street in the style of the 1920s. The workshop needed a coat of paint and the petrol pumps hadn't yet been changed over to decimal currency. The alarm cable didn't work when I trod on it and an old dog lying in the sun between the air hose and a rusted watering can that seemed to serve as the radiator water supply didn't even scratch himself as I walked past him.

I went up to the workshop and peered inside. An old Holden was up on jacks in the middle of the floor which was littered with tools, car parts and other equipment. A battered work bench was in the same condition. I called out and nothing happened. Another yell and a door opened at the back of the shed and a man came through it carrying a teapot and an enamel mug. He moved carefully, picking his way through the litter like an actor obeying chalk marks on a stage. He had been tall but had lost inches from years of bending over cars. He wore thongs, old grey flannel trousers and a brown cardigan over his bare chest. His grey felt hat had been all the rage when Don Bradman was a boy. I moved forward into the shed and heard a growl behind me. The dog was bristled up and baring its teeth six inches from my ankle.

"Easy, Josh," the man said. "Back off, boy."

I let the shiver run its way down my back and legs and stood still. The dog growled again then jogged off to the shade of the petrol bowsers.

"Is your name Bert?" I asked.

He moved closer and took a good look at me. It was impossible to judge his reaction. The nose was a bit purple and the face hadn't been shaved today, yesterday or the day before. The smell coming off him was strong—motor oil, tobacco and underarm. I dropped back a fraction.

"What if it is?"

"Got a niece, Noni?"

"Yeah, you a cop?"

"You expect one?"

"Where Noni's concerned, yes." He beckoned me further into the workshop and peered over my shoulder as I came in.

"What's wrong?" I said, turning to look out toward the street.

"Nothing." He poured tea into the mug and sipped it. "Just looking. Abo hanging around earlier." He blew steam off the tea. "Sorry I can't offer you a cup, only got the one mug. A cop you said."

"No, I didn't. Don't worry about the tea."

He looked at me over the rim of the mug. His eyes were pale blue dots amid a mass of wrinkles and puckered flesh.

"If you're not a cop what are you? Bookie's mate?"

He was off on a new tack and sketching in areas of Noni's past life. She was probably in trouble with the Commissioner of Taxation and hadn't renewed her driver's licence.

"Noni's missing," I said evasively.

He shrugged and finished his tea in a long gulp. He began patting his pockets in the age-old manner of the tobacco cadger. I handed him my packet, papers and matches. A cigarette took shape between his fingers; he didn't look at what he was doing as if that was against the rules. He lit up and handed the makings back.

"Thanks, son." His voice was friendly, almost wheedling but there was a guarded, semi-hostile undertone to it.

I let my eyes wander about the shed and spotted something in a far corner. He saw me looking.

"When did you last see Noni?" I asked.

"Years ago."

I sauntered over to the rear of the shop and kicked at a tarpaulin-covered lump on the ground. It clanged and I eased the tarp away to show a cage of silver-frosted bars, the frame from Lorraine's ute. I started to turn back and stopped when I saw that he'd moved across to the work bench. He fumbled behind him and his arm swept around but he was much too slow and I ducked to let the heavy spanner fly over my head and crash into the metal frame. I moved in on him fast and crushed him back against the bench. He wasn't as old as he looked and he was quite strong but he had no confidence. He pushed against me briefly but I pulled him forward and then slammed his spine back against the bench and the fight went out of him. I slapped the side of his face lightly.

"Why'd you try that, old-timer? What's it to you?"

He didn't answer so I slapped him again. I don't like hitting people older than me, but then there's a lot of things I do that I don't like.

"Come on! What's it to you?"

Still no answer. I hit him two jolting slaps. His face blotched suddenly and took on an unhealthy rubicund glow.

"You'll have a heart attack," I said. "Natural causes." I pulled my hand back for another slap. He wriggled a bit but wasn't really trying; his breath was coming in short, wheezy spasms like an emphysema case in the last stages.

"OK, OK," he gasped, "you're right, me ticker'll give out. I'm too old fer this. I can't take this many frights so quick."

"Noni's bloke?"

"Yes. Shit, what a hard case. He dumped the frame and took some plates off a wreck out the back."

"You let him?"

"He showed me the gun. That was enough for me."

"Where did they go?"

An impulse to lie and a touch of fear came into his face. The fear won.

"Gone to see Trixie Baker."

"Who's she?"

"Woman in Macleay. She was in on some trouble Noni had a few years ago. Good few years now."

"Tell me about it. Sit down."

He sat on the bench and watched me while I made a cigarette. I got it going and put the makings away.

"You're a sick man," I told him. "It's bad for you. Let's hear the story."

But I'd somehow lost the initiative. Perhaps he saw in my eyes that I wouldn't push him into a heart attack or maybe he just didn't care. He swore at me and told me nothing. I raised my voice and then thought of the dog outside the shed but he didn't give the dog a whistle. He shut up and didn't do anything, just put up a total defence of silence. Then I took another look at the Holden, it was an FX in the last stages of restoration. Repeated cutting and polishing had brought the duco up to a mirror finish and the chrome gleamed in the dim light like sterling silver. I pulled open a door and glanced at the upholstery; it was leather, flawless and luxuriant. Bert watched me as I circled the car. I came back to him.

"Just two questions, Bert."

Silence.

"Where does Trixie Baker live?"

Nothing.

"Tell me about the Abo?"

More nothing.

I swooped down and picked up a gallon tin which had fluid of some kind splashing about in it. I smelled it. Petrol. I pulled out my matches, jumped over the car and held the tin and the matches up near the driver's window.

"Hate to do it, Bert." I put the can on the car roof and struck a match. He jumped up and his mottled face was pale and working.

"No, wait . . ."

The passion was in his face and the truth would be in his

mouth. I dropped the match and scuffed it out. The words came flooding out of him like extinguisher foam.

"Trixie's got a farm, ten miles north. Sallygate road, first farm past the bridge, you can't miss it. I don't know what the old trouble was, I don't honest."

I believed him.

"The Abo?"

"Young bloke, tall, caught him in here early this morning. Scared the living shit out of me."

"Was this before or after Noni was here?"

"After."

"What was he doing?"

"Sleeping, back there." He pointed to a heap of bags half-hidden by the side panel of a car at the back of the shed.

"Why so scared? Just a drunk or something."

"Not him. No fear. Stone sober."

"What did you do?"

"Told him to shoot through and he did, but like he was going anyway, you know?"

I put the can down and stuck the matches back in my pocket. I couldn't waste any more time on Bert. Noni and her companion weren't too far ahead. I asked him how far and he told me they'd left about four hours ago. He didn't seem to object to the extra question. I rolled him a cigarette and lit it for him. He inhaled gratefully.

"Thanks, Bert," I said: "You've been a great help. Now, you're going to drive me out to Trixie's. You drop me there and forget the whole thing. OK?"

He protested but I overrode him. We went around the FX and out the back door to where an ordinary-looking Valiant was parked. Bert climbed in and started it up and it didn't sound so ordinary. He'd modified it in ways that I couldn't understand which had turned it into a high performance car. He explained this to me in taciturn grunts as we drove; cars were at the moral centre of his life and he was prepared to talk about them as about nothing else. I listened to his technical explanations in silence, thinking. Noni and the man had pushed hard to get this far and it seemed logical that it would be the last port of call but I had no idea what it added up to.

The drive seemed to relax Bert; he looked better somehow at the wheel, more physically in charge of himself and any nervousness he betrayed could easily be put down to uncertainty about my behaviour or that of the man with the gun. I put just one question to him on the drive and the answer was no, he'd never seen the gunman before.

Ten miles out from Macleay we passed over a wooden bridge and the metal road changed to dirt. Bert drove in second gear for a hundred yards and stopped where the road took a right-hand bend.

"Trixie's place is just around this corner." He jutted his bristled chin in the direction he meant. "If I was you I'd take it easy. That bloke with Noni looked jumpy and mean to me." His eyes opened as he saw me pull the .38 out of the coat pocket. "Jesus! You too. You said I just had to drop you here." His hand was on the gear stick, ready to move.

"That's right." I opened the door and stepped out. "You wouldn't be the sort of man to go to the police telling tales would you, Bert?"

"Not me."

"One thing interests me. You don't seem concerned about the girl. She's your niece, isn't she?"

"Not really. I was married to her mother's sister once. She doesn't mean anything to me."

I nodded and stepped back. He put the car in gear, U-turned neatly and drove off. I held the gun under the coat and moved along the side of the road. She didn't mean anything to me either, but here I was with a loaded gun going up against another loaded gun and not a friend in sight. I had the negative, defeated feeling that I wouldn't like to die up here in all this lush vegetation and so far from home. I fought it down and turned the bend.

The farmhouse was set back about a hundred yards from

the road at the end of a dusty drive. Some straggly gums grew along one side of the track and I came up through these to within spitting distance of the house. It fell short of colonial elegance by a long way, being basically a one-pitch wooden shack that had been added to by side and back built-ons. What paint was on it was white. There were wheel-marks on the drive but no car in front of the house where the drive ended. I skirted around the house, keeping under the windows and close to the walls. No car. Behind the house, about fifty yards back was a big iron shed. A road ran up to it from the eastern boundary of the farm. There was no cover between the house and the shed so I dropped the coat, took a grip on the gun and ran, weaving and keeping low.

I made it in creditable time and circled the shed. Plenty of wheel marks, old and new, but no car. The shed's sliding door was half open and I went in. There were a couple of long trestle tables and lots of wire netting racks suspended about head high from the roof. Over in one corner there were a dozen or so big green plastic garbage bags, bulging full. I went over and untied the top of one. There was enough grass inside to turn on every head between Berma-gui and Byron Bay.

I worked my way carefully back to the front of the house. There was no bell and to use the knocker I would have had to step inside because the door was standing open inside a fly wire screen. I rattled the screen and waited. A fly battled against the wire trying to get out. I let it out and went in myself. The house had the low hum—made up of re-frigerator motor, dripping taps and the ghosts of voices—that all empty houses have. I walked through the nonde-script rooms and passages on the way to the kitchen which was poky and dark with blinds drawn and flies buzzing. The buzzing was loudest over in a corner near a walk-in pantry.

A foot and half of a leg in a pale beige stocking were sticking out of the pantry. I went across and crouched down. A woman was lying with one leg extended and the other tucked up under her. One side of her face was a dark, crumpled ruin. Flies were gathering around the dried blood. Her features were reconstructable from the undamaged side—thin mouth and high forehead. She wore a severe blue linen dress that looked expensive. As I reached for her wrist I heard a noise behind me and I turned bringing the gun up but I was too slow and the business end of a thin-bladed knife was tickling my ear while the gun was still pointing nowhere.

"Drop the gun."

Two men with swarthy complexions, Italianate suits and stockinged feet were standing over me. They looked strange in the neat suits and socks but I didn't feel like laughing. One of them, the taller, said something in Italian and his mate moved back out of the kitchen. He returned with their shoes and they slipped them on, the taller guy still holding the knife close to my head. My joints were creaking and I made to straighten up and felt the knife go into the ear flesh a fraction. I sank back.

The Italians had the build of men who knew how to move and what to do when they got there. Ideas of taking them were out of the question. They conferred in Italian and weren't talking about *pasta*. I pointed at the woman.

"She's dead," I said stupidly.

They didn't even look at her. The knife artist retracted the blade with a click and while I was listening to it the other one stepped forward gracefully and clouted me on the side of the head with something thick and black and hard. I slid down and then he hit me again and a bright flare of pain went through my skull and spread and took away the light.

11

I woke up inside a small, gloomy room with points of light stabbing in through the roof. The floor was rough planking with heavy metal strips binding it down. The light was about the same as in a cinema just before they start showing the ads. The room was drafty. It was also moving. My head throbbed viciously when I moved and I dropped back down on the pile of sacking and carpet scraps where I'd been thrown. I closed my eyes and let myself adjust slowly to the surroundings. When the headache had settled down into sync with the noise of the engine and the wheels I admitted to myself that I was in the back of a small, enclosed truck. I crawled and lurched about the cabin checking the walls and rear doors. Tight as a drum. Through a chink in the floor I could see the road rushing past at a steady pace, but there's no way to tell from moving bitumen which way you're headed. I pounded on the wall near the driving end of the truck and got no response. I was locked in as safe as the crown jewels and nobody was going to do a thing about it. I wadded up the packing, put my head down, and drifted off to sleep.

I dreamed I was crushing rocks on the Long Bay rock pile and then I got over the wall and made it down to La Perouse. The crowd around the snake pit was immense; it flowed over the road and up the grassy slope toward the houses on the hill. I pushed my way through the throng which was mainly made up of blacks until I got to the fence. The pit was full of snakes of all sizes and hues writhing about and rearing up to strike at the audience. Penny was in the middle of the pit with a python coiled about her and she was screaming for help. I was trying to get over the fence and the people around me were laughing because a big black snake was waving its head in front of me, darting at me and holding me back. I yelled something and woke up drenched with sweat and clutching at the empty air.

I sat in the truck while it cruised along for what seemed like ten hours. My watch had stopped at eleven a.m. and if there's any way to tell the time from inside a closed truck I don't know it. The traffic noise picked up at one point indicating that we were passing through a town. I heard the rattle of a train a bit later—that still put us anywhere on the east coast. I was edgy from tobacco withdrawal and almost hallucinating from the effects of two hard blows on the head within twenty-four hours. Also I was scared; there were a few bodies in shallow graves, courtesy of the grass producers and I didn't want to join them. I tried to quell the fear and kill the time by sorting out the parts of the case so far.

Noni was on the run, maybe semi-unwilling, with an unidentified man who was prone to violent solutions of his problems. What they were running to was a mystery. A woman named Trixie Baker was involved, fatally as it turned out. There was something in Noni's past that connected her to the live man and the dead woman and I wouldn't begin to unravel the affair until that secret was yielded up. I gave it away at that point and concentrated on my thirst. I thought about exactly what sort of drink I'd like to have in what circumstances and settled for a middy of old with a double Teacher's on the side. The saloon bar of the Imperial Lion with Ailsa along for company would be nice. I went to sleep again.

The truck stopped suddenly and threw me against the wall. I swore and struggled to get up, then the doors opened and a blaze of electric light flooded and blinded me. I crawled to the edge of the tray and stopped there like a rabbit transfixed by a spotlight. I heard a snigger and then an accented voice told me to get down. I dropped off the end of the truck and my knees buckled when I hit the ground. I heard the snigger again and thought it would make a good target for a fist if I ever felt strong enough again to make one.

My eyes adjusted to the light and I took in that I was in a warehouse of some sort. The ceiling was high and the floor was hard cement. Two hundred-watt bulbs hung down close to my face like lit-up heads in nooses. Four men were standing near a new, green Fiat sedan parked beside the truck. I'd seen three of them before, the two who'd taken me in Macleay and the one in the camelhair overcoat. He'd been in Trueman's watching the Moody workout. The fourth man was dressed the same way as the others in a suit with highly polished shoes. He had a frizz of dark curly hair around a bald top. I didn't know him.

The one in the two-hundred-dollar coat spoke with a guttural voice in an accent that was almost stage Italian.

"Mr. Hardy, you're putting me to a lotta trouble. Why you sticking your nose in my business?"

"What business would that be?"

"You're smart, an investigator," he drew the word out ironically, "you think it out."

"You're the olive oil king," I said. "You're going to rough me up for using peanut oil to fry my chips."

One of the Macleay boys stepped forward and slammed me in the gut. I felt the breakfast of God-knows-how-long-ago rise in my gorge. I straightened up.

"I don't know what your business is Mr. . . . . ?"

He laughed. "That's better. No jokes. Coluzzi. You were at the gym watching the black, Moody. You go to see Ted Williams, you see Sunday in La Perouse, then you go to Macleay."

"I went to the toilet in between."

He struggled to keep his hands and feet still. "I told you no jokes. Why you hanging around these people?"

"What's it to you?" I was puzzled that he hadn't mentioned the marijuana. He was prepared to use muscle on me but not to go all the way. He was talking to me for some reason rather than having me kicked into paraplegia—that gave me some leverage but it was hard to judge how much. I snapped my fingers.

"I've got it, you're the boomerang king . . ."

The knuckle man moved again but I was ready for him this time. He swung his foot and I went down, got hold of it, lifted, twisted and flipped. His arms flailed and he went over and belted his head into the bumper of the truck. He groaned, rolled over and lay still. His mate exposed a knife but Coluzzi motioned him to stop.

"My business is fighters, Mr. Hardy . . . one of my businesses. I'm interested in the black fighters. I want to put them in against my boys, the Italian boys. We could get terrific houses, no? A lot of money to make."

"Honest fights?"

He spread his hands apologetically. "We see. Maybe. You could do yourself some good."

"How?"

"First, you tell me who you working for and what's the angle."

Some light dawned. Coluzzi figured he had competition and he wanted to know more about it. He was a shrewd guy who wanted to sew the whole thing up neatly before he put any time and money into it. Maybe he did have competition. In any case my skin seemed to depend on him continuing to think so.

"Did you have me bashed outside a pub in La Perouse?"

"No."

"You had someone watching me in Newcastle?"

"Sure."

The man I'd thrown was on his feet again looking very pale around the edges. The man with the blade was looking anxious to have a go and the priestly character was very quiet and still. If I was going to get out of this without any more of the physical stuff this was the time to talk.

"I heard a whisper that something like this could be on," I said.

"Yeah? Who from?"

"Tickener, the reporter. I don't know his sources."

"What you snooping around for—Redfern, Macleay, La Perouse, the black belt?"

The priest sniggered and Coluzzi spoke sharply to him in Italian. At a guess he was telling him to shut up or he'd do something unpleasant to him that would cramp his style with the ladies. Coluzzi repeated the question angrily.

"I'm looking into it for Harry," I improvised. "I haven't got on to much yet but I've got no axes to grind. I could keep you informed. I've been in the middle so far, copping it from both sides. Maybe it's time for me to come off the fence."

"How do you mean?"

"I got bashed in La Perouse as I said. My guess is that was your opposition."

Coluzzi scratched his jaw and turned aside to talk to the bald man. The bruisers stood flapping their ears and I listened to the flow of Italian, catching a word here and there but not making much sense of it. The bald man did most of the talking and Coluzzi did a lot of nodding. He swung back to me.

"Adio's got a good question. If you help me and I get ridda this opposition you talk about and you talk to the reporter, where does that leave me?"

It was a good question. I looked at Adio with respect and he gave me a tight, sardonic smile. I took out my wallet and showed him the money in it. Twenty-three dollars.

"I've got about twice that much in the bank. I could use some more. You don't pay tax on money you win on fights."

He didn't look convinced but the money argument was intelligible to him.

"What about Tickener?"

"He doesn't own me. There'd be one condition though."

"What?"

I looked at the two enforcers in their padded shouldered suits and narrow crocodile skin shoes. They looked well fed, they were probably pampered by their women and generous to a fault with their kids. In Coluzzi's service, though, they were vicious thugs and their indifference to the dead woman in Macleay suggested that they'd done worse things than hit peole on the head. I pointed to the taller.

"Give me a free swing at him with the blackjack."

Coluzzi laughed gutterally and rapped out some more Italian. The other two men smiled, the tall one didn't smile. His face lost a few shades of colour and his mouth twitched as Coluzzi dipped into his mate's pocket and lifted out the blackjack. I gathered that the tall man's name was Carlo. Carlo stood stock still and ground his teeth together. He seemed to be setting his bones and gristle and tensing his flesh against the cruel bite of the cosh.

I tossed it in my hand; a short, palm-sized hard rubber grip with about six inches of whippy, lead-loaded rubber attached. Carlo screwed up his eyes and swayed just a little. I pulled back my arm and stretched out my other hand to touch him on the left ear. He flinched a fraction. I swung hard at his head and let the blackjack go just before my hand got in range; it sailed over his shoulder and crashed against the tin wall. Carlo sagged slightly at the knees. His face was dead white and his eyes were hard with hate. I slapped him lightly on the face and let out a harsh laugh that didn't sound as nervous as I felt.

Coluzzi echoed the laugh with more feeling. Some of the tension evaporated and I asked him for a cigarette. He snapped his fingers and a packet of king size Chesterfields was produced. I took one and Carlo's off-sider lit it. I sucked the smoke deep and expelled it in a long stream, it floated up and hung like ectoplasm in the harsh light. A few more vigorous bursts of Italian between Coluzzi and Adio settled it. Coluzzi came forward and looked hard into my face; he was a few inches shorter than me and had to tilt his head up to do it. The skin stretched over his jaw and pulled taut around his neck. I saw for the first time that he was old, wrinkled by age but without a spare ounce of flesh on him. He looked like a Corsican bandit, hardened by years of sun and rain, good for a fight until the day he died.

"Alright, Mr. Hardy," he said, "you're on. I want to know what you find out. Everything."

"How do I reach you?"

He reached into his waistcoat pocket and pulled out a card; Adio produced a gold pen and he scribbled a number on the back of it. He handed the card to me. On it was printed "Aldo Coluzzi, Merchant," and an address in the city. He hadn't mentioned the marijuana. I wondered why but wasn't about to raise the question now. The less said about that the better. Coluzzi looked pleased with himself and rubbed his hands together.

"So, Mr. Hardy, she's arranged. We understand each other. Now you show a little trust and take another ride in the truck."

I was expecting tricks, double-crosses, anything, but this looked a little too obvious.

"Why?"

"You don't know where you are. I want it that way."

He sealed it by handing me my gun. Then he turned away and he and Adio got into the Fiat. There was no question of argument. Carlo and the other hood had an unsatisfied look about them that I wasn't anxious to test. I climbed up into the back of the truck. Its doors closed. I heard a heavy sliding door being opened and then we were bumping over a rough surface for a while before getting onto a road. I checked the pistol—empty breech, empty clip. We drove fast for what felt like an hour and then cruised to a stop. The doors swung open and the lights of the night flickered outside.

"Out," said Carlo.

I got down and stood uselessly in the middle of a small lane running between two high factory walls. The Italians didn't speak. They shepherded me over to the left-hand wall and motioned me to press my face into it. I did and waited for the sap or the kidney punch. Nothing happened. They got back into the truck and drove off. I didn't even get the licence number. I turned around and stood with my back against the wall and waited until the sweat running down my chest reached body temperature. I started walking and found that I was in Annandale, quite handy to home. I hailed a taxi and was there in a few minutes.

I used a key I kept hidden under a half brick behind a pot plant to get inside the house and smelled the familiar odours, even if a bit stale. From habit I'd picked up the newspaper and taken it with me. A glance at the date reminded me that I had no idea of the time. It was two a.m. This whole thing had started a bare forty hours ago and I'd already covered a lot of territory for Tarelton's money. But there are no prizes for that. As of now the trail was cold. It was time for some brain work. For that I needed help. I found some stale tobacco in the house and rolled a couple of cigarettes. I got a flagon of wine and a soda syphon out of the refrigerator and sat down with an ashtray and a glass. After finishing the cigarettes and lowering the level of the wine considerably, the pattern of things still eluded me. I seemed to have two different problems on my hands.

One was Coluzzi and the fight game. Well that was nasty with the knives and all, but there was nothing much in it for me. I'd have to discuss aspects of that with Harry Tickener. And I still worried about the marijuana farm. Maybe there was some connection between Coluzzi and the mess Noni Rouble was in. That had two sides to it—a black and a white—and I was sure they were connected. There was something up there in Macleay, some time back and involving money, only money. A pale, flabby, violent man had been told to forget about it. I didn't think he would. I was beginning to get a feeling for what that money trouble might be, and I didn't think it concerned a map to Lasseter's lost reef.

That was as close as I got to clarity. I thought about the list of great black fighters who'd come out of the game with nothing to show for their scarred eyes and broken hands and slurred speech. I thought of Jimmy Sunday and Penny Sharkey, and I thought about Harry Tickener again.

I finished the drink and went upstairs. I got out of my pants and shoes and sweater and sprawled on the bed pulling a blanket over me. The light was on but it didn't bother me a bit.

12

The telephone woke me. I caught sight of the clock as I rolled over to grab the receiver—six-thirty a.m. I put my head back on the pillow and tried to unscramble reality and dreams. I grunted into the mouthpiece and it sputtered back at me like a firecracker. I sat up.

"Easy, easy. James?"

More sputtering and incoherence on the other side of the wire.

"Stop it," I yelled. "Shut up, take a breath and give it to me clearly."

A pause, a long one, then the actor's voice came through, still with a note of panic but under control.

"Noni's been kidnapped. I've just got a note."

"At six-thirty?"

"I couldn't sleep, I was up early and found the note taped to the door."

"What does it say?"

I heard a rustle over the line and then James's voice, shaky, reading.

"We have got the girl. Five thousand dollars gets her back."

"Is that all?"

"Yes."

It didn't figure. Ted Tarelton could raise twenty times that. Why hit James? My silence made him panicky again and he almost stammered, asking if I was still there. I said I was.

"What should I do?"

"Can you raise it?"

"The money? Yes, just."

"Will you?"

"Yes, of course, of course."

"Stay put. I'll be right over."

I hung up on him, jumped up and took a quick shower. I was pulling on some clothes when the phone rang again. I made a bet with myself and won. Madeline Tarelton.

"Mr. Hardy? Just a minute. My husband wants to speak to you."

I heard a click, waited and then Ted's rich voice came in.

"Hardy? My girl's been snatched."

"I know. You got a note?"

"Yes, how . . . ?"

I told him how and asked him to read out the note. It was the same as James's except that it asked for a hundred thousand dollars and said a contact would be made at five p.m. the following day. Ted's voice vibrated a bit and the idea occurred to me that he'd be on the Courvoisier a bit earlier today. I promised him I'd be over as soon as I'd seen James. He wasn't too happy about that, claiming an employer's rights but I soothed him. He seemed impressed that James had said he'd raise the five thousand, as if it was a bride price. I suppose it was, in a way. My cool competence was dented a bit by having to ask Ted for

James's address. I'd forgotten that I didn't have it, but he gave it to me without seeming to take it amiss.

My perfectly good car was sitting in the Newcastle airport parking lot and it was raining again. I got a taxi to James's place in Darlinghurst. It was a terrace house with a door that let straight out onto the street. It was painted white and had some new iron on the roof but it hadn't been made over into anybody's dream. A yellow Mini with a cracked rear window, taped up, was parked outside. I knocked at the door and James opened it with a buzzing electric shaver in his hand. Half his face was shaven and half not. He looked terrible. He ushered me in and started to gabble. I reached out and clicked off the shaver. That shut him up.

"Let's see the note," I said.

He went out to the kitchen and I followed him. The house wore the same look all the way through, pleasant enough but as if no one cared. He pointed to a piece of paper on the table and I picked it up. The words he'd read out were printed across a cheap piece of notepaper in capitals. A black ballpoint pen had done the writing and there were no idiosyncrasies in it that I could see. Across the back of the paper, which had been folded in three, was a strip of cellulose tape. James resumed his shaving, wandering about the little room stroking his jaw. He was wearing drill slacks and an orange-coloured thing I think is called a shaving coat. He would. I waited until he'd finished shaving and turned the motor off, then I told him about Tarelton's note. He ran his hand over his smooth face and frowned where he found a missed spot. I pushed the shaver out of reach and leaned on him.

"How soon can you get the money?"

"Today. I'd have to see my family's lawyer, but I'm sure it can be arranged."

"Good. Do it. Don't tell anyone else." I started for the passage but he came after me and caught me by the arm.

"God, don't just walk out. What do you think of it? What's going to happen?"

"I don't know," I growled. "I'll talk to some people, then we'll play it the best way we can."

"It all seems so strange—I mean for this to happen so long after she disappeared. It seems—I don't know—oddly managed."

"You're the theatre man," I said.

I brushed him off and left the house saying I'd call him at the theatre when things had been decided. I caught a taxi to Armstrong Street and wondered why I'd replied the way I had to his last remark. I didn't know. Maybe just to be rude.

Madeline Tarelton opened the door again. She was wearing a lime green trouser suit today and nothing about her had deteriorated since I'd seen her last. She seemed to be bearing up under the strain and her voice was edged with contempt when she spoke.

"Ted's still in bed. He'll see you there."

"Where's the room?"

"Upstairs, in front."

I went up. The room was big with two glass-paneled doors letting out onto a balcony. The water was visible through them, shining dull and grey under the thick white sky. In bed Ted was not nearly as impressive as he was when up and around and properly togged up. The skin around his jaw sagged, his rumpled hair looked thin and his body under the bedclothes was lumpy and powerless. The room had pale candy striped wallpaper and a deep pile carpet; it was too fussy and frilled, with fringed lampshades and a brocade bedcover, for my taste and Ted looked uncomfortable in it. I sat on a bentwood chair cushioned with satin while Ted folded up the newspaper and pulled himself straighter in the bed.

"Bad business this, Hardy," he said. "Fair knocked me. I took a bit of a turn. Crook heart." He placed his hand over his chest. I nodded.

"Got the note?"

He produced it from the breast pocket of his puce

pajamas and handed it over. Identical to James's except for the extra information.

"I was up early. Meeting on today at Randwick. I went for the papers and there it was, stuck to the door. Madeline had to bloody nearly carry me back here."

The experience had swept away his usual bluster; I couldn't tell whether he was most upset by the kidnapping of his daughter or the reminder of his own mortality, but it was obviously the right time to pressure him a bit.

"You can raise the money?" I asked.

"Easy. Reckon I should?"

"Yes. But there's something weird about this. It doesn't smell right."

"How do you mean?" he said listlessly.

"Could the girl be shaking you down?"

Colour flooded his face and he looked about to sound off at me which he undoubtedly would have done if he'd been feeling his usual, successful self. Now he flopped back against the pillows and fidgeted with the quilt.

"Possible, I suppose," he said lamely. "Is that your theory?"

"I haven't got a theory, just a feeling. It's a strange one. I never heard of two ransoms being asked before. Complicates things. Not that they're not messy enough already."

"Madeline told me you'd rung the other night. By complicated you mean about the Abo? What's happened since then?"

I gave him an outline leaving Coluzzi out and not going into details about Noni's reputation in Newcastle. He couldn't help on that score; he'd practically lost all touch with the girl from the time his wife had left to when Noni turned up motherless. Ted's instincts, bred in betting and sly grogging, were to avoid the police, so he fell in with my suggestion that we keep the police out of it for the time. I had a feeling, which I was backing, that the girl wasn't in danger. But the cops wanted to talk to her in connection with Simmonds's death and if they started poking around and stirring things up it could all turn sour and Noni might suddenly become dispensable. I gave Ted the gist of this and he agreed to raise the money and wait for the contact.

"I think that's just plain stupid," Madeline Tarelton said from the doorway. She came in carrying a glass of water and some pills on a tray. She set them down on the bed and gestured at her husband to take them. He did. I pocketed the note and got up from my chair.

"Just a minute," Madeline said quickly. "This is insane, you must go to the police."

"I don't think so," I said. "And your husband agrees with me."

She snorted. "You're playing games. I have my doubts about you, Mr. Hardy. This is a mistake."

"Keep out of it, Madeline," Ted said sharply. Maybe the pills had done him some good. Madeline swung round on him, surprised, but he cut her off.

"You don't give a damn about the girl, she's nothing to you. Alright, fair enough, but she's my daughter and I want her back safe. We'll do it Hardy's way."

"That's not fair!" Her composure was disturbed which looked like a rare event. "That girl is a menace, the dregs, she . . ."

"Shut up!" Ted roared. His face turned purple.

"Don't shout, you'll have another attack."

I left them to it and went down the stairs and out of the house.

I pulled up the hood of the light plastic parka I was wearing and walked through the drizzle to Oxford Street where I caught a bus to the city. On the bus I read yesterday's paper. Simmonds's death got a small notice on page four in between an item on rail fares going up and the birth of an elephant at the zoo. The police appealed to the blonde woman who'd found the body to come forward. The Chev Biscayne was described. The woman and the car were the police's only lines of investigation. I couldn't imagine the La Perouse blacks identifying Noni to the police, however much they disliked her, but some back-tracking by the cops could turn her name up soon and then the heat would be on me.

I got off the bus outside *The News* building and bought the morning paper. There was nothing more on Simmonds but the discovery of an injured woman on her farm near Macleay got a mention. The woman was in a critical condition in Macleay hospital and police were anxious to interview a tall dark man wearing light-coloured clothes and carrying a dark coat. If they were any good it wasn't going to take the local police long to trace that man from his taxi to his breakfast to his shave. I'd used the name Colin Hocking for the plane ticket but a quick scout about at Newcastle would turn my car up and then I could expect visitors. On the sporting page there was a preview of the fight coming up between Jacko Moody and Tony Rosso. It would be the first main event for them both. They had good, rather similar records, but Moody had KO'd two men whom Rosso had only decisioned and he was favoured to win. It reminded me that I had to get tickets from Harry Tickener for Ted Williams.

The News building is a standard glass, concrete and plastic tower which creates a canyon without and neuroses within. The lobby was hung about with glossy blow-ups of press photographs that showed politicians with beer bellies and worn-out smiles, football players spattered with mud and fashion models of unbearable thinness. I went up to the fourth floor where Harry shares some cramped office space with thirty other reporters. They steal each other's cigarettes and listen to each other's phone conversations. I wound through the desks and wastepaper bins. Harry's typewriter was blasting.

"Hallo, Cliff—hang on a second." He pushed a lock of his thin yellow hair back and stabbed at his keyboard with long, tobacco-stained fingers; three of them.

"Carry on exposing," I said. I sat down in the hard chair drawn up in front of the desk and rolled a cigarette. The old tobacco had tasted bad enough last night; this morning it was disgusting. Tickener stopped pounding and stretched both hands up in the air. Nothing creaked, he was still young.

"What can I do for you, Cliff?"

"Two things; tickets to the Moody fight—a pair. OK?"

"Yeah, no trouble. You coming with me?"

"I hope so. I've got something on but it should be worked out by then, one way or another. Remember the guy we met at Trueman's?"

"Oh yeah, the actor. His bird was missing. Flushed her?"

"Not yet. Now the other favour."

He looked quickly down at his typewriter, picked up a pencil and made a note on the copy.

"Are you sure you've got the time, Harry? I'd hate to throw your schedule out."

He looked embarrassed. "Shit. Sorry, Cliff. It's this piece on Moody. I want to get it right."

"Read A. J. Liebling. Who's your top crime man?"

"Garth Green."

"Good memory? Knows the files?"

"Steel trap."

"Will you introduce me to him?"

"Sure, when?"

"Now."

He looked relieved and jumped up from his chair.

"Steady," I said. "Are you sure he'll be in?"

"He'll be in." Tickener came around the desk. "He works till two p.m. and drinks till two a.m. Let's go."

I followed him. There were a few people walking about in the corridor and a small clutch of reporters was grouped talking in a doorway. They parted like the waters when a six-foot girl with close-cropped red hair walked through the door. She was wearing boots, a long dark skirt and a tight-fitting jacket and she carried her head like a Queen. She had a high, proud nose and big dark eyes in a face as pale as a lily. I gaped with the journos but Harry seemed not to notice her and kept on his way. I wondered about Harry. He knocked on a door which had stuck to it a file card with the name garth green typed on it in lower case.

Tickener pushed the door open and I went in after him. A big man in shirtsleeves with heavy striped braces was sitting in a swivel chair looking out the window. With his grizzled balding head and meaty arms he looked like a cop which probably helped him in his calling. Looking out the window was probably a good idea for a crime reporter, too. As sure as hell there'd be some of it going on out there. He turned slowly round to face us.

"Hello, boy wonder," he said.

Harry laughed a little more heartily than he needed to. "Garth, this is Cliff Hardy, he . . ."

"Private man, I know." He leaned forward to shake hands. "Glad to meet you." I trusted him with my hand and he gave it back to me undamaged.

"Hardy's on a case, Garth, and he could use some help. I thought you might have something for him. OK?"

Green waved at him and pulled a cigar out of his shirt pocket.

"I've got a piece on the run," Tickener went on. "I'll just get back to it."

Green waved again and Harry gave me a nod before he scampered off.

"Good bloke, Harry," Green said. He lit the cigar. "Doing well too. What can I do for you? Who do you want the shit on?"

"Not like that. It's criminal history I'm after."

"Why don't you ask your mate Evans?"

"You're well informed."

"Good memory," he grunted. "Read Harry's stuff on the Costello case. You've got the right contact there. Evans is an honest cop."

"That's right and so I can't use him right now. I'm in a bit too deep and there's things I'd rather not say."

He grinned; his big, boozy face broke up into amiable creases and more grizzled grey hair poked out of his nostrils. "I get like that myself sometimes. Let's hear it. I'll help if I can."

I reached over and stubbed out my cigarette in the half tobacco tin he used for an ashtray. "It's pretty general. What do you know about crimes, solved and unsolved, up around Macleay way?"

"A bit—when are we talking about?"

"Twelve years ago, maybe longer."

He leaned back, took a drag on the cigar, sucked the smoke in and blew it at the ceiling. The action brought on a coughing fit which left him red in the face and clutching the edge of his desk. "I've tried everything . . . fucking pipes . . . these things." He waved the cigar. "All the same, I have to do the drawback. All I want to do is smoke fifty plain Turf a day like I used to."

"Why don't you?"

"Too scared." He put the cigar down; a thin column of smoke rose up from it like an Apache signal. "Macleay . . . not too hard to name the big one, bank job in . . . sixty-six."

"What happened?"

"Two men did a Commonwealth bank on a Friday. Took away fifty thousand dollars."

"Never caught?"

"Not a sign."

"The money?"

"Never found. The bank put up a big reward but heard nothing."

"That's strange. Did you cover it yourself?"

Green picked up the cigar again. There was a faint curl of smoke coming from the end and he sucked it into life, blowing out an enormous cloud. He looked at it virtuously. "Yeah. I went up there and looked around. Thought I might get onto something and make a big man of myself. Nothing doing. It was a pretty amateurish job. They got away on foot. Dead lucky."

"How did the cops figure it?"

"Same as me, two roughies who got lucky. The cops dragged in everyone they could think of but got nowhere. I wrote a piece on it . . . hang on."

He lumbered over to a battered filing cabinet under the window. He pulled out a drawer and riffled through the folders standing up inside it. He took one out and back to the desk where he opened it and leafed through some foolscap sheets with news cuttings pasted to them.

"Yeah, here it is." He handed the sheet across to me and I ran my eye over the columns of newsprint. It was a straight recital of the facts including a description of the bandits who'd worn stocking masks and carried sawn-off shotguns. I pushed the sheet back across the desk. Green fiddled with his cigar and looked at the wall over my head. His eyes screwed up and he let out a tired sigh. His first drink was still a good way off.

"Yes?" I said.

"I remember now, there was a whisper about it. They were trying to fit someone up with it, a standover man with some local form."

He butted his cigar and a smell that would soon be a vile reek started to sneak across the desk toward me. I thought that it might help his anti-drawback campaign if he smoked better cigars. I was about to say so when he started drumming his fingers on the desk.

"I'm slipping," he grumbled. "Can't remember his name. Look, Hardy, I'm rambling. This of interest to you, this the one?"

"It could be—missing money sounds right. What about the standover man?"

"The name's gone but he went up for rape in Newcastle, young kid. He got ten years."

I heard something click inside my head like a combination lock tumbler coming into place. I sat up sharply. Green looked amusedly at my reaction.

"That's right, they didn't have anything much on him for the Macleay job as I recall, just something about the company he kept. The cops were just as happy to do him on the rape charge. It was open and shut." He leered at me and I winced at the joke. He laughed. "Now you look interested."

"I am. I see a connection. How can I get some dope on this rape case?"

"I thought you were interested in lost money."

"Yes, and lost women. Let me get it straight before I go off half-cocked. What was that about the company he kept, the rapist?"

"Jesus, Hardy, it's twelve years ago. I might be confusing it with something else." He picked up the sheets of paper, aligned them and tucked them back in the folder. Handling the relics of the time gave him assurance. "I think it was just that this bloke, whoever he was, used to hang about with an Abo up Macleay way."

"So what? There's lots of them up there."

"That's right but you didn't read the story very thoroughly did you?" He handed it back to me and I read it word by word. One of the tellers said that one of the bandits looked dark under the mask, like an Aborigine. The thing was coming together now. I passed the cutting back.

"Pretty thin."

"That's what I said," Green barked. "Macleay's a racist hole; was then anyway, probably still is. It wasn't much to go on but it was the only whiff the coppers had." He blew a kiss at the wall. "But it died on them."

I leaned forward, excited. "I'm sorry to press you, but the names are important. Is there any way to get on to them?"

"Sally Fitch would be your best bet. Get at it from the rape angle. What she doesn't know about criminal fucking isn't worth knowing. I'll take you along."

We left the room and he moved along the corridor in that light, fast way that some big men can. He must have weighed sixteen stone and no one got in his way. He nodded to people and I kept an eye out for the crew-cut redhead but she didn't show. Green poked his head through a door then went in and I followed. It was another thirty-desk room with a good deal of noise and screwed up paper. Green ushered me across to a corner where a pot plant, a hat stand and a filing cabinet sheltered one desk a bit from the hurly-burly. He introduced me to the woman behind the desk; they ribbed each other about their drinking, smoking and other vices. Green shook my hand again and went away.

Sally Fitch was a lean blonde in her thirties. Her hair was rather faded and she showed signs of wear and tear; there was a scar running down the left side of her face that she covered with make-up. She was a good-looking woman, nonetheless. She lit a cigarette and looked me over with steady green eyes that wouldn't be surprised at anything, not even if I leaped up that minute and threw myself out the window.

"What can I tell you that Garth can't, Mr. Hardy?" she asked. "Like those virtuous private eyes I can say I don't do divorce work."

I laughed. "I do when I can get it. It's getting rarer."

Her eyebrows went up. "Divorce is?"

"No, the dirty work those virtuous private eyes say 'I don't do' to."

She tapped ash off her cigarette and pushed it about in the glass ashtray. "Good thing, too. Mine was as dirty as you'd hope to see. Well then, what?"

"I want to know all you can tell me about a rape case in Newcastle around 1966 or '67—all the names, all the details. I don't have time to look up the papers and my guess is it wouldn't have made the papers anyway."

"Why?"

"If I'm on the right track, the girl involved would have been a juvenile, very much so."

She drew on her cigarette and let the smoke trickle out through her nostrils, an unusual thing for a woman to do. On her it looked amusing and I grinned. She didn't notice. She scribbled "1967" and "Newcastle" on a blotter in front of her and drew lines around it. She embellished the lines, producing an ornate, curly doodle, then she got up and pulled a drawer out of her filing cabinet. Two drawers and some vivid swearing later she lifted out a thin manila folder. A glossy photograph slipped out and I bent to pick it up.

"Hold on!" She came around the desk and retrieved the picture. "I don't just hand this stuff out willy-nilly." She smiled and softened her voice. "Anyway, don't steal my thunder."

I nodded and waited while she looked through the papers. There wasn't much to it and it didn't take her long. She closed the file and looked up.

"I think this is the one you want. The girl was fifteen, Newcastle, May 1967. It was a bit out of the ordinary; the girl knew the man who raped her. She knew the woman he lived with better. And the girl reported the rape to the police herself. There was a short piece, no details, in the Newcastle paper. No reporting on the trial, that's the law.

"Yes. You've got the names though?"

"Uh-huh. The girl was Naomi Rouble, the man was Joseph Berrigan. The woman he lived with was Patricia Baker."

I nodded. "That's it. It makes sense in a crazy way. What about the photo?"

"The girl. It was taken when she came out of the police station—suppressed of course." She slid it across the desk. The hair was wild and disheveled, the eyes were puffy from crying and it was eleven long years ago, but the face was unmistakably that of Noni Tarelton.

13

By the time I'd thanked Sally Fitch, looked in on Tickener and cleared the building (no sight of the redhead), it was midday. The streets were crowded with people doing their lunchtime shopping and gawking. George Street was a solid wall of bodies coming the other way and I gave up the battle and ducked into a pub to drink my lunch and do some thinking. I had a steak with the wine and turned the case over in my mind. A constant stream of smooth-voiced chatter from the businessmen pushing out their waistcoats with expense account lunches didn't help, but then there wasn't much to think about. Noni Rouble-Tarelton was on the run with a man who'd raped her eleven years before. He'd killed one person since getting out of jail and savagely beaten two more, both women. Now it looked like he was a blackmailer. There were still questions on all this but a few answers were coming in; the bank robbery and fifty thousand dollars was part of it. On the ethical side was the question of when to let the police in. That troubled me. It always does.

I walked up George Street through the thinning ranks as the slaves went back to work. The rain had cleared away and a pale sunlight was dappling the footpaths and glinting on the oil slicks on the road. I hailed a cruising cab and said I wanted to go to La Perouse. The cabbie was a chunky, greying veteran who looked as if he'd been born behind a steering wheel. He was reluctant about the trip.

"It'll cost you."

"La Perouse," I repeated. "You could get lucky."

He grunted and dropped the flag. He was sour at the possibility of having to drive back to town without a fare, but every profession has its perils. I settled back and endured his company. The traffic was light and we made good time. Long Bay didn't look too bad in the sunlight, especially with the new outside walls. Inside them it was a different matter. I directed the driver through La Perouse's neglected streets and we found the pub where I'd drunk with Jimmie Sunday. I tipped the driver and he forced out some thanks before slamming the door harder than he needed to.

A dark woman was behind the bar. She was sitting on a stool smoking and reading a magazine. Apart from her the bar was empty. I went up and laid a five dollar note on the counter and ordered a middy. She pulled it.

"Jimmy Sunday around?" I asked before she could get her hand on the money. She drew on her cigarette and expelled smoke over my head.

"Might be."

"Will you have one yourself?"

"Tah," She flicked out a glass and slid it under the gin bottle in a smooth, practised movement. I waited while she splashed tonic into the glass, dropped in some ice and made change from the five. She took a sip of the drink and sighed appreciatively.

"You know Jimmy?" she asked.

"A bit. I was drinking with him here the night before last. Thought I'd run into him again."

"What's your name?"

I told her. She drank some gin and pulled on the cigarette, it burned down to the filter and she dropped it at her feet. She was a big woman wearing a blouse and jeans. A packet of cigarettes was in the top pocket of the blouse resting on the shelf of her big, stiffly brassiered bosom. She pulled out the cigarettes and got another one going.

"Jimmy's around. Could give 'im a ring if you like."

"Thanks." I drank some beer while she went off to the

telephone at the far end of the bar. I wandered over to the wall and looked at the sporting photographs that are a part of the decor of all genuine Australian pubs, symbolising some mystic connection between athleticism and alcohol. The pictures were mostly of racehorses, stretched out near the winning post and standing in the victory ring with flowers around their necks. One of the winning jockeys was an Aborigine but none of the proud owners was anything but true-blue Caucasian. There was a collection of boxing pictures and a cartoonist's attempt at capturing the mystique of the Sands brothers: Dave, Alfie, Clem, George and Russell stood in a ring with their gloved hands clasped above their heads in the fighter's victory salute. There was a close-up of dark little Elley Bennett landing one of his famous knockout punches on "Mustard" Coleman and another of Bobby Sinn, face wrinkled with concentration, picking off a bewildered Jimmy Carruthers with a classic straight left.

I turned when I heard the door to the bar slapping shut. I suppose I'd expected Sunday and had arranged my face in a grin but it slid away when I saw who'd come in and what they were doing. Ted Williams was slamming home the top bolt on the door. His companion was making shoo-ing gestures at the barmaid. She ducked under the bar and went out through a back door. I heard a key turn in its lock. Williams's mate was an Aborigine, very dark and not young. He couldn't have been more than five-foot-six tall but he must have weighed fifteen stone. He had massive shoulders and a chest like a grizzly bear. He was wearing thongs, jeans and an outsize black T-shirt; his black, wavy hair was slicked down with water as if he'd got out of the shower in a hurry. Williams hadn't changed a bit which meant that he was still a black Goliath. The only difference was that he'd left his smile in Redfern. I opened my mouth to say something but Williams cut me off.

"You said your name was Tickener, mate. Now it's

Hardy. We don't like gubbs who hang around bullshitting us, do we, Tommy?"

The bulldozer shook his head and shuffled forward a few inches.

"No, suh, wese don't."

I tried to smile but the joke wasn't for me and my mouth was desert dry. I backed off toward the bar with my near-empty glass in my hand. I wished it was a gun. I wished I were somewhere else. Tommy looked me up and down and came forward again, this time with the light, balletic step of a trained fighter. His massive arms swung loose at his sides and he turned them over like a man cranking a car engine. The bar top ground hard into my spine and there was nowhere else to go.

"Who're you?" I croaked. "I was expecting Jimmy Sunday."

He grinned and slammed one fist into a palm.

"Jimmy's busy," he growled, "I come to take care of you meself."

"You know Jimmy?" I was desperate, using Sunday's name as a talisman.

He moved closer and from the way he moved I could tell that he wasn't planning to waste any more breath on words. It wasn't a negotiable situation. I wished I had Carlo's blackjack. The glass in my hand felt as useless as a yo-yo. His eyes under heavy bushy brows were focused on my hands and feet the way every barroom heavyweight knows to do. To hell with the look in the eyes—if you know your business that's going to be fear. I slid along the bar just to stop myself from freezing up and to give him a moving target. But I had to stop somewhere and I did so where the bar met the wall. I let him get within punching distance and made a shaping-up gesture with about as much threat in it as a pas-de-deux. His punch came in hard and fast but he was a little bound up by fat and I leaned away from it. He lost balance for a fraction of a second and I clipped him on the ear as hard as I could while on the retreat. If I thought that'd

101

win me a little respect I was wrong; he rushed at me like a bull crowding a matador into a *barrio*. He half-caught me but I twisted free and ground my elbow into the same ear. It didn't seem to bother him; he circled with his arms outstretched and seemed to cut off half the room.

I backed away and cornered myself again over by the table where the elders had been playing cards. I stumbled against a chair and he came forward and threw a right at my belly. He was more than half a foot shorter than me and the punch was straight and full-forced. I rode back from it a bit but it knocked wind out of me and jellied my legs. He came on and I cocked my right for a haymaker to the head. He couldn't have cared less and kept coming. I braced myself and swung my foot short and hard up into his crotch. He doubled over. He'd expected a fancy fist fight and I didn't give him a chance to correct his mistake. I shuffled fast and delivered the foot again to the same spot. He started to crumble and I bunched my fingers and drove into his fleshy neck below the ear. I felt the muscle under the skin resist and then the knuckle bit into the veins and cartilage. He dropped in a heap and crashed his head on a table edge on the way down. As he fell, the breath wheezed out of him and I had a flash of memory about the sound. It was like the noise I'd heard in the car in the split second before my head caved in.

Williams hadn't moved from the door. I eased my way out from the table and went across to the bar. I reached over it and pulled up a schooner glass which I filled with beer from the tap-gun the woman had left lying on the rusty tray. I took a deep drink and waited for my heart to settle back to a normal pace. Tommy was lying with his feet drawn up to his bulging belly. I set the glass down next to him. His eyes were open and he was concentrating everything he had on his pain. His dark skin had a yellowish tinge and some veins had broken in the whites of his eyes, making them a murky pink. The harsh breath was coming regularly but with enormous effort. I was safe from him for at least ten minutes. A sound behind me made me turn as the barmaid came through the door at the back of the bar. She stared down at the man on the floor and then up at me with a new respect.

"Jesus," she breathed. "What did you hit him with?"

"This." I held up my fist which was swollen from the neck-punch and bleeding around the knuckles from the earlier tap.

"Jesus, do you know who that is?"

I looked at him again and tried to imagine him years younger and without the fat, as a chumky welterweight perhaps. But I couldn't place him.

"No. Fighter was he?"

"That's Tommy Jerome," Williams said quietly.

I let out my breath in a whistle and felt back for the support of the bar. The jelly feeling had come back into my legs and I suddenly felt very, very tired. Tommy Jerome had killed two men in the ring and had beaten others so savagely that he'd run out of opponents. He was number one contender for the Australian welter and middleweight titles for a couple of years but he never got a shot at the titles because no fight manager wanted his meal ticket wrecked that badly. The championships changed hands a couple of times while Jerome sat there at number one. I'd read that he'd gone to England and lost a few fights there which could have only one explanation. That was ten or more years ago and he'd gone to seed badly. Still, I was glad I hadn't known who he was before I hit him.

"I got lucky," I said to the barmaid. "He thought I'd fight fair."

"Lucky? Fair or unfair, you're lucky to still have teeth." She lit a cigarette and looked across at Williams. If it was a challenge he wasn't taking it up. There'd been enough talking, now I had to get something done. I reached for my change on the bar and detached two dollars. I went around the bar and made her a gin and tonic and pulled a middy for Williams. I gave them the drinks and dropped the money on the till. There was a rattle at the locked door but we ignored it. Neither Williams nor the barmaid was happy with the situation but they seemed to have run out of ideas. They took the drinks.

"Right. Now I want Jimmy Sunday. Where is he?"

They drank but didn't answer.

"Look," I said to Williams. "I gave you a wrong name. OK, I'm sorry but I had reasons. Get Sunday here and you'll see what I mean." I jerked my thumb at Jerome who was lying crumpled and still. "What do I have to do, eat his kidney fat?"

"I'll get Jimmy for you." The barmaid moved off to the phone.

"Where is he?"

"Sharkey's."

"Call him."

She did. A voice came on the line and I grabbed the phone. Sunday didn't sound surprised to hear me and said he'd come straight down to the pub. The barmaid had picked up a cloth and begun polishing glasses. She was humming "Get me to the church on time." I went over and slid down the door bolt and opened the door. Sunday was jogging easily down the street and I stood back with the door open and waved him in. The barmaid flicked some money out of my change and pulled a beer. She slid it along the counter to Sunday who grabbed it and went over to look at Jerome. He'd straightened up a bit and was trying to prop his back against the wall. He made it and massaged his crotch with both hands. A vein was throbbing hard in his forehead and there were bubbles of saliva at the corner of his mouth. I stepped quietly across and handed him the two-thirds-full schooner. He wrapped a big, dark hand around it and lifted it to his mouth.

"This is the guy who bashed me the other night," I said to Sunday. "He came back for a second go and got careless." I took Sunday by the arm and steered him to a chair. I got the makings out, made a cigarette and put the tobacco on the table like a peace offering. "Now, you tell me what's going on around here," I waved to indicate the room and the world outside, "and I'll tell you what's going on in here." I rapped my bleeding knuckles against the side of my head.

Sunday looked at my fist and took a long pull on his beer. "Silly bastard Tommy," he said. "I told him you were alright."

"You're a fuckin' Uncle Tom, Jimmy," Jerome rasped out from his position against the wall. "Always were."

"Will you knock it off," I snarled. "Jimmy, can you tell me what all this heavy stuff is in aid of?"

Sunday mused for a second, then lifted his hand. "Sadie, four beers and a drink for yourself. You've got a say in this. Come on over here." He reached into his pocket. The barmaid got the drinks and carried them over on a tin tray. She asked Jerome if he could get up.

"Yeah, if I have to." He pulled himself up from the wall and eased his bulk into a chair. I reached down for the schooner and put it on the table. He drained it in a gulp. He still hadn't spoken to me. Sadie distributed the drinks and Sunday rolled a cigarette from my makings.

"Ever heard of a bloke named Coluzzi?" he asked me.

"Heard of him and met him," I said.

"Doesn't surprise me one bit," Jerome muttered. Sadie hushed him. "Let him talk."

Sunday drew in smoke and gagged on it. "Shit, this stuff's terrible. Well, this Coluzzi's trying to take over the fights. Reckons he can get boxing back on TV. Whole thing's been very quiet lately."

"Yes," I said, "since that Yank was killed."

Sunday nodded. "Right, well we're all for more fights, but we hear this dago wants to set it up all his way."

"He told me he wanted to match Italians and Aborigines. Good for the gate."

"Yeah," Jerome snorted, "how many do you reckon the Kooris'd win?"

"He was vague on that point," I admitted.

"I'll bet he was," Sadie spat. "I've got a son, he's just starting in clubs, they tell me he's good."

Jerome and Sunday nodded solemnly.

"I hate bloody boxing," Sadie went on. "I reckon it's ruined more good men than anything except the war. Still, my Chris's dead keen on it and I want him to get a fair go. He'll have to lose more'n he'll win if this Coluzzi gets hold of it."

"It's nothin' new," Jerome said bitterly. "Everyone has to throw a few on the way up . . . used to, anyway. I threw 'em on the way down."

"That's right, Tommy," Sunday said soothingly. "That's why it's got to change, especially now."

"Jacko Moody," I said.

They nodded and everyone drank. It was like a salute but not a cheerful one.

"Jacko's a champion for sure," Sunday said. "You'd agree with that?"

"With luck and good management, yes."

"He's fucked before he starts if Coluzzi gets him," Jerome said.

"He hasn't got a contract has he? He's barely out of the prelims."

"He's barely out of the bush, too," Sunday spoke slowly. "He's got a sort of contract with Trueman, he signed something. He was so anxious to get into the game he did what Trueman told him. He doesn't know exactly what he agreed to. What's sure is that Trueman's in with Coluzzi and he'll do a deal on Jacko if the money's right."

"So will this bastard," Jerome grunted.

I slammed my glass onto the table top. "Well, let's talk about that! What brought you down on me, Jerome?"

Jerome knocked back some of his beer and scowled at me across the table. Physically he was almost a monster but his brain appeared to be working well enough. He held up thick fingers with enormously broad nails as he made the points.

"You were at Trueman's gym when Coluzzi was there and you stopped a row. You lied about who you were to Ted here and one of Coluzzi's boys escorted you out of Redfern. Then you fuckin' come down here pokin' around and looking for Ricky. I didn't trust him either. That was enough for me. You admit you know Coluzzi."

"I can explain it," I said, "but it's a long story and not much of it is to do with what we're talking about now."

"Double bloody Dutch," Jerome growled.

"Easy, Tommy," Sunday said. "I told you this Hardy was alright, you didn't need to bash him."

"You wouldn't take me like that again, Hardy."

"I know I wouldn't, Jerome. But if we can get over all that we could do something useful about this fight business." I could feel the racial disharmony mounting and the need for some practical, immediate proposal to deflate it. I'd been ready to sell Coluzzi out the minute I was sure I could get away from him alive. This was a bit earlier than I'd have chosen and it was hard work dealing with a hot-head like Jerome. Sunday was in better control of himself though and I felt I could work something out with him.

"We can do our own planning," Jerome said.

"Sure you can, but could you get Coluzzi and his mob in a particular place at a particular time?"

"No way," Sadie put in. "Those dagoes are dead scared of our boys. They carry guns, too."

"OK, OK," Sunday said impatiently. "We'd have trouble getting close enough to Coluzzi to smell the garlic. What's your idea?"

"I'll look into Trueman's connections with Coluzzi and if there's anything in that I'll give it to Tickener. He'll screw them in the paper. And I'll set up a meeting with Coluzzi and have Jerome and a few others along, that should be fun."

"It sounds a bit fancy to me," Jerome said.

"Yeah, it's fancier than hitting people over the head with boomerangs, but where did that ever get anyone?"

Sadie laughed. "Drink up and I'll shout. I reckon it sounds alright. Jimmy?"

Sunday and I drained our glasses. Sadie and Williams did the same. Sadie put them on the tin tray.

"I'm on," Sunday said quietly. "Ted?"

"Me too. I'll go and see Jacko and word him up a bit. He's a nervy bastard Jacko and he's worried about this Rosso."

"Why?" I asked. "He can beat him."

"I reckon, but he says Trueman's teaching him some trick or something." Williams's voice trialed off vaguely.

"Sounds fishy,' Sunday muttered. "Jacko wouldn't need any tricks to take the Italian."

Sadie came back with the drinks. Jerome grabbed his and downed it in two swallows.

"It'll be the death of you, Tommy," Sadie said.

Jerome wiped his mouth. "Yeah, what a pity. Well, I gotta go."

With a little imagination I could include myself in the farewell. I decided to and to follow it up.

"Before you go, can you tell me why you don't trust Ricky Simmonds?"

"Don't?"

"Slip of the tongue. Didn't, then?"

Jerome looked at our faces in turn and let his eyes rest on mine. Then he shook his head. "I'm not talking personal about one of ours to you, Hardy. You might be alright like Jimmy says—we'll see." Pain shot through him and he winced when he stood up. He kept himself straight though and walked out of the pub. The door slammed behind him and Sunday let out a long, relieved breath.

"It's lucky you're a good talker, Hardy," he said. "Wouldn't have fancied your chances in a re-match."

"You're so right." We drank and didn't say anything for a few minutes. The door opened and two men came in brushing water off their clothes and swearing about the weather. Sadie got up and went behind the bar to serve them. I could hear the swish of tyres on the road outside. The fine day had caved in, the way it can in Sydney, in a few minutes, without warning.

14

I signalled to Sadie for another round. "This'll do me," I said. "I've got things on tonight, I can't be pissed."

Sunday nodded, then he tapped himself on the forehead.

"Got a message for you. Forgot with all this boxin' business going on. From Penny. She wanted to get in touch with you. Reckoned she saw Noni."

"Where?"

"I dunno. Not around here. Penny moved out the other night and went into town somewhere. She phoned me and wanted to talk to you. She'd forgotten your last name. I said you'd be in the book. Are you?"

I didn't answer. Sadie came with the beer and I drank automatically although thirst had long since been defeated. It sounded odd, help from an unexpected quarter at this stage of the game. Again I got the feeling that events were being stage-managed, directed from on high but why and by whom I didn't know. Noni on the loose fitted in with the feeling I had that she wasn't in direct danger, but the further involvement of Penny I hadn't anticipated. Images of the two girls, black and white, formed in my mind. The black girl, young and clean, nursing a corroding hate of the white girl with the murky past. Sunday snapped his fingers in front of my face.

"Hey! Hey, Hardy! You there, man?"

I came out of it. "Yes. Just thinking. Did she say where she'd seen her? Noni?"

"No, we didn't chat. Seemed like it was just then, this morning about ten, but that was just a feeling. Listen, you've got to take it easy with Penny, Hardy."

"What do you mean?"

He drank some beer and pulled on his thin cigarette. It burned fiercely and unevenly down one side and he flicked the ash off into a beer puddle. Williams was sitting massive and still beside him. I thought I had never seen a man so passive but it was a menacing passivity, like a reservoir of emotion, dammed up, able to be burst.

"Penny's got a lot of guts, you know?" Sunday said jerkily. "She's real determined. Anything she wants she goes after and nothin' stops her. Some people down here say she's a bit cracked."

"I could see she was out of the ordinary. Why cracked though?"

He leaned back in his chair and expelled smoke through the battered gristle and bone that had once been a nose. My feeling was that Sunday saw himself as a leader, a wise and respected man, and was building up that role little by little every day. That was the way it was done and one mistake could ruin it all. He knew me for what I was, a functionary, a weapon of white society and he wanted to keep me trained on my own kind, but he needed to reveal a little of what he knew to hold me that way.

"Down here there's three kinds, much the same as up in town. There's the ones that don't give shit. Just get pissed, do what they have to do and die. There's the whingers and bludgers who moan about bein' black and disadvantaged and do fuck all about it. Then there's the goers who try to change things, don't piss their brains away, don't whinge."

"You're a goer?"

"Bloody oath I am. Penny is, too, but in a different way. She's a bit of a loner, reckoned she wouldn't take any

110

government money. Make it on her own then hit the whites for everything she could, that was her idea. She was starting to study law. Get the idea?"

"I think so. Why do you talk as if this was all in the past?"

"Well, that's the trouble. She used to go on with all this stuff, get people's backs up too, but a lot knew she was talking sense. Then she fell for Ricky . . . bad—you know? And Ricky's nothing special, bit of a no-hoper like his Dad. Penny reckoned she could reform him but he didn't pay any attention, and people laughed at her then. I mean Ricky just didn't fit in with Penny's ideas about life. That made Penny crazy on the subject of Noni. You probably saw that yourself?"

"Yes."

"She's been heard to say she'd kill her."

I let out a breath. "That'd be all we need. I better call my answering service to see if she's left a message." I was pretty sure there'd be no message. What Penny wouldn't trust to Sunday she wouldn't leave with an impersonal recorded voice. I got up to go to the phone and something Sunday had said came through the channels again. I leaned over him resting my hands on the table.

"Don't take this wrong, it's all in confidence, but what did you say about Ricky's father?"

"Said he was a bit of a no-hoper. Right, Ted?"

Williams nodded and there was something collusive in that nod. I had the feeling that whatever information I got about Ricky's father, it wouldn't be the whole story.

"He did some time," Sunday went on. "Small stuff. He's dead now."

"Sure of that?"

"Must be. Vanished years ago." He opened his hands.

"Were he and Ricky close?"

Sunday sighed and I knew I was pushing it. "No," he said.

"How was that?"

111

"Dunno. Ricky's old man went off him when he was a nipper. Happens."

"Not often."

Sunday shrugged.

"Have you ever heard of a man called Joseph Berrigan?"

"No." He enveloped the word in smoke.

"You don't seem sure."

"It rings a bell. Can't place it, though. Something to do with Ricky."

I shook my head. "Jesus, this is getting complicated." I went over to the bar phone and rang my service but there was no message. I got money out and reckoned up with Sadie. The bar was starting to fill up and my fighting hand was throbbing and the beer had made my thinking thick and sluggish. I felt that one more piece of information might make the pattern clear to me, might explain why a girl was running with a man who'd raped her. And fifty thousand dollars was a lot of money to be still missing. Age would not weary it nor the years condemn.

"What's this about, Hardy? Where's Noni?"

"Kidnapped, Jimmy, that's the way it looks anyway."

Sunday traced a design in the spilt beer. "Always thought it was wrong, Noni and Ricky and that. What's her chances, Hardy?"

"I don't know. Is there anything you can think of that might help?"

"You don't think one of us done it, do you?" Williams said gruffly.

"No, but there's missing pieces everywhere. Ricky, he's a real mystery."

"Why?" Sunday snapped. "Flash young bloke, bad boxer, good fucker who liked white meat."

"So I've heard. What was wrong with his boxing? Ted here said it was too much bed not enough sleep."

"Not altogether," Sunday said. "That was part of it. You see him fight, Ted?"

"No. Just in training, sparring."

112

"Yeah, well he was fast enough, his legs were alright and he was game but his left was no good, stiff like. He was in a car crash when he was young, got spiked through here." He indicated the left side of his chest.

He seemed about to say something more but he stopped himself. I was aware again of their suspicion of me. They held back as a matter of experience and pride. Pride is a hard quality to deal with in an investigation—it holds secrets and distorts facts.

"One last thing, Jimmy," I said slowly. "Where do you put Ricky in that list of yours?"

"Ricky doesn't go on a bloody list," Williams said harshly. His emergence from passivity gave his words unusual force. "Rick was different, he had . . . power."

"Power," I said.

"Yeah, some people say he was a bit mad after that accident." He was sorry as soon as the words were out and ended lamely. "He wasn't mad, he had power."

I nodded and knew I had all I was going to get. Sunday gave me the Sharkeys' telephone number and I said I'd be in touch. Williams grunted goodbye without committing himself.

The rain was a fine mist, veiling the buildings and traffic. I hunched my shoulders against it and ran for a bus stop. After a half hour wait I caught a passing taxi. The alcohol, the tension and the fresh air had done strange things to my brain. I felt I had two heads: One of them was thinking about Sunday, Coluzzi, Moody and boxing; the other about Noni, Berrigan, blackmail and bank robbery. I tried to switch off the first head as we ripped along the freeway back to the second head's problems.

15

It was close to five o'clock when the taxi dropped me in St. Peters Street. I skipped through the rain and used my key on the door of my office building. The other tenants had cleared out for the day. Trade was bad. I went up to my office, picked up the mail from the floor and settled down behind my desk. The one cheque in the collection was small enough to remind me that I had to get some more money from Tarleton. The bills could wait. I dropped them into a drawer. A fat, colourful envelope offered me the chance to win a split-level home north of Townsville with a stud farm, Mercedes sedan and power boat thrown in. I looked at the pictures; nice, pretty house, pretty horses, pretty beach. I fished out five dollars and started to fill in the ticket blanks, then I noticed that it said "No cash. Cheques or money orders only." I screwed the stuff up and dropped it in the waste bin. Then the phone rang.

"Cliff? Grant Evans."

I dragged my hand wearily across my face. "Shit, don't tell me the building's surrounded and there's no escape."

"Knock off the bullshit. I thought you were going to report in?"

"Who said that?"

"That was my understanding."

"You misunderstood, mate."

"Like that, is it? Look, this is not time for games, Cliff. This thing is hotting up."

I made a non-committal noise and he went on.

"You're on the scene up Macleay way, we hear. You get around all the best murders, don't you?"

"She's not dead."

"Bloody near it. I suppose you saw the grass?"

"Is *that* what it was?"

"Lot of it, Cliff, and there's an enquiry on."

"I know."

"Do you know two Italians, one tall, one short?"

"Yeah, Primo Carnera and Carlo Ponti."

"Terrific, Cliff, you're a ball of style and you've told all the jokes. Now I'm going to tell one. Heard the one about the private detective who lost his licence for withholding information from the police?"

"No."

"Yeah, he's a bus conductor, makes a hundred and fifty bucks a week and gets to wear a nice green uniform. Meets a lot of people and travels all over town."

"Sounds nice."

"He misses the glamour. Listen, Cliff, I'm serious. We're under real pressure to look good with these enquiries on. I'm appealing to your better nature."

"I can't tell you anything yet, Grant. Give me twenty-four hours, maybe thirty."

"No."

"You have to. You owe me."

There was a silence, then he said: "I owe you one. Are you calling it in?"

"I have to, Grant."

"OK." He paused. "Thirty hours."

"Thanks. And one thing—where's Simmonds's body?"

"Just around the corner from you, cock. Glebe morgue."

He hung up. The line buzzed emptily and I put the receiver down. I swiveled around on my chair and looked out the window at the city. The light was just about gone and the buildings were drained of colour. They were all grey, and it didn't matter whether they were insurance offices or churches, they were just shapes. The tops of the park trees were waving in the wind like dark, threatening tentacles. It was a good night to be with someone you knew well, in a place you liked with some good food and wine. The air in the office smelled old and stale as if it had been packaged and put there and was due for a change.

I called Saul James at home and got no answer. They pulled him out of a rehearsal at the theatre and he told me that he'd have the money tomorrow. I said I'd collect it. Madeline Tarelton answered the phone again and said that Ted was out. He'd left a message for me that the money would be ready by noon tomorrow. I told her I'd be around to wait for the call. She seemed to want to talk but I wasn't in the mood.

"What will you do between now and then?" she asked. There might have been a hint of invitation in that, but I didn't want to know, not then.

"Investigate the living tonight. Tomorrow morning I'm going to look at a dead black man. A shotgun took his face away."

It chilled her and she rang off. I left the building.

I caught a bus back to Glebe and had it to myself for most of the way. I got off near the pub, bought wine, and walked the rest of the distance. Harry Soames next door had guests. That meant they would smoke a lot of grass and sit around listening to music through headphones. Soames had installed headphones in the bathroom, in the garden. I didn't know what sort of music he listened to any more and that suited me fine. I went into the house, drank wine, showered, drank wine, cooked an omelette and drank more wine. By nine o'clock I was as ready to break the law as I'd ever be.

I had on sneakers, dark jeans and sweater and a denim jacket. The wine glow lasted through the bus ride to the university and the tramp across the campus into Newtown. It lasted while I waited for the stragglers to leave the pub across from Trueman's gym and there was just enough of it left for steady hands and quiet feet as I skeleton-keyed the lock to the old building. I went up the stairs by the thin beam of a pencil torch and the keys took me through the door into the gym as if I owned the place. It wasn't my first burglary or my tenth, but I was nervous. There aren't any faithful bobbies on the beat checking the doors and windows these days, especially in Newtown, but unusual lights or noises can still draw attention and I had no excuses. Trueman hated my guts and if I was caught at this he'd play it for all it was worth.

The gym smelled of the day's sweat and smoke as I sneakered through to the office. The door wasn't locked. Sammy wouldn't keep any money here and that accounted for the absence of burglar alarms, too. Sammy had had a little celebration it seemed; a Scotch bottle stood empty on the battered pine desk and beer cans and plastic cups were strewn around. The room had a heavy, rich odour produced by liquor, tobacco and human bodies. The party mess only added to what was already a mess. Trueman kept papers on spikes, in drawers, on top of chairs and on the floor. Pictures of past fighters were Sellotaped to the walls and papers were slid in behind them; letters were stuck between the pages of racing guides and bills and receipts bristled from the pocket of an old raincoat hanging on the back of the office door. It looked so unsystematic as to be burglar proof. I wasted minutes flicking through the relics of Sammy's past failures and found nothing more recent than a picture of Tony Mundine captioned wishfully "The next cruiserweight King."

I sat in Sammy's chair and thought as well as my noisy heart would let me. Maybe there was nothing here. Maybe I'd have to try Trueman's house. That would be a very different proposition; Sammy had a few boys from the country living with him always and I didn't fancy padding about in the dark in a house full of fighters. Ted Tarelton had a lot of money and I'd probably be covered for the bridge work and jaw wiring, but they say it alters the shape of the face and I was fairly content with the face I had. I fiddled with it now the way you do when you're thinking hard; moved sections of it about and pulled bits of it. There was no way of getting inside Sammy's mind to crack his system and that was a disgusting thought anyway. Its whole area was probably occupied by beer, boxing and bathing beauties. That led me alliteratively to books and to the one example of the animal in the office—a half-dead copy of Ray Mitchell's *The Fighting Sands* and that led me to Jacko Moody's contract. Or copies of it.

They were carbons, folded down the centre and tucked inside the book which was lying on top of Medibank forms. The contract tied Moody up for two years and was due to expire in a month. It was the standard thing; Trueman collected expenses and fees out of Moody's purses and had sole rights to OK and veto matches. It was hard to see what the fighter himself could have been getting out of his penny-ante preliminary earnings. It was legal and binding as far as I could tell but the expiry date made Trueman vulnerable. That is, if another contract hadn't been signed. With Coluzzi's schemes still in the planning stage, that seemed unlikely. I took one of the copies and put it in my pocket.

I was straightening the papers when a noise out in the gym made me freeze. I clicked off the light and the tiny noise sounded like a gunshot. Four steps took me over to the door which I'd left open and I peered out into the darkness of the big, pungent room. I could hear feet shuffling on the floor and harsh, stifled breathing. I slid out of the office and along the nearest wall. No weapons came to hand and the torch was slim, elegant and useless. There was a muttered curse in the darkness and a floundering, stumbling noise and I used the cover of it to make it across to the locker bay. I pressed myself back against the cold metal and ran a hand across the top of the set of lockers feeling for a weapon. Nothing . . . just dust. I was fighting against a shattering sneeze when the light over the ring came on.

A man was standing in the middle of the ring holding his hands up above his head. As a picture of athletic triumph it was spoiled by the bottle in his hand. He kept one hand raised, brought the other, the one holding the bottle, down and took a long, gargling drink. He walked carefully over to the red corner and set the bottle down on the stool. Then he moved back to centre ring and began to shadow-box. He was as drunk as an owl and his movements were a broken, uncoordinated parody of the boxer's grace. He blundered into the ropes, fell and crawled across to the stool. The sleeve of his coat had come down across his hand; it was a cast-off coat, a derro coat, and he fought for what seemed like minutes to get clear of it and to get hold of the bottle. He made it and took a quick slug. He pulled himself up by the ropes and struck the attitude of a fight announcer. He mimed pulling a microphone down from the roof.

"Ladeez an' gentlemen," he bellowed, "fifteen roun's of boxing, for the lightweight champeenship of th' world. In th' red corner," he pointed to the bottle, "at nine stone nine pounds, Taffy . . . Taffy Thomas." He flung out his arm, lost balance and collapsed to the floor. He tried to pull himself up again but thought better of it. He crawled to the corner again and used the bottle. It fell from his hand onto the apron of the ring and off to the floor. He pitched forward, rested his head on his arms and went to sleep. I came across to look at him; the ear showing was cauli-flowered and his body was pear-shaped and dumpy inside the formless coat. I'd never seen him fight but I'd heard about him. It wasn't that long ago.

I doused the light and left the gym.

16

It was after midnight when I got home. The house next door was dark and quiet; no one around to spot Raffles sneaking back with His Lordship's silver. I'd forgotten to check the mailbox earlier and I reached into it now and pulled out an airletter. I read it over a cigarette and a glass of wine. Ailsa was in Samoa and missing me; I was in Sydney and missing her and Samoa. I distributed the papers I'd taken from Trueman's office among the pages of the three volumes of Bertrand Russell's autobiography. Cyn had bought me the books, one by one, as they'd come out, and written inscriptions in them. I didn't read the inscriptions. There was dust on the books and I opened and closed them hard, blew on them and put them back on the shelves. I didn't spend enough time at home to get around to dusting bookshelves. There were probably silverfish, too, maybe mice. It would be a good house for mice, nice and quiet with just the occasional scrap of food around. I went upstairs to bed, quietly, so as not to disturb my mice.

The city morgue is in the basement of a low, long building the colour of dried blood. The building houses the Coroner's Court and the Forensic Medicine division; the live people go in the front off Parramatta Road, the dead ones go in the back off Arundel Street.

The desk attendant was thin and hatchet-faced. He wore a narrow black tie, a brilliantly white shirt and an even whiter coat. I showed him my licence and told him my business and he didn't like any of it. His voice was a thin bleat: "I haven't the requisite authority to show cadavers to members of the public."

"I don't want to see your whole collection—just one."

"The rule applies."

"I'm investigating his death."

"Not officially, and you have no proof of that."

I needed a name. Not Evans. He wouldn't bail me out of this. I reached around in my mind and came up with it.

"Dr. Foster, the police forensic man will OK it," I said. "Call him and see."

It was bluff and weak as a politician's promise but it did the trick. He didn't want to bother the brass.

"Very well. Take this down those stairs and show the man at the door." He scribbled the time, date and three initials on a card and pointed to a set of stairs descending into the bowels of the earth. I went down three flights. It got cooler and the tiles got bleaker and my steps rang sharply in the still, clinical air.

The man at the door was the exact opposite of his counterpart upstairs. He was red-faced and cheerful, overweight and scruffy around the neck and lapels. He took the card and stuffed it into the torn pocket of his coat.

"Through here, mate," he chirped. "Keep your breakfast down, won't you?"

I said I would and followed him through a set of heavy perspex doors. The room reminded me of a changing room at a swimming pool. It had a concrete floor and mirrors at either end. It was white-tiled with a green strip around it at shoulder height for a touch of gaiety. The fluorescent light was harsh and instead of the swimming pool's smell of chlorine and sweat this place reeked of formaldehyde. There were steel handles sticking out of the walls, waist high at six-foot intervals. We stood in the centre of the room by a bench that had straps attached to it and a shallow basin mounted beside it. A gutter ran from the basin to a channel in the floor. The attendant asked me who I wanted to see as if he was in charge of a theatre dressing room. I told him.

"Ah, yes," he crooned, "black beauty." His voice was still chirpy and his step was jaunty. I expected him to break into a dance routine.

He went over to the far wall, pulled on a handle and a seven-foot long, three-foot wide tray slid out soundlessly.

The attendant twitched the calico sheet aside. The naked body was pale under the harsh light, scarcely darker than a suntanned European, but it was the same colour all over. I looked down at the corpse but it wasn't like looking at a person. There was no face. The mangled head had been sprayed with something which made it a dark, featureless blob. I leaned over and looked closely at the left side of the chest. The flesh had been burned and shattered by the shotgun blast. Bone and other matter obtruded from the hundreds of small wounds which added up to a massive injury. The attendant looked at me oddly.

"Something?" he asked.

I straightened up. "I wanted to see whether he had a scar on his chest, here."

"It should be on the report. Oh, I see what you mean. I'll get the report anyway. Finished?"

I said I was. He slid the tray back and we left the room. In the cubicle at the foot of the stairs a couple of rows of clipboards with papers affixed hung on hooks. He reached one down and scanned the top page.

"Male Aboriginal, aged . . . about twenty-five years . . . ah . . . no, . . . scar on leg . . ." He flipped the page. "Autopsy . . . massive haemorrhage . . ."

"Any mention of an old chest wound?"

"Ah . . . no, but then you wouldn't expect it, would you, not with that lot."

I said I supposed not and thanked him for his help. He gave me a cheery smile and ducked back into his cubicle. I had my foot on the first step when he stuck his head out.

"Here, take your card back. The old chap who came to see him nearly left his here, too."

I went back and took the card.

"What old chap?"

"Old Abo. Down here . . . let's see . . . yesterday. Had a police pass. Relative of some kind. He just took one quick look and left. They're superstitious about the dead, aren't they?"

"Yeah. So am I. About this man." I described Rupert Sharkey to the attendant but he shook his head.

"No, nothing like that. This man was short and stocky . . . an' older than what you're saying."

"What was the name on the card?"

"I don't remember. He'll have it up at the desk."

I thanked him again and went up. Hatchet-face looked displeased to see me but showed off his efficiency by producing the black man's police pass within seconds. It carried the name Percy White and an address in Redfern. I handed my card in and left the place puzzled, unenlightened—but alive.

I celebrated my condition with a beer in the Forest Lodge hotel up the street from the house of the dead. I bought tobacco and smoked a few cigarettes and let the fumes of liquor and weed take away the stink of death.

Halfway through the second beer I called Sharkey's number in La Perouse. Sunday was there and I filled him in with what I had on Moody's contract with Trueman. He said Williams had seen Moody and warned him not to sign anything further and the fighter had agreed. Nothing more had been heard from Penny. I asked Sunday about Percy White but he'd never heard of him. As far as he knew, and that was pretty far, Simmonds had no such relative. The description I had could fit a hundred men in La Perouse alone. I asked him if Ricky Simmonds had a scar on his left leg. He laughed.

"I never knew an Aborigine who didn't—falls, burns, sores, insect bites, you should see me."

I grunted something and rang off. I finished the beer, left the pub and walked across to the university library. A quick

123

check of an old city directory told me that the address "Percy White" had given in Redfern didn't exist.

This heavy detecting took me until midday. I bought some Vogel bread sandwiches outside the library and stretched out on the lawn that overlooks Victoria park. The buildings around the quadrangle loomed up behind me, solid and gothic and echoing to the footsteps of the learned. The neophytes gathered on the lawn giving me, an outsider, a wide berth. Almost to a man and a woman they wore jeans, forbidden dress at university back in the days when I'd played briefly at the experience. Otherwise nothing much had changed; the sexes basically grouped apart with only a few of the stars from each side coming into collision. But the lawn lunch-eaters weren't representative. Behind closed pub doors and in smoky studies the drinkers and hairy politicians gathered to plot the overthrow of society within the next semester. The deadly swots were still in the library and the smooth-talking professionals who would control this place and most others like it in a few years, were debating, or running the tennis club or sipping sherry somewhere with their masters. I ate the sandwiches and watched a pair of tight-jeaned women parade slowly across my field of vision. Their breasts jogged gently under linen shirts, their bottoms rode high and tight and their legs seemed to go on forever. I sighed, got up and brushed grass off my clothes. I was sweating. It was a fine day. Maybe I was too warmly dressed.

17

I caught a taxi to Paddington and was met at the door by a flushed and anxious-looking Madeline. She had a couple of dresses over her arm and there were shoes on the floor in the passage behind her.

"Leaving?" I asked.

She bit her lip. The white chunky teeth went into the moist purple lips and sent a sexual shiver through me. She saw my reaction and it didn't throw her one degree off course.

"I am, if you must know. Ted's impossible. All that money for that worthless slut . . . the police . . ."

"She's his daughter."

"Maybe—if her mother was anything like that who could say?"

It was nothing to me except that men being left by their wives are apt to act irrationally and Ted couldn't afford to. I said so and she spun away and started to gather up shoes. I came a couple of steps into the passage and tried to keep my mind off the yard of deadly stocking she was showing under a white crepe dress. She saw me looking, straightened up and smoothed the dress down. My mouth went dry.

"You haven't the time," she said softly. "Ted got a call half an hour ago. He was to wait for another call at his office. He's there now with the money—off you run, Mr. Hardy."

"Where's the office?" I croaked. She walked off down

the hall; she'd spent hours on the walk and it was worth every minute. She came back with a card and I took it.

"Don't leave," I said. "See it through. You're being childish. See how it looks after we get the girl back."

She threw the dresses down and burst into tears. She dumped the shoes and ran off down the hall.

Well done, Hardy. Terrific work. So subtle. I closed the door quietly and backed out to the gate. A white Celica was parked outside the house with some clothes on the back seat. The key was in the ignition and Madeline's perfume was in the air. I slid behind the wheel, started the car and drove off toward the city. I didn't like the new twist. It had an amateur feel. It's easier to watch a house than a city building, easier to spot reinforcements. Then I swore at myself for not scouting Armstrong Street. If there had been a look-out he'd have got the message loud and clear. Maybe it wasn't an amateur play after all.

Ted's office was in a tower block across from Hyde Park. The Celica had a sticker on it that let me drive into the car park under the tower and almost got a salute from the attendant. Ted's suite of offices had a lot of shag pile carpet, stained wood and tinted glass. Here he was Tarelton Enterprises and looking like he could spare a hundred grand, but you can never tell.

An ash blonde stopped pecking at her typewriter and showed me into Ted's lair. The carpet was deeper and the wood more highly polished than outside; there was an interesting-looking bar at the end of the room and that's where Ted was standing. He greeted me and dropped ice into a second glass and built two Scotches. He walked back to his quarter-acre desk and set the glasses down carefully; it wasn't his first drink and it wasn't his second. He waved me to a chair; I picked up the Scotch and sat down—it was a drink to sit down with.

"Got the money?" I asked.

"Sure." He reached down, missed his aim and had to steady himself on the desk. He pulled up a black, metal-bound attache case. "Wanna see it?" He was aping confidence and assurance but it was a bad act.

I nodded. He sprung the locks and pushed the case across the desk. The money lay in neat rows held by the case's straps. It looked what it was—a hell of a lot of cash.

Ted said the call was due at four o'clock and we were twenty minutes short of that. I drank and looked at my employer. He seemed to have shrunk inside his clothes; the expensive tailoring hung on him indifferently and his patterned Establishment tie was askew. Normally Ted had a high colour—the product of good health, good times and good brandy. Today he was pale with a couple of vivid spots. Bristles that had survived a shaky shave outcropped on the pale skin. His hand shook as he scrabbled a cigar out of a box on the desk. I rolled and lit a cigarette. We drank and my nerves started to twang in the silence.

"I pinched your wife's car," I said. "I think she was planning on leaving. Why don't you ring her?"

"You a bloody marriage counsellor now?"

"Just an idea. You're going to need help through this."

Panic leaped through the liquor and into his eyes. "Why? You don't think they'll . . . they won't kill her?" He looked at the money.

"You can't tell. I don't think so, but it might not be easy getting her back."

"You're saying she's in with them? I told you that's crap. I don't want to hear any more of that."

"Mr. Tarelton," I said wearily, "this is nice Scotch but this isn't a nice job. You don't know your daughter, you don't know the first thing about her. I've found things about her that'd make your hair curl. That's my job. I rake muck and mostly I keep it to myself when I can. Sometimes I can't and this looks like one of those times. Please don't tell me what you don't want to hear. It doesn't help." I'd started to raise my voice. Now I dropped it back to as comfortable a tone as I could manage. "I think it would be a good idea if you called your wife."

He was in no shape to fight. He drained his glass and took a long pull on the cigar. "Alright, alright, you know your business. Jesus, I thought I knew about strain but there's nothing to touch this."

He was getting gabby and I had no use just then for the full story of his life. I pointed to the phone and he picked it up and dialled. He held it to his ear for a minute then slammed it down.

"Engaged," he snarled. "At least she's still there. That blasts your theory . . ."

The intercom buzzed. "I said no calls," Ted barked. He flicked the switch. "No calls till four!" The black box spoke back: "I'm sorry, Mr. Tarelton, it's your wife on the line, she sounds upset."

"Put her through." Tarelton picked up the receiver and swung half-away from me. He suddenly jerked upright in his chair.

"What!" His voice broke and he stammered, "What? What?"

I mouthed at him to play the call through and he flicked switches clumsily. Madeline Tarelton's voice cut harshly into the room, its elocution-lesson tones pared away by fear.

"Ted, Ted," she gasped, "there's a man here with a gun." Her voice was cut off by a short scream and Tarelton yelped into the phone. "Madeline, Madeline, what does he want? Do what he says."

There was a pause and she spoke again, fighting for control. "He just wants me to tell you to do as you're told." The line went dead. Tarelton looked at the receiver in his hand. He was clutching it as if he could squeeze more information from it. I got up and took it away from him. Then I picked up his glass, went to the bar and made him another drink; he had another phone call to get through and he wasn't going to do it without help. I went back and he took the glass.

"What does it mean?"

"They're making sure. It doesn't change anything."

He sensed my uncertainty and turned his cornered frustration on me.

"It's your fault, you took her car, she'd have been . . ."

"Where? Would you rather that? It's not true anyway. They'd have moved when they were ready. She'll be alright. Shut up and let me think."

He bridled. "Don't . . ."

I flapped a hand at him and he subsided, then the box spoke again.

"A call for you, sir. It's just past four o'clock."

"Thank you," Tarelton said weakly. "Put it through, please."

"Pay-out time, Ted." The voice was male, not rough, not educated. Australian, not foreign. Tarelton croaked something indistinct.

"The money, Tarelton. Have you got it?"

"I've got it. It's here. Let me talk to Noni and if you harm my wife I'll . . ."

"Shut up and listen. The girl's alright. You'll see her tonight. I don't know nothing about your wife. Who's helping you with this—a lawyer, a friend or what?"

"Nobody. You said . . ."

"Don't give me that. You'd have someone. He there with you now?"

"Yes."

"What's he look like? Describe him."

Tarelton looked unseeingly at me. His colour was bad and he was working at his shirt collar with one finger.

"Tell him," I said.

"He's tall and dark . . . thin," Tarelton said desperately. "Thin . . ."

"Yeah, I caught that. How old?"

"Late thirties."

"What's he wearing?"

"Dark trousers, grey pullover, light blue . . ." he searched for the word, I gave it to him: "Parka."

"Blue parka."

"What the fuck's that?"

"A sort of jacket. Look, can't we settle this reasonably? Just let my wife go and . . ."

"I told you, I don't know a bloody thing about your wife, now shut up! Send this character with the money to Elkington park in Balmain at six o'clock sharp. Got it?"

"Yes."

"Before he goes tell him to ring Saul James—here's the number . . ." He gave it in a firm confident voice. "Just tell James he's acting for Tarelton. He'll know what to do. Oh, one last thing. Tell your man to go to the park by taxi. That's it."

"But . . ."

"But nothing. Do as you're told and the girl'll be alright. Slip up and I'll cut her bloody throat."

He broke the connection. Sweat was pouring down Tarelton's face which had settled into creases and lines that aged him ten years. He reached for his drink and gulped it.

"Take it easy," I said. "You don't look well. You could have a long wait and you can't keep sucking that stuff down the whole time—you'll crack up."

"You're right," he pushed the glass away as if he meant it. "What do I do next?"

"Call your wife."

He did. The phone must have been snatched up the second it sounded. Their voices over-rode each other and a great gust of relief filled the room.

"He's gone, Ted. He just walked out a minute ago."

"He didn't hurt you?"

"No, he didn't touch me, not really. I couldn't have stood it, either." There was a note of horror in her voice of a kind I'd heard before so I wasn't surprised when she said: "He was black, Ted. An Aborigine."

"Shit," Tarelton said.

"Ask her if he was stocky, middle-aged or older, carrying weight."

He did and she said it was an accurate description. I

thought of "Percy White" holding a gun on a flower of white womanhood in the hundred-thousand-dollar house. It was a bizarre, cinematic image, unreal, but it had been real enough to terrify those comfortable people through to the marrow. It had been totally effective in securing Tarelton's consent to the kidnapper's terms, but the man on the line had affected to know nothing about it. He was either very tough, a good actor or telling the truth. Either way it was confusing. Tarelton found it so, too. He promised his wife he'd be home within the hour and she rang off. Apparently her thoughts of leaving home had been dispelled. Tarelton stroked his jaw as if to reassure himself that the old familiar truths were still intact.

"What's with the Abos, Hardy? I don't get it."

I picked up the bag and started for the door, then I noticed that I had an inch of Scotch in my glass and I came back and drained it.

"I told you, Noni ran in rough company. This is part of it but I don't know how it all ties together yet. I've got some ideas but this comes first." I held up the bag. "Marked the money?"

"Yeah," he looked ashamed. "That is, I've got a list of the numbers."

"That'll do," I said. "I'll be in touch as soon as I know anything."

He nodded and I went out. I was in the car park before I remembered that I hadn't asked if I could use the Celica. Neither had I asked for more money but I was carrying more than I'd ever seen in one go in my life, and it hadn't seemed like the right time.

The Celica took me to Darlinghurst in five minutes. I parked outside James's house and rang the bell. James opened the door and ushered me in. I could hear voices.

"Television," James said apologetically. Maybe he thought I was one of those people who disapprove of tele-viewing in the daytime. Maybe I was. We went through to the kitchen. He was wearing the same sort of clothes I'd seen him in before; soft shades and fabrics to match his character. His hair had recently been combed when wet and I noticed that it was receding a little at the forehead. I slung the briefcase down on the table.

"What's that?"

"Ted Tarelton's hundred grand. Got your share?"

He blinked at the harshness of my voice. "Yes, here." He pointed to a blue airline bag on the floor.

"Got a list of the numbers?"

He looked surprised. "No, why?"

"So the money can be traced after the pick-up."

He arranged his face virtuously. "I don't care about the money."

I grunted. "Up to you. Got anything to drink?"

"Vodka. In the kitchen."

"I'll fix it," I said. "Want one?"

"Yes, I suppose so, thanks." He slumped in his chair and lit a cigarette. I went out to the kitchen and got the bottle. Smirnoff. Actors always drink vodka. Maybe it makes them feel like Raskolnikov or maybe they just don't like people to smell booze on their breaths. I poured two hefty slugs, chopped bits off a lemon and dumped some ice into the glasses. To my mind the recipe should then read: "Pour down the sink and open a bottle of Scotch" but it was no time to be choosy. I went back into the living room and handed one of the drinks to James. The second he touched it the phone rang and he dropped the glass. The liquor splashed onto the rug and spread about in drops and rivulets like runaway quicksilver. He bent to recover the glass.

"Answer it!"

He stumbled across the room and snatched up the receiver. His face was drained of colour and his knuckles were tight and blanched where he clenched the phone. He opened his mouth to speak and was cut off by a quick, staccato flow of sound across the wire. He nodded once, looked up at me and said:

"Yes, yes, he's here."

More nodding, then: "The rotunda . . . toward the water. Yes, I'll tell him. Taxi, yes . . . Look, is Noni . . ."

I heard the click from across the room. Decisive man with a telephone, this character. James put the instrument down slowly as if he was still obeying orders issuing from it.

"You're to leave the money . . ." he began.

"In the rotunda and walk toward the water. Yeah, I gathered that."

"Don't bite my head off."

"Sorry," I said grudgingly. "It's just that I don't like this set-up. It stinks of double-cross for one thing and there's a phoney feel to it."

He flushed angrily. "What do you mean phoney? Kidnap, ransom." His anger dropped suddenly away as if he was incapable of holding any strong emotion for long. A dull stupefied look on his face made me wonder whether there was any centre to his character at all under the histrionic

133

shell. He went on lamely: "Do you mean it's all too, well, dramatic to be real?"

"Not exactly." I couldn't tell him what I meant. I didn't really know myself. I'd been on the sidelines in one kidnapping that had ended the worst way a couple of years back and I'd talked to men who'd been involved in others. I remembered, and had got from participants, a sense of desperation and urgency that wasn't here now. Still, the terms were clear and so was my responsibility.

"What do you think will happen?"

"I know what you're hoping for," I said tightly. "You're hoping I'll drop the money and that your girl will come walking out of the mist and I'll bring her back and you'll live happily ever after."

His face twisted into a grimace that was part self-pity, part something else.

"You think I'm soft, don't you?"

"It doesn't matter what I think. I'm trying to tell you that kidnapping almost never works out sweetly. Someone nearly always gets hurt and people get changed by the experience. Some people begrudge the ransom money for the rest of their lives."

"I've told you, I'm not worried about the money."

"Maybe not. That's not the point. You're not listening to me. Get ready for something rough. If all I hear about this girl is true, you're in for a bad time whatever shape she comes out of this in."

The half-hearted anger came back in the form of a pink flush.

"What the hell do you mean by that?"

If I'd thought he was working some kind of deal on the case, some tax dodge or any one of the hundred or so reasons people have for setting these things up, I would have tried to break him with the information I had on the girl's past. But I didn't think that; he'd accepted a lot of things about her that would have sent most people off in the other direction, fast, and his concern for her seemed

134

genuine, if immature. This was no time for self-discovery. I suspected that the events of the next few hours would stamp him as perpetually young or force him to grow up fast.

"Never mind," I said. "I've got to go."

He looked alarmed. "You'll be too early."

I juggled the car keys in my hand and reached for the briefcase and the bag. James moved quickly to block me.

I brushed him aside roughly. "Look, there are no rules in this game no matter what they say on telly. It's a game of chance. You can't tell what's the right thing to do and what's not. But I'll tell you two things I'm not going to do. One, I'm not going to walk into a park in Balmain after dark carrying a hundred and five thousand bucks without having a look around first. And two, I'm not going to leave myself stranded there with no transport. Sit down. Look, I'll drive to Balmain, scout around and then get a taxi. Got it? Have another drink. Have a couple."

He looked relieved. "Sorry. I didn't mean to tell you your business."

"You've got a right," I said more gently. "It's your girl and your money." He started to speak and I held up my hand. "I know, I know, you don't care about the money. I've got to go. I'll call you when I know something."

Thick dark clouds had blotted out the fine afternoon and heavy rain was falling when I climbed into the Celica and stowed the money on the back seat. A strong wind was whipping the rain around and the spray from the other cars cut down the visibility. I crept through the city and picked up speed over the Glebe Island bridge where the lighting was good and the roads were clear. I reached Terry Street half an hour before the appointed time, parked the car in a lane and worked up to the edge of the park using whatever cover I could. The wind bit in through the light parka and the thought of leaving that much money in the car nagged at me. The .38 inside the jacket where I'd slashed the pocket and reinforced the lining was heavy but a comfort. It was slow to get at it but it was there.

The park runs down from the road to the water and ends in a narrow peninsula with steep, rocky sides. It's bounded by a residential street on one side and by the Dawn Fraser pool and some gardens on the other. The park is about six hundred yards deep and is sixty or seventy yards wide at its broadest point. The rotunda sits in the middle like a salt dish on a table. I hadn't seen it for years but I remembered its vandalised wall linings and smashed fittings and it was unlikely to have changed. I moved up from the street to a point behind a toilet block at the edge of the park and peered into the gloom.

Nothing was moving except one of a pair of swings which creaked like a door in a Gothic mansion. The slides and turnabouts were weird, inter-steller shapes against the harbour mist and drops of water splattered down on me for ten minutes then eased back down to the street. I went back to the car, got in and wrote down the serial numbers of the money in Saul James's bag, then I transferred Tarelton's cash to the soft bag. I walked up to Darling Street holding the bag and trying to feel confident. A taxi U-turned at my whistle and pulled up beside me, splashing water on my legs.

The driver pushed open the front passenger door. "Sorry, mate. Where to?"

I got in and took out a two-dollar note. "Around the block and drop me at the entrance to the park. It's a two-dollar ride."

He looked at me quickly, the Sydneysider's suspicion of parks and perverts showing in his eyes but he shrugged and slipped the car into gear.

"You're the boss."

He did the circuit in second and I tried to push an unwanted image from my mind—it was a picture I'd seen of ex-President Gerald Ford looking bulky and unsure in a bullet-proof vest.

I paid off the cab outside the arched sandstone entrance to the park. The pistol butt was cold and hard in my right hand

and the plastic handle of the bag was slimy in my left as I went down the short flight of stone steps.

My rubber soles squelched on the wet path as the darkness of the park closed around me. I stared hard ahead of me and around but there was nothing moving that shouldn't have been. The path sloped down slightly to the basin occupied by the rotunda. I could sense eyes on me and the wind seemed to be carrying the sound of harsh breathing and the smell of fear. I went up the steps to the rotunda. It hadn't changed, except to be even more dilapidated. A crazy network of slats hung down from the roof and one of its brick pillars was now a pile of rubble spilling out toward the centre of the concrete floor. A pool of water about six feet across and a few inches deep gleamed in the middle of the circular space. I set the bag down in the centre of it and straightened up slowly.

"Very funny, mate." The voice was harsh and thin like a fingernail across a blackboard. "Take the hand out of the jacket and keep it in sight."

I did what he said. The voice seemed to be coming from the front of the rotunda, low down, beneath my eye level. There was a gap between the floor and the railing with plenty of space to see and to shoot through. I held my hands out wide and empty.

"OK. Out you go and walk down to the water. Don't look back or it'll be the last thing you do."

The voice, still harsh and tight, was steady and sounded as if it meant what it said. This was the part I didn't like. I backed out, walked around the side of the structure and started down to the harbour. I thought I might have a chance at him when I'd moved down a bit because it was too dark for good shooting and there was some cover beside the path. The idea died when I heard the voice again. It was much closer. He'd moved around and stood at the top of the path, positioned where he had me in a shooting gallery for a hundred yards, targeted against the lights where the peninsula begins to narrow down. He said "Keep going" and I

137

did, concentrating on getting to the lights without any bullets in my hide. I'd gone about forty feet when I heard a noise like a scuffle behind me and I instinctively dropped down. A muffled shout and a sharp crack and a bullet whined off the concrete ahead of me and to one side. I pulled the gun out and started to crawl to a tree. A bullet thudded into the trunk I was headed for and I twisted round and fired back at the rotunda, aiming low. For no reason I could think of I shouted a word:

"Berrigan!"

The response was a hissing curse. A shape loomed up at the centre of the rotunda, a dark menacing shape that flashed fire at me. I felt leaves and dirt kick up into my face and I fired again and there was a scream and metal rang on concrete.

I rolled off the path and crawled behind a tree. I screwed up my eyes and strained them through the darkness but I couldn't see any movement up ahead of me. The park had swallowed up the sound of the shots and the whisper of the trees and the wash of the sea took over again and restored the quiet, normal rhythms of the night.

I got to my feet and approached the rotunda, keeping off the path and using the trees for cover. Moon and park light gleamed on metal. I looked down at the big gun and left it where it lay. I hoisted myself up over the railing and came into the circle from the rear. A man was lying on his back in the middle of the pool of water. Water had splashed out all around him from the impact of his fall and a section of the pool was nearly dry where the water had seeped into the man's clothes. I put my fingers on his wrist and waited to hear the blood pumping through, but there would never be long enough to wait. He was dead. There was no sign of the airline bag. I lit a match and held it up to make sure. The flickering light caught and danced over his face; the skin was stretched tight over the sharp, hawkish cheekbones. Bony, bat-winged ears stuck out from his close-cropped skull. The coat of his suit had come open and exposed his tiny bony chest covered by a woollen shirt. I struck another match and bent over him. The shirt front was a sodden, oozing mess that glistened thick and oily in the match-light.

I walked up to the road feeling only marginally like a member of the human race. Each killing of another person diminishes your share in the common feeling that unites civilised people and my stocks were running low. Military service is supposed not to count in this process but for me it did. As I walked I realised that my hand was clenched tight around the butt of the Smith & Wesson and I recalled other pistols I'd fired at other men in this city and other guns, all shapes and sizes, growing hot in my hands as I pumped bullets at human flesh. Small soldiers, their hats festooned with jungle camouflage, danced before my eyes and I sweated as freely as I had back in those Malayan jungles.

I found a phone booth and called Ted Tarelton and told him what had happened. I couldn't tell him anything about the girl except that I'd have to report the whole thing to the police now and her name would come out. He accepted it better than I expected. He didn't try to talk me out of it and I wondered what he felt now about the girl. His wife had answered the phone and handed it straight to him without comment; even over the impersonal wire I could sense their reconciliation and maybe that's what mattered most. The money certainly didn't matter a damn. With Saul James it was harder; he showered me with abuse and almost broke down. When he recovered he put one question coldly:

"She's dead, isn't she, Hardy?"

I still didn't think so and that's what I said but it made no impression on him. He hung up on me. They had one thing in common—neither of them cared a hoot how many men I shot to death.

The Balmain police station is tucked up next to the town hall like a bedmate. I parked the Celica outside, went in and asked for the duty officer. A uniformed constable with pimples asked my name, inspected my licence and wanted to know what it was about. I told him briefly and he showed

139

me through to a cold, cream-painted room with a table and two chairs. I sat down, rolled a cigarette and waited. I stuck my head out of the door to ask for coffee but there was no one to ask. I memorised the cracks on the walls and the cobwebs hanging from the roof. I took my gun out and put it on the table in front of me. I swore at it and the little black hole at the end of its muzzle stared me down. I put it away.

After fifteen minutes the door opened and two men came into the room. One of them was the new style of copper with a modish, broad-lapelled suit, collar-length hair and a Zapata moustache. His type imagines it can efface itself at a rock concert but it always sticks out like a bull's balls and never gets offered a joint. The other man was cast in the traditional mould; his face was shaped by grog and collisions with fists and the cut of his hair and clothes owed nothing to vanity. He spoke with the rasping whisper that comes from years of hushed conversations in pubs and stilted evidence-giving in court.

The young one stationed himself by the door, the other swung his leg up and perched on the end of the table across from me. His eyes dropped to my trousers and stayed there. I noticed for the first time that they were smeared with blood. For no reason my reaction to this inspection was cheek.

"You better go down to the park. Someone might take him home as a souvenir."

The older man turned around to grin at his mate.

"Pathetic, isn't it? Give them an investigator's licence and they all think they have to be smart." The younger cop nodded on cue. The veteran settled himself more comfortably on the table.

"Oh, I'm sorry, Mr. Hardy, I'm forgetting my manners. My name is Carlton, Sergeant Jim Carlton and this is Sergeant Tobin."

I said nothing and re-lit my cigarette, which had gone out.

"Yes, well, now that we're all introduced I think we'd

140

better get on." Carlton's voice was friendly in a dangerous way. I prepared myself for the boot that would knock the chair from under me or the slap that would send the cigarette flying, but nothing like that happened. Carlton went on, showing his great weakness: he loved to talk. I relaxed.

"You know, I really dislike men in your game, Hardy—I always imagine they've got beautiful, rich mistresses and good ins with high-up coppers. I know it's not true. I know you're all seedy little losers scratching a living around the divorce courts. The reality makes me happy but the image gets up my nose, know what I mean?"

I grinned at him. "You're an intellectual. Eloquent, too. I'm sorry to disappoint you."

"You don't," he said. "You're just right. You haven't got two bob and you're up to your balls in trouble."

"You could be right, Carlton," I said. "Why don't you pick up the phone and talk it over with Grant Evans? He'll be interested."

Tobin looked alarmed. "Evans?" The modish moustache twitched. "He's all right, Evans. Jim, what d'you think?"

Carlton sighed and rubbed his hand over his bristled face. He'd seen it too often before—influence, names, interference. He looked resigned, then angry. He banged his fist on the table.

"Alright, you know a Chief Inspector. Big deal, he can't cover you for this."

"I don't need cover. I just have to tell you what happened and I'm willing to do that."

"How nice," Carlton sneered. "Talk away."

"Don't be silly. I've been through this before. You take a statement now, stenographer and all, with my solicitor present, or we go down to the park in a friendly way and I'll tell you about it. I don't know the derro scene in Balmain too well, but I imagine you could have some bad cases of alcoholic freak-out if you let corpses lie around in the parks."

141

"Stop being clever, Hardy. We've checked out the park, the body's being taken care of. I want to hear what you've got to say."

He was throwing his cards away and the younger man could see it. He levered himself off the wall and came forward to lay a hand on Carlton's shoulder.

"Easy, Jim," he said. "Let's play by the book. We're getting nowhere."

Carlton shook the hand off irritably like a dog shedding water. The difference in their ages and the sameness of their rank was eating at him like a cancer. He bulled up from the table and jerked a thumb at me in a gesture that was meant to be tough but lacked all authority.

"OK, Hardy, we'll play it your way. Guys like you and your tame Chief Inspector make me sick."

I got up slowly and watched him stalk out of the room. He was probably an honest cop and that couldn't be any easier in Balmain than elsewhere. The honest ones were edgy and this sometimes prompted them to behave like the dishonest ones. It's an old trade. Tobin let him go and waved me through the door.

"Have you got rich, beautiful mistresses too, Hardy?" he asked as I passed him.

I grinned. "Just the one."

We went out into the night and got into a police car. The uniformed man at the wheel gunned the motor and U-turned violently, throwing Tobin almost into Carlton's lap. The older man swore and pushed him away. The night had thickened and the rain was falling steadily. Carlton stared gloomily out of the window and refused a cigarette from Tobin. I took one and he lit it with a nice-looking gas lighter. Three puffs and we were at the park. We piled out of the car and the driver pulled police issue slickers from the boot. We trudged down toward the rotunda like a set of spies, all distrusting each other and caught in a ritual over which we had no control.

Two heavily built cops were sheltering the rotunda. One

of them stamped out a cigarette as we approached and his companion plodded out into the rain.

Carlton marched up to the body and looked down at it. The corpse had about as much emotional impact on him as a pound of potatoes.

"Let's see your gun," he grunted.

I handed it over and he sniffed it. He fiddled with it for a minute and seemed unfamiliar with its mechanism.

"We'll hear your excuses later. You shot him. Where from?"

I retraced my movements up the path and pointed to the approximate spot. "I shot *at* him," I said.

"One shot?"

"Two."

"Why?"

"He was shooting at me."

"How awful." He prowled around the path and the body and I heard him cursing the rain and the wind. Tobin came forward and squinted back down the path to the shadowy structure.

"Pretty good shot," he said, "given the conditions. What was the angle?"

"I was flat on my belly and I was shit-scared."

"Yeah, I would be too." He squared his shoulders and marched back to the rotunda. I leaned against a tree with my shoulders hunched against the rain. I heard muttered voices and then one of the cops scurried up the path to the road. Tobin came out of the gloom and joined me under the tree.

"You've got a licence for the .38?"

I told him I had.

He drew in a deep breath and raised his cigarette to his lips. It had gone out in the rain. I looked at the damp butt between my fingers and we threw them away simultaneously.

"There must be quite a story to this, Mr. Hardy."

"Why so?"

"The dead man isn't holding a gun and there's no other gun around that we can see."

19

It took more than two hours of questions, coffee, cigarettes and hot tempers to get it all sorted out at the station. Carlton and Tobin went through their version of the heavy-soft routine, but their hearts weren't in it. They didn't like me, they didn't like me dealing with kidnappers and they particularly didn't like me doing it in Balmain. But they didn't think I'd criminally killed Berrigan. I told them who he was and how he was connected to Noni Tarelton. I told them about the Baker woman in Macleay but I didn't make the connections for them, I just had to clear myself on that count. Tobin tried to tie it all together.

"This Berrigan was a nutter, right? He was still hung up on the girl and he killed the Abo who was screwing her. Then he went to Macleay after the money but he didn't get it. He bashed the Baker woman, then he dreamed up the idea of getting some cash by ransoming the girl. Maybe she was in on it—yeah, that'd explain it."

I was tired and would have agreed to anything but he didn't need the encouragement. Carlton was sneering at him from across the room and that was enough to spur him on.

"It looks bad for the girl," he continued. "It looks as if she was in on the whole thing and then double-crossed Berrigan. She scooted with the money."

He was the original wrap-it-up-and-post-it boy. The theory had some merit; I was pretty sure I'd seen two figures at least in the park and the gun and the money couldn't have flown away. There were some things I didn't like about it though: I wasn't sure that the relationship between Berrigan and Noni would have permitted this development. I wasn't sure the girl would have been cool enough to pick up the money and gun and fade into the night. It looked full of holes, but perhaps I just didn't want to look failure squarely in the face as I'd have to do if I accepted Tobin's scenario. Ted Tarelton and Saul James were out a hundred and five thousand dollars and still no girl. I was out a few hundred myself. If I'd belonged to a professional association of private detectives, I'd have deserved drumming out. Carlton broke in on my musing.

"That the way you see it, Hardy?" The sneer was still on his face. It was also in his voice.

"Yeah. I suppose so." I hadn't told them about Coluzzi or the blacks or Noni's drug habit. They were little private pieces of worry that didn't need airing. Still, it didn't say much for Tobin's power of mind that he didn't ask how I'd got back from Newcastle or how I'd been spending my time. Mentally, I threw his theory out the window.

"Right," said Tobin. The word came out smugly. He turned to Carlton and waved him in like a football coach calling a reserve off the bench. "Jim, how do you see Hardy's position now?"

Carlton looked as sour as a green lemon. The look he shot at Tobin suggested that if the younger man ever got an inch out of line Carlton would pour it straight into the official ear sooner than he could spit. The enmity between them explained the unworkability of the team; Carlton too sour to be imaginative, Tobin too ambitious to be careful. It was a brilliant sadistic pairing and had to mean something within the police set-up. Not my problem.

Carlton glared at me. Cigarette ash had fallen on his waistcoat and his dark stubble was shadowing his cheeks and doubling his chin. He didn't look spruce and he knew it. He knew that I knew it. Tobin, elegantly arranged against the wall, looked fresh and bright. He got out a cigarette and lit it with a snap of that fancy lighter.

"I still don't like you, Hardy," Carlton grated. "Your type shouldn't be running around with licensed guns. You're a menace."

I let it pass. It was just guff, old, stale, defeated air. He took out a notebook and began checking items.

"One, failing to give information concerning a felony—the Simmonds killing. Two, failing to report a felony—the Baker woman. Three, conspiracy in a felony—this ransom balls-up."

"I'm illegally parked outside the station, too," I said.

Tobin grinned. He'd contrived to do all the smart talking himself and left the silly, hack stuff to his partner. Suddenly I felt vaguely sorry for Carlton and a sharp dislike for Tobin. But I had to stick with the strength. I shrugged and squashed out a cigarette I hadn't wanted when I'd made it.

"Book me on it, then. I'll call Cy Sackville and we can all go home to bed."

Carlton dusted off his hands to release some aggression and worked his body off the table. "Get out, Hardy. Piss off."

I held out my hand as I got to my feet. "Give me my gun back."

He shook his head. "No way. It's evidence for an enquiry. I might get you delicensed yet. Why? Do you need it to get from here to your cute little cottage?"

"You never know. I lead a dangerous life. That all, then?"

Carlton ignored the question and left the room. Tobin barred my way with a stiff arm across the door.

"Aah, you might mention to Evans that you got a fair shake here."

He was the second cop to ask me for the same favour in forty-eight hours. It made me feel like a pimp for a venereal whore. I brushed the arm down.

"I might," I said.

At lease he didn't thank me. I walked out of the station, got in the car and headed for where there would be consolations—cold, wet and alcoholic.

It was close to ten-thirty when I got home. I left the car in the street rather than do the fancy backing and filling it takes to get into the courtyard. The bushes and shrubs whose names I don't know were heavy with water and I got some of it on me as I brushed past them. A voice hissed my name from the shadows near the front door. I crouched and slapped my hand to where the gun should have been, then let it drop uselessly at my side. I was a sitting target, caught in the glow from the street light and my stomach lurched with the knowledge. Then she stepped out of the shadows, slender as a wand even wrapped up in a donkey coat.

"Mr. Hardy, it's Penny Sharkey."

She moved into the light and her finely-shaped head picked up a sort of aura. She was wet and breathing heavily; I should have heard that from the path, but it wasn't my night for professional standards.

My initial feelings were completely erotic. Extreme tiredness can do that to you. I wanted to hurry inside with her and let everything go to hell except sex. The fantasy lasted perhaps a tenth of a second before the veneers of civilisation and notions of professional conduct and God knows what other inhibitions crowded it out. I took hold of her arm and I could feel her shaking. I hung on hard, got the key in the lock and opened the door. She stumbled ahead of me into the passage and threw her hand up over her face when I turned on the light. I clutched her harder, perhaps out of fear that she'd run away, perhaps from lust. She wrenched her arm back and I felt that pain shoot along and affect her voice.

"You're hurting me!"

I said I was sorry and let her go. I went past her into the house turning on lights and leaving her to follow me if she wanted to. I opened the refrigerator and got out some wine.

"Drink?"

"Yes, thanks."

I poured the drink and set it down on the table. I didn't look at her too closely. I was conscious of the slenderness of my hold on her and she was the only tangible thing I had left of the Noni Tarelton case. If she was part of it at all. Suddenly I was sure that she was. She stood in the middle of the kitchen dripping water on the floor from the soaked nap of her coat. I sat down at the table.

"Take your coat off, Penny, and sit down. I'm sorry I hurt your arm, I've had a rough night and I'm not thinking too straight." I mustered up a smile from somewhere and made unbuttoning motions with my hands. She undid the coat, slipped out of it and dropped it over a chair. A stream of water ran off and made a pool on the floor. She sat down and drank three inches of wine in one steady pull. The tiny breasts pushed up under her white skivvy and I tried to distract myself with the wine. I drained my glass and poured some more. I held the flagon enquiringly.

"No, this'll do." She sipped the stuff as if it had a name and an age.

"Why are you here, Penny? What's going on? Sunday told me you wanted to contact me."

She curled her hands around the glass and wouldn't look at me.

"I saw Noni. Just by accident. In Balmain. I tried to tell you."

"Why didn't you call again?"

"I couldn't. They left the cafe. I rang Jimmy while they were eating."

"What were you doing in Balmain?"

"I got a job there, in a solicitor's office. I started yesterday. I won't have the job now, I haven't been in today."

"Why?"

"I've been looking for you, waiting for you."

"Why me?"

"I want to see Noni in a box. You said you'd let things work out the way they had to. Noni's with a man who'll kill her. I'm sure of it."

I described Berrigan and she nodded vigorously. "Yes, that's him!"

"Tell me what happened."

"I was in this cafe having coffee and reading the paper. I was hidden by the paper when they came in. They sat down a couple of tables away and ordered food. I could just hear what they were saying."

"Which was?"

"They were having an argument, about plans or something. His plans and her plans. And about money. I couldn't catch the details."

"Then what did you do?"

"I tried to get you through Jimmy. I got a bit closer to them when I came back . I was wearing these big shades and Noni didn't look at me. She wouldn't recognize me easily anyway. She hasn't seen me often enough."

"What did you hear this time? Where was this by the way?"

She named an all-night cafe on Darling Street. "I heard him say that if it all went alright they'd have the money anyway. She was saying they'd missed the money or something like that."

I drank wine and thought about the story. It sounded alright, a bit too pat perhaps but she'd had time to get it straight. It fitted the facts as far as I knew them but it didn't lead anywhere.

"Anything else?"

She drank some more of the wine, a little nervously, I thought. She stood up, went across to the coat on the chair and dipped into a pocket. She came up with some filter cigarettes and I lit one for her. She puffed at it and fiddled with the spent match.

"I know where he . . . where they're going after the plan is finished, whatever that is." She drew in smoke and expelled it through her finely-shaped dark brown lips. The hand holding the cigarette was shaking and she was staring at my face as if willing me to do what she wanted, including, maybe, believe her.

I tried to keep anxiety out of my voice. "Where would that be, Penny?"

"I'll tell you if you promise to take me with you and let me in on whatever happens."

I shook my head. "No, it could be rough. Besides, I'd have to search you for concealed weapons."

"Nothing like that," she said fiercely. "I promise. I just want to be there. I could help."

I was sure she wasn't telling me the whole truth, but I could only guess what she'd left out. I was sure that she didn't know of Berrigan's death. That meant we'd both be heading into a tricky situation with only partial knowledge of the background facts. That sounded like a recipe for misunderstandings and disaster. But in the plan that was slowly forming in my head she could certainly be a help. In fact, the more I thought about it, she was indispensible. I couldn't take her on without checking her story though. That done, I could risk it. I had to, anyway.

"Alright, I'll take you. Where?"

"Macleay. I know where in Macleay, too, but I'll tell you that when we get there."

I grinned. "You're an old pro. Fair enough, I'll check the flights." I got up and started to move out to the kitchen. "Got any money?" I said over my shoulder.

The airline informed me there was a flight north at seven-thirty a. m. I booked two seats. When I got back Penny had tipped the contents of a small embroidered purse over the table and had arranged things in piles. The money didn't amount to much of a pile. "Twenty three dollars, thirty eight cents," she said quietly.

"I've got about a hundred. We'll need more. I'll have to go out tonight and get some."

"Don't go out." I looked up, surprised at the different note in her voice. She was pushing her hair back with both hands. Her figure was lean and flat but definitely female. I felt the juices flowing again and she came around the table to where I'd sat down. She leaned over and pushed the wine away, then she bent and kissed me on the lips. She tasted fresh and salty like a clean stretch of sea on a clear day. I hooked my arm up around her neck and pressed her head down for another kiss, a long one. I felt my tiredness drop away. I felt eighteen years old and I wanted her. I stood up and put my arms around her. She was slim and firm like a young tree. It seemed to me as if my arms could go around her twice and I was feeling younger by the minute. I was hard and breathing fast and she was pressing her hips forward at me and then suddenly it felt all wrong. I was twice her age and a few years more, and she was alien and strange. The bones of her back felt fragile under my hands and I felt clumsy and old. I eased her away.

"It's not a good idea," I croaked.

She looked incredulously at me. "You want to, you're hard as a rock."

"I know, but I don't go to bed with teenagers. It doesn't mean I don't want to."

"Bullshit." She embraced herself, crossing her arms, and pulled off her skivvy. Her tight trousers had a silky sheen and they shimmered as she flipped out of them and let them slide to the floor. I watched her thumb down her pants and the hard, spare lines of her brown body cut off my breath. She squeezed her miniscule breasts together with the spread fingers of one hand.

"Come on, I like you." Her teeth shone in her beautiful dark face but her eyes were as hard as agate. I was suddenly aware that she was giving a performance, a good one but a cold one and I resisted the knowledge but it took over and gripped me. I reached for the wine.

"No," I said hoarsely. "Come back in five years."

She laughed a bit unsteadily. "Don't be silly. Where's your bed?"

She whipped around and I heard her feet dancing up the stairs. Carefully carrying a full glass of wine, I followed. She'd turned on a lamp in the bedroom and was bending to pull back the cover. In the lamp glow she looked like an Egyptian maiden of infinite grace performing some domestic task. She slid into the bed except for one bare arm which she arranged outside the covers and alongside her. She lifted the arm and let it fall.

"Get in."

She'd have tempted Gandhi and I knew that if I moved an inch toward the bed I was done for. I raised the glass and drank some.

"Go to sleep. If it's any consolation to you I'm going to get drunk."

I started back to the stairs. She was laughing when I reached them but the sound stopped very soon.

I didn't get drunk. Not then. I let myself quietly out of the house and caught a taxi back to Balmain. The all-night cafe was fighting the darkness with a pale, flickering neon sign and droning, toneless canned music. I pushed the door open and went in to the smells of burnt bread and over-fried oil. There were about ten tables in the place and solitary men sat at three of them. One of the men had his head on his arms and the other two weren't far off it. A heavily built man wearing a large apron came from the back of the place when the door slammed behind me. He went behind the counter and leaned forward over the espresso machine. His hair was black and curly above a round olive face. The thought crossed my mind that he was the same nationality as Coluzzi, but that's where the resemblance to that predator ended. This was a soft, comfortable man.

"Yes? You want something, sir?"

I asked for coffee and held out a five-dollar note. He pushed the cup over to me and I gave him the money.

"You can keep the change for a little information."

He held his fingers poised over the keys of the cash register like a typist waiting for her nails to dry.

"Information?"

"Nothing dangerous. Were you working here yesterday morning?"

"Sure, I own the place. I'm here all the time."

I handed him the picture of Noni Tarelton. He looked at it and shrugged.

"Maybe. Lots of girls like that around here."

Balmain, it's the only place to live. I described Berrigan to him and he nodded so hard his chin wobbled.

"Sure, sure, I remember now. Ears like this." He fanned his ears out the way Lorrain had; it must have happened to Berrigan all his life and it was a bad thing for a criminal to be so recognizable. He should have tried another trade.

"That's him. What did they do?'

"They had breakfast—eggs and toast and coffee."

"Did you hear them talking?"

"No, too busy."

"OK. Now this is the important part. Who else was here?"

He laughed with the rich, high notes of the Italian tenor. The guy slumped at the table jerked up and looked around, then his head fell back.

"I couldn't tell you, Mister, the place was full. It's my busy time like I said."

"I appreciate that, but you should remember this one—a black girl, young, very good-looking."

"Ah, the blackies, sure I remember them."

"Blacks? Did you say blacks?"

"Yeah. The girl, must be the one you mean, and a man, youngish fella, a tough guy."

I felt the excitement rise inside me. He pushed my coffee cup forward on the counter.

"It's getting cold."

"Forget it," I said, more sharply than I meant to. He looked offended and I picked up the cup and took a sip. "Terrific. Tell me about the girl and the man, what did they do?"

"Are you the police?"

"No, private enquiries. Look. I showed him the licence and drew another five out of my wallet.

"Is it about dope?" he asked quickly. "I hate dope, sloppy people, dirty . . ."

"So do I. Yes, dope's part of it. Just tell me about the girl and the man." To encourage him I finished the coffee. He pulled out a packet of Gitane filters and offered them to me. I refused and he shook one out and lit it; the acrid smoke overwhelmed the cooking smells and gave the place a conspiratorial, secretive atmosphere. I fiddled with the note, folding it and tapping it on the counter.

It got to him and he screwed up his eyes against the smoke, visibly searching his memory. "The man was here first, yeah, that's right. He had just had coffee, over there." He pointed to the deepest, darkest corner of the cafe. Then he thumped himself on the head and his curls bounced. "No, no, I've got it wrong. The girl, the blonde, and the man with the ears came in first. They sat here." He indicated a table near the door. "I didn't see the black come in. He must have come in the side door. It's open at the busy time." The cafe had a lane running beside it and a door let out onto the lane. I nodded and he went on: "He was just there, the toughie, in there where I said. I remember because he paid me when I brought him his coffee. That's not usual, you know?"

I knew, I said. "What about the dark girl?"

"She didn't stay, didn't buy anything. The blonde and the man with her paid and went, then the young guy went after them. The girl came in the front—they were all going out the side, see? She just went straight through after them. She came back here later and had coffee . . . yeah, I think it was her."

"You've got a good memory."

"I sing, opera you know? I have to remember the words and the movements. You like opera?

I hate it. "Yes," I said. I gave him the other five and he tucked it away in his apron.

"Thanks, I'll buy a lottery ticket. The big one, you know?"

"Yeah, good luck."

"It's bad luck for those people, isn't it?"

"Why do you say that?"

"Don't get me wrong, it's nothing personal, but I got a sense, you know? You're a bad luck man and the chair told me anyway. The one with the ears, he sat in the bad luck chair."

"What's that?"

"Don't let this get around, eh? But there's a chair in this place that's unlucky. People sit in it and they have bad luck. A friend of mine, his daughter died, and a woman I know, she got hit by a bus, right out there." He pointed out into the street. I took a last look around the cafe. Nobody had moved. Nothing had changed. It was just a little bit later and the air was a little bit staler. And for the men at the tables the park was just so much nearer.

"Why don't you move the chair?" I said.

"I do, every day. It's over there now." He waved his hand with the cigarette in it to the far wall. "You think I'm superstitious?"

I shrugged. "I don't know, could be. Why don't you try an experiment?"

He looked interested. "Like what?"

"Try the chair on someone you don't like."

"There's no one I don't like that much."

"You're lucky. I've got to go. Thanks for the help. Goodnight."

"Goodnight, Mr. Hardy."

He was quick. I grinned at him and went out.

The house was quiet when I got home. The bedroom let out a soft glow and Penny's coat and clothes were still in the kitchen. I tossed the clothes onto a chair and fought down the impulse to go upstairs. I needed help in the fight so I rooted around and found a bottle of rum, half-full. I got out ice and chopped up lemons and settled down in the front room with the bottle and the fixings. I worked steadily through the liquor and started on *Flashman* for the third time. I remember reading "Possibly there has been a greater shambles in the history of warfare than our withdrawal from Kabul . . ." and taking another drink of the rum and thinking what a shambles the Tarelton case was in and then nothing more. The couch was big enough and soft enough and I was drunk enough. I slept.

20

When I woke up Penny was standing over me with a cup of something emitting steam in her hand. I groaned and pulled myself up on the couch. I took the cup and sipped it. Instant coffee. Not the worst thing for my head just then but not the best. I ungummed my eyelids a second time, enough to see Penny had put her clothes back on. Not that it mattered. I was in no condition to take her up on her offer of the night before if she should repeat it. Her hair was damp from the shower and her skin shone like polished copper.

"You look terrible," she said.

"Thanks. What's the time?"

"Six-thirty. The taxi's due at seven. You've got time for a shower."

"Thanks again." I set the coffee down on the arm of the couch and swung my feet off it. My head rang like a J. Arthur Rank gong. I headed unsteadily for the shower. The water helped a bit. I felt better still after a shave and ready for a drink after I'd dressed. In the kitchen Penny was sinking a big fat tooth into a piece of toast. I shuddered when she offered me some and got the white wine out of the fridge. When a tall glass of riesling and soda was fizzing in my hand I felt well enough to compliment her.

"Don't work in offices. Go on television, advertise things, make yourself some money."

"I might," she said and knocked back half a pint of orange juice.

Carrying the drink with me I went from place to place

collecting things. I packed a cassette tape recorder and a pair of binoculars into an overnight bag. An old credit card Ailsa's firm had issued me and not cancelled went into my wallet and an unlicensed Colt automatic went into the lining of the parka where the .38 had been. She had her coat on and the glasses and plates cups were rinsed and stacked when the taxi honked outside. We went out of the house into a neutral and uncertain dawn.

We preserved silence on the drive to Mascot. The airport preliminaries weren't any more complicated than usual and I still had a few dollars left after buying tickets, papers, and magazines. Unlike most people, Penny was easy to travel with; she was there when she was needed and not in the way when she wasn't. We got looks, usual I suppose for couples of mixed colour: half curiosity, half hostility. Penny noticed me glowering at the lookers.

"Don't worry," she said, taking my arm, "your lot have been staring at us since you got here."

Flying was a novelty for her and she enjoyed the rituals of it all. I sat in my seat and obeyed orders slavishly out of some dark belief that this would keep me safe. When we were airborne Penny stared out of the window at the few flashes of green and brown that showed through that high-flying fog. We were half a hundred people flying blind, trusting our lives to a few fuses and valves. I tried to concentrate on the papers but couldn't. Penny read in a desultory fashion for a while and then I felt her go tense beside me. I sneaked a look across and she was gnawing her lip.

"What's wrong?"

"I'm frightened "

"Of flying?"

"No." She waved strong men's traumas away with one thin hand. "No, of course not. It's nothing, flying. I thought it would be more exciting. It must be boring after the first time."

I nodded. "Well then . . . ?"

"All this. How's it going to end? You haven't even told me what's happening."

"You're holding out on me, too."

"Where they're going? I told you I'll tell you in Macleay." She glanced around the cabin. "I suppose I can tell you now. We're not going anywhere else."

"It can wait," I said sharply. "I think I know anyway. No, you're holding back something else, but I'm not going to press you. In fact I 'll tell you things and not ask for anything from you. OK?"

"Why?" she said warily.

"I have reasons. Partly because I have to. I want you to do something for me and it won't make sense unless you know what's going on."

I filled her in on some of the details—on the ransoms for Noni and who paid them and how the police were in on the whole thing now. I didn't tell her about Berrigan's death or about "Percy White." She'd heard a little about Coluzzi and the fight game from friends. I expanded on that a bit and kept away from the subject of Ricky Simmonds until I mentioned Trixie Baker. Penny looked interested in the name.

"I've heard of her," she said, "from Ricky I think. Doesn't she have a farm or something?"

"That's right, just out of Macleay. Ricky talked about her?"

The smooth brown skin on her forehead wrinkled. "I think so, once when he was a bit drunk, not so much about her as about someone who worked for her, one of us."

"An Aborigine?"

She snorted. "I don't mean a Hottentot."

"OK, OK, keep your hair on. What did he say about this person of your own race?"

She looked at me to decide whether to take offence or not but I'd arranged my face in its most winning shape and she let it pass.

"I told you Ricky always seemed to be looking for

158

someone. Well, I asked him about it this time, when he was full and he said 'I'm sure that was him, at Trixie Baker's' or something like that. I didn't push him, it didn't make sense to me. Does it mean anything to you?"

"I think so. Ricky was looking for his father, I reckon. I think his father and Berrigan robbed a bank in Macleay in 1966. Berrigan was connected with Trixie Baker, maybe Ricky's father was too. Perhaps Ricky got a lead on him but couldn't clinch it. Anyway, this is where you come in—I have to ask the Baker woman some questions and I haven't got a chance in a million of getting in to see her."

"Why?"

"The police already dislike me for leaving the scene of the crime—her bashing that is. I did, but I had no choice. That's sort of been squared now in a way, but I'll still be very unpopular around Macleay."

"What do you want me to do?"

"Done any acting?"

"A bit, street theatre, black theatre stuff."

"That'll do—this is a cinch for you. I'm going to get hold of a hospital cleaner's uniform. Dressed up in that you should be able to sneak around the hospital and find Trixie Baker. It can't be a big place. I want you to take this in," I tapped the bag with the tape recorder inside, "and ask her some questions. The right answers will sort this mess out. Will you do it?"

She seemed about to ask a question, an important question, but she bit it back.

"Yes," she said quickly, "of course I will."

"There's another thing. Is there anyone in Kempsey, one of you, I mean, who'd know all about the Aborigines in the area—who's who and when and where?"

She didn't have to think. "Yes, Charley Gurney, he was initiated, he's old, a clever man. That means . . ."

"I know what it means. I've read Elkin. Would you take me to see him?"

She nodded. "Anything else?"

159

"That's all for now, except to warn you that you're in for a rough time. I expect all this to sort out, but I don't expect it'll come out neat and pretty."

She shrugged. "We'll see."

"Yeah." I picked up her hand. In my yellowed, scarred claw it looked like a soft brown orchid. "I'm sorry as hell I had to refuse you last night, I didn't want to."

"You were right, I think, but I'm sorry too."

I put her hand back on the seat rest. "It's better we didn't because we're on opposite sides of this even if you do help me. I want to get Noni Tarelton back home to her rich Dad in one piece and you're not going to stop me. I'll flatten you if you try."

She looked quickly at me. I wasn't smiling and neither was she. It was a risky declaration because the help she would be giving me would be substantial and things could get into a hell of a mess without it. Maybe they would anyway. She had a right to know the rules I was playing by but I hoped it wouldn't come to an outright conflict between us. She had strength and guts and would fight hard. Also there was something between us, a connection, part sexual, part temperamental. It would be a nasty falling-out if it happened.

The plane swayed around like a mast in a high wind on the last hour of the flight and Penny didn't seem quite so blasé about flying. I didn't enjoy it myself and then I had to face a moment of tension when I presented the out-of-date credit card at the car hire desk. It passed muster and there was a white Datsun waiting for us in the company bay outside the airport building. The air was warm and dusty. A haze in the sky suggested that the day would get a lot warmer. I unlocked the driver's door and threw the bag into the back seat. Penny stood by the passenger door sneering at me as if I was some inferior and unpleasant exhibit in a zoo. I didn't like that look. I settled myself in the seat and turned on the air-conditioning. She tapped on the window. I wound it down.

"Yes?" I said

"Let me *in*, Hardy."

"A girl like you wouldn't ride in a big, fat, Nip capitalist car like this would she? Take a bus, I'll meet you behind the pub."

Her eyes blazed at me and I could hear her breath coming in short, hard bursts.

"Let me *in!*"

I flicked the door open, she got in and sat down hard staring straight in front of her. It was a bad start.

"Don't be so touchy," she said.

"I'm sorry. Look, we need a car for this job. They're all rubbish, they're all too expensive and they fall apart too soon, but we need one and this'll do. Alright?"

"Yes," her voice was tight and small.

I swung the beast out of the car park. I wanted to tell her to get ready for some lying and shooting, but I didn't know how.

We drove in silence along the dusty roads into Macleay. I hadn't liked being there the last time and I didn't expect this time to be any better. Penny sat with her arms wrapped tightly around her thin body as if trying to physically contain her resentments. The car handled well, a bit squashy and soft compared with the Falcon, but it would be fast if that was needed. The air-conditioning worked, cooled me down and smoothed the edges off my temper. Penny took her coat off and threw it on the back seat. We exchanged small smiles as she did so. She hit the radio button and got some country and western music which she turned down very low.

I drove into Macleay and cruised slowly past Bert's garage. Penny looked out at the place with the rough-painted sign hanging over the petrol pumps and nodded. "You *did* know where they were going."

"Yeah. The thing is, are they still there?" The garage looked closed although it was after ten a.m. and a piece of cardboard with something written on it was hanging on the handle of the office door. I drove past again and could see at least two cars parked in the alley beside the garage. I found a phone booth and located Bert's number in the directory. I called it. The phone rang twice, then it was answered by the voice I'd heard telephonically at Ted Tarelton's. I asked for Bert and was told he was sick. I asked when his place would be open again and the voice said "tomorrow." He hung up.

The way to the hospital was signposted and the building couldn't have been anything else; it was like hospitals everywhere, all clean lines, light and airy, set in lawns and trying not to look like a place where people died. We parked in the visitors' area and Penny got out of the car. "Wait here," she told me.

I did as I was told. I rolled a cigarette and fiddled with the tape recorder. It seemed to be working alright, drawing power from the batteries and responding to all buttons. I smoked and waited while the morning heated up. Sweat was soaking my collar when Penny got back. She climbed in and unrolled a bundle.

"Chic, isn't it?"

She held up a pale green, front-buttoning, belted dress with yellow piping.

"Terrific. Your size?"

"Close enough. We'll have to go back to town, I'll need a scarf and some sneakers."

We drove back to the shopping centre and bought the things and a pillow case and a plastic bucket. On the way there I showed her how the tape recorder worked. She nodded, wrapped the machine in the pillow case and put it in the bucket. She changed clothes in the back of the car and left her platform soles, slacks and top on the back seat with her coat. I drove to the service entrance of the hospital and let her out. She stood beside the car while I told her what I wanted to learn from Trixie Baker. I gave her two hours and she didn't argue about it. She pointed to a park bench near a small copse artfully contrived by a landscape gardener.

"There, in two hours." The sheer confidence in her voice made me look at her carefully. She'd moved into the role already, her shoulders were slumped and she carried the bucket as if she'd forgotten it was there. The uniform and the scarf and the sneakers toned her down. She'd pass as a menial as long as nobody got a good look at her fierce, alert face and beautifully tended nails. She slouched across to the heavy plastic doors of the service entrance and slipped through.

I drove slowly back into town, turning the next steps over in my mind, looking for snags and dangers. There were dozens of both. It took me nearly half an hour to pick my spot from which to watch Bert's garage. Behind the building and across a narrow lane was a shop that had been burnt out. The blackened brick shell still stood and an iron staircase took me up to the second story which was intact apart from many missing floorboards. Crouched by the back window I could get a good view through the binoculars of the back doors and windows of the garage.

It was hot, boring work. I didn't want to send smoke up into the still air in case the watched were also watching and I hadn't brought the cooler and the chilled beer with me. For a while nothing happened and as my eyes adjusted to the light and the shadows and shapes I began to be aware of a fine mist drifting out from one of the windows. Coming from a motor garage that could mean only one thing—spray painting. This was confirmed when a man wearing overalls came out into the yard pushing painter's goggles up onto his head. He was short and stocky and dark—very dark.

He took a few deep breaths and some more mist came floating out of the open door behind him. Then he ducked back into the garage and came back a minute later with a welder's torch. He gave it a few experimental blasts and took it back inside. The set-up wasn't too hard to figure and I had to admire it. You've got a hundred thousand or so dollars in ready money but it might be marked. You've got cops in Sydney and Newcastle looking for you. And you're black. So what do you do? Fix up a truck, really fix it up with bars and secret compartments and a new spray job and take to the roads. Get out into the bush where you can camp, spend the money carefully, spinning it out, while the heat dies down. You can come out in Perth or Darwin or wherever the hell you please. Not bad. It was a pity to disturb it but I had to. Fixing a truck in the way I imagined they'd be fixing it would take time and that was what I needed.

I watched for another hour but nothing changed. I fiddled with the adjustment mechanisms of the glasses, trying to get a clearer focus on an oil drum near the back door of the garage. Something about that drum disturbed me, but it was in shadow and I couldn't pick out any details. I backed away from the window and went down the staircase and out to the car. My shirt was a wringing wet rag when I got there and I took it off and draped it over the roof of the car while I rolled and smoked a cigarette. The shirt was hot and stiff after a couple of minutes. I put it back on and drove to the hospital.

Penny was waiting on the seat when I drove up. She ran across to the car and threw the bucket savagely into the back.

"Easy," I said. Then I noticed that she was carrying the tape recorder. I took it from her and settled it gently on the seat. "How did it go?"

"No trouble," she said tightly. She got into the back seat and began changing her clothes. I resisted the temptation to watch her in the rear vision mirror. She stuffed the uniform, sneakers and scarf into the bucket and clambered over into the front seat. She put the tape recorder on her lap and patted it.

"Want to hear it?"

"Not now. How's Trixie Baker?"

"Bad. I don't think she wants to live."

"Upset about all this?" I nodded at the machine.

"Not really. I think she's a bit relieved it's all come out."

"How about you?"

"Doesn't change anything for me. What have you been doing?"

"Watching the garage. They'll be there till night time I

164

reckon. We've got time to see the clever man, how do we find him?"

"Stop the first boong we see and ask." I looked quickly at her. The hospital encounter had got to her and the tough indifference was a pose. Her features were all drawn tight and there was tension in every line of her body. The bitter remark was hard to interpret. I had too little experience of her moods, but she was seething inside, fighting some deep battles in which her pride and her colour and her loyalties were all taking a hand.

21

We picked up some sandwiches in town and Penny talked briefly to an Aboriginal girl in the shop while she was waiting for the food. I lurked in the car. About fifty pairs of male eyes followed her as she trotted across to where I was parked. She got in and handed me a paper bag.

"Thanks. Got the address?"

"Yes, and directions. You'd better get moving. It's out of town a fair way."

We ate as I drove. I wanted a drink badly and said so.

"You'll have to pick up some grog for the old man anyway," she said. I could hear the disapproval in her voice. Drink for her was synonymous with broken heads and blood or maudlin sentimentality that wasn't the same thing as love. Nothing to show for the rent money but a reeking breath. I'd seen it too but managed to overcome the prejudice. I stopped at a pub on the outskirts of town and bought a dozen bottles of beer. I cracked one and swigged it as I followed Penny's directions. Her voice, as she gave them, was muted with contempt.

We got clear of the streets and houses and passed through a strip of forest and a patch of fifty-acre farmlets. The road got dusty and narrow and when a couple of vehicles came from the other direction, I had to put the bottle down and steer cautiously. We went over a hill and crossed a bridge across a sluggish creek. Around the bend a small weatherboard cottage appeared. Its front gate was about three feet back from the side of the road. I swung the car down a rutted track that ran along beside the house. An ancient Holden ute was parked under a lean-to at the end of the track. Rusted car bodies and unidentifiable bits of ironware lay around like corpses. A thick bush grew all over the place; it straggled up the peeling walls of the house and ran around the front and tackled the decrepit verandah.

We got out of the car and Penny put her hand on my shoulder.

"Let me do the talking. I'll have to introduce myself and that'll take a while."

"What about the beer?"

"Leave it in the car for the moment. Tobacco will do for now."

We went around to the front of the house. The verandah boards creaked under my weight but held. Penny knocked on the door. The house wore a guarded, cautious air with curtains drawn across the narrow windows and a blind pulled down over the glass pane in the door. Penny knocked again and we heard shuffling footsteps inside. The blind flew up and an old, thin Aborigine looked at us through the glass. His deep-set eyes ran over Penny and then pierced into my face. I had to look away. His eyes were like lasers searing through to the back of my skull. He released the door catch and pulled the door inward.

"Gidday. Come in." His voice was like the rest of him, smoky dark and seamed with experience. He wore grey trousers and a white shirt pressed into razor sharp creases. Veins and sinews stood out in his arms like a network of thin ropes. The verandah and the floor of the house were on a level. So were his eyes and mine. That made him six feet and half an inch tall. I wondered if I would still measure that in my seventies. He ushered us through to a small sitting room occupied by a threadbare couch and some old padded chairs, a scrubbed pine table and a glass-fronted case. Penny and I sat on the couch and he lowered himself into one of the chairs; his feet were bare so he was taller than me. His hair was thick and grey, waving over his neat skull like a finely worked helmet. I searched my memory for the face his reminded me of and got it—Robert Graves. He had the same beaky nose and sunken eyes, old as time.

Penny set about introducing herself. It involved references to Auntie this and Auntie that and towns in this part of New South Wales and gatherings held over the past twenty years. Gurney nodded and smiled at the familiar names. While this was going on I looked around the room; the case held photographs, elaborately framed, and sporting trophies. There was a picture of the Queen on the wall above the fireplace. Penny finished talking and the old man leaned back in his chair and beamed at her with what looked like a full set of genuine teeth.

"Well, I'm pleased to meet you, girlie. I never knew your dad but I heard of him. Who's your friend?"

I got up and leaned forward, sticking my hand out. "Cliff Hardy, Mr. Gurney. Glad to know you."

We shook. His hand was as hard as iron and a joint of his little finger was missing.

"Hardy, eh? What's your game, Cliff?"

I told him and rolled a cigarette while I spoke. I offered him the makings and he took them.

"Thanks. How can I help you?"

"Penny here tells me that you know all there is to know about the Aboriginal people in this district."

"S'right. Lived here all me life, never been to Sydney even. I was put through up by Burnt Bridge in 1919."

"Initiated? Can't be many around like you."

"I'm the last one." He got his cigarette going and pierced

me through again with those eyes. "What do you want me to tell you?"

"All you can about Albie Simmonds."

"Albie in trouble?"

I nodded.

"What sort of trouble?"

"Bad. Kidnapping. Gun trouble."

"Why should I help you? You huntin' him?"

"Not exactly. I want the girl he took. If I know certain things maybe I can stop more people from being killed. Two men're dead already."

"Albie kill 'em?"

"I don't know. I don't think so. That's one of the things I've got to find out."

He leaned back and blew smoke at the roof. There wasn't an ounce of spare flesh on him; his belly was flat and the skin around his throat and jaw stretched smooth and tight. He had authority. If he'd said no and told me to leave I'd have gone. He was that sort of man.

I felt as if he was putting me through some kind of test only I didn't know the rules and the proper way to conduct myself. I sat there and tried to look honest and strong. He looked at me so long I thought he was going into a trance. Then he came out of it and nodded sharply.

"All right." He took a draw on the cigarette. "I can tell you a bit about Albie. Mind you, he's had a few names in his time. Not too many people know him as Albie Simmonds."

"Percy White?"

"That's one. Terrible man for the grog, Albie, that's no secret."

"That reminds me, I've got some beer in the car, would you like some?"

"Too right."

"I'll get it," Penny said. She left the room. Gurney watched her appreciatively. So did I. I wondered if he lived alone. There was no sign of a woman's touch in the room we were in.

"Where d'you want me to start?"

"Just tell me about Albie, from the beginning."

"Yeah, well, Albie wasn't a bad lad. Too much grog around the family always, but that wasn't his fault. He got into bad company and a fair bit of trouble with the coppers. Small stuff though."

"Is he a full blood Aborigine?"

"Pretty nearly. Like me. Why do you ask?"

"His boy, Ricky, wasn't very dark, I just wondered . . . what about his mother?" He looked at me again, as if he was testing the quality, the very grain of me. "Nellie? Half and half," he said slowly.

"I see. Go on, Mr. Gurney."

"Albie moved around a bit . . . up here . . . Sydney. Couldn't settle. Nellie just had the one kid, Ricky, and she died young. The boy went to people in Sydney."

"Did Albie see much of his son?"

"No."

"Why not?"

"That's something you'd have to ask him."

"Fair enough. Did Albie work for Trixie Baker?"

"Sort of—aah good girl!" Penny came back into the room with a tray. Two open beer bottles were on it and three glasses. She poured a glass for the old man and half a glass for herself. I filled a glass and we all said cheers and drank. The beer was warmer than it should be but still not bad. Gurney sighed and emptied the glass in three long gulps. He filled it again and watched the head rise and settle.

"Where was I? Albie and Trixie, yeah. You couldn't say Albie worked for her, he was a mess then, drinking fierce. He was calling himself Carter then—this is a few years ago."

"Why all the names?"

"Police trouble, I s'pose. We all knew who he was but the whites around didn't. It's a bit like that up here."

"Do you know if his son got in touch with him at that time?"

"He tried."

"What happened?"

"Albie ducked him, went bush."

"Why?"

"I'm not sayin'. Personal to them."

"I suppose you won't tell me about Albie's relationship with Trixie Baker either?"

"That's right. Sorry. I haven't been much help. I will say this, you seem to know a thing or two about Albie and the boy."

"Not enough."

"You know some. It's dangerous. I'd keep out of it if I was you."

"I can't." I finished the beer and got up. Penny had hardly touched hers and she didn't give it a glance now. She shook hands with Gurney and he and I exchanged nods. I'd intruded too far on a matter that excluded whites or should, in his view. It was too delicate to be trusted to me with my clumsy, money-motivated ways. He'd decided that and exercised just as much of his authority as he needed to keep the knowledge from me. He knew that I'd go on, that he couldn't stop me. He accepted that, but he didn't want to shake my hand again.

"Thanks for the beer," he grunted.

I said something polite and we trooped down the passage and out into the raw sunlight.

"Not very helpful," Penny said as we walked to the car.

"Could have been worse. I got some things out of it by implication."

"Trixie Baker told me she and Albie Simmonds were lovers. It's on the tape."

I nodded. "I thought so."

We got in the car and I noticed that three of the beer bottles were still on the seat. I pointed to them.

"That was for him."

"Not good for him."

"I know what he'd say to that. Has he got a wife by the way?"

She grinned. "I heard he has three."

We drove off and Penny yawned a couple of times and knuckled her eyes. I pulled over under a tree and stopped.

"Have a sleep if you want to. I'm going to listen to the tape."

She nodded, took her coat with her out of the car and settled herself on the grass using it as a pillow. I made a cigarette and lifted the top off one of the beer bottles. The liquid frothed out and the stuff left behind was warm but I sipped at it anyway. I pushed the "play" button.

PENNY: "Mrs. Baker, can you hear me?"

VOICE: "Yes, I can hear you, who're you?"

PENNY: "My name is Sharkey, Penny Sharkey. You don't know me, but I know who hit you—Berrigan."

BAKER: "How do you know that, I never told . . ."

PENNY: "I'm working with a man who knows all about it. He wants to fix Berrigan, will you help?"

BAKER: "I dunno, Berrigan . . . he might come back . . ."

PENNY: "Hardy says he won't. He guarantees it."

BAKER: "Hardy? Never heard of him. What is he, a cop?"

PENNY: "He's a private detective . . ."

BAKER: "Shit, no, nothing doing . . ."

PENNY: "I trust him."

BAKER: "Well, good for you . . . Something about you. Can't see with all these bloody bandages. What are you, a darkie?"

PENNY: "I'm an Aborigine, yes."

BAKER: "I like Abos, good people. I had a good man once. (Cackling laugh) Could be one of your tribe— Albie Simmonds, know him?"

PENNY: "I knew Ricky, his son."

BAKER: "That right? Well, well." (Laughter) "Yeah, well that's another story. What's in this for you, girlie?"

171

PENNY: "I want Noni."

BAKER: "How's that?"

PENNY: "Noni Tarelton. She's with Berrigan now. I hope he kills her. Anyway, she's up to her neck in this. She'll go to jail if I have anything to do with it."

BAKER: "Now you're talking! That slut Noni. Tarelton you call her? She was Rouble when she was fucking everything in sight round her. You reckon this Hardy's good, he'll get Berrigan?"

PENNY: "I'm sure of it, but he needs to know the story to put the pressure on. I don't really understand it myself Mrs. Baker, I just have to ask you some things."

BAKER: "All right, ask away."

PENNY: "You've answered one—you and Albie Simmonds were lovers?"

BAKER: "Yeah, when he was off the grog."

PENNY: "Hardy said to ask you about the bank job, Simmonds and Berrigan, Noni and the money."

BAKER: (Laughter) "Shit, he does know a thing or two. Smart bugger is he? Alright, this is it. Joey and Albie did the job. Fifty thousand they got. Nearly killed them. Well, me and Joey weren't getting on so well, on account of me and Albie, see? They gave me the money, but Joey got real rough one night and I decided to do him. I got Noni to get off with him and charge him with rape. I paid her a hundred dollars." (Laughter) "Funny thing, I never had to pay her all of it because she got put away for moral danger, you know?"

PENNY: "Yes."

BAKER: "Well, Joey got sent away. Albie went to see him. They'd been mates for years, and I don't know what Joey told him, like, but Albie wasn't never the same again. He went on the grog like you've never seen. He took his boy to Sydney. Nellie, the mother, she was dead by this time, and he stayed down himself a while. He came back from time to time but he was never much good. Nice bloke though, Albie. What's his son like?"

PENNY: "Bit wild."

BAKER: "Yeah? Albie was quiet, real quiet, drunk or sober."

I stopped the machine, re-wound the tape and played the last two passages again to make sure I had it right. Then I let the tape run on.

PENNY: "What about the money?"

BAKER: "I moved it, got about thirty thousand for it. I sat on it for a while, then I got the farm and started to set up . . . you know about that?"

PENNY: "No."

BAKER: "Doesn't matter then. Oh shit, this pain in the side of me head, I can't stand it."

PENNY: "Are they giving you something for it?"

BAKER: "Yeah, doesn't help though. I reckon I've got something bad. Growth or something. They won't listen, nobody'll listen . . ."

PENNY: "Why did you stay here? You must have known Berrigan would come back."

BAKER: "Yes, I did. Well, I've got some money put away. I was going to give it to him, it'd be his share of the job nearly. And there's big money coming. Was, anyway, before this. But I hadn't reckoned on him looking up the girl and finding out it was me set him up, see? It's a long time ago but he was wild, crazy. When I didn't have the whole fifty grand to give him he went off his head. Noni just watched while he worked on me. Christ it hurt, still hurts . . . Well, that's it, that's what your man wanted to know?"

PENNY: "I suppose so. Is there . . . anything else?"

BAKER: "No. That's enough isn't it? Jesus what a mess. He wouldn't let me explain. I wonder if Albie seen him?"

PENNY: "Do you think he might have, Mrs. Baker?"

BAKER: "Ah, I dunno. Albie was up here not long ago. He was talking about Joey and his boy. Pissed, though. Didn't make much sense."

PENNY: "I'll have to go. Don't worry, Mrs. Baker, I'm sure nothing will happen to you."

BAKER: "Good luck to you, girlie, you're game. I'm not worried . . . doesn't matter . . . I'm not going to leave here alive anyway."

22

I woke Penny up and we got on the road again. I was tired and edgy from the heat and the traveling and the unraveling of people's private lives. And this was just the beginning; the real sortings-out were ahead. I smoked and the tobacco tasted like old spinach. Penny looked at me as I swore and threw the butt away.

"What's the matter?" she said. "Is the tape alright?"

"The tape's fine. I feel lousy."

She looked and smelled fresh. The breeze was in her Afro mop and there wasn't a drop of sweat on her.

"Too much beer," she said shortly. "Have you thought what you're going to do next?" She clicked her tongue. "I can't see how that tape will help you."

I wasn't quite sure myself. It had confirmed things I'd sensed, things about a quiet, dark man who'd dumped his son, parted ways with another man and gone to pieces. Twelve years ago. If I was going up against a talking situation the more I knew the better. Trouble was, it might be a shooting situation. I was afraid of that; I didn't trust Penny not to do something independent and dangerous under those conditions. I considered calling in the cops but rejected the idea quickly. To do that would up the chances of shooting starting. That is, if the cops didn't just run me straight out of town. Macleay cops would feel about an armed private detective wandering about with an Aboriginal girl calling in on the hospital and the black citizens, like they would about a drop in pay. I didn't say anything. I thought and sulked and drove.

It was nearly four when we got back into town; long shadows were starting to drape themselves over the streets and the air had cooled. The sky was like a sheet of pale blue silk stretched over the frame of the world. It would be a good night for taking a walk, or going to a drive-in or doing almost anything other than what I had to do. I drove up the back street and stopped by the derelict shop.

"We watch for a minute from there," I told Penny.

"Then what?"

"I'll phone the place and start bargaining."

"For Noni," she sneered.

"Right. Come on."

The street was empty. A factory faced the shop from across the road and nothing seemed to be going on there. I grabbed the binoculars and got out of the car. Penny followed me as I picked my way through the rubble of the shop's ground level. I took a quick look at the back of the garage before going up the staircase and what I saw made me stop in my tracks. Penny bumped into me and swore.

"Shut up," I hissed. "I don't like this."

"What?"

"See that car, the yellow one?"

The yellow Mini was parked at the back of the garage. I could see the tape holding the rear window together. I'd seen the car before—in the street outside Saul James's terrace house in Darlinghurst.

"I see the Mini. So what?"

"It belongs to Noni's boyfriend, actor named James. He's the last person I need around just now."

"Isn't that nice?" she purred, "Noni's boyfriend. Tough character is he?"

I laughed. "Just the reverse. Soft as mush."

"Is he in on it, the kidnapping?"

"I can't see how." I considered it. "No, no chance. He's blundered into it somehow and it screws it all up."

"How?"

"He's a potential hostage for one thing, and if he was thinking of coming up here he might have told someone else. He might have told Tarelton. The army could be on the way.

"Your precious Noni could get hurt," she crooned.

I lost my temper and rounded on her. "Drop it, Penny! This is serious, I've got bad feelings about what's going on in there. It's not just Noni who might get killed. Another man's dead, anyway."

"Who?" There was panic in her voice. "What are you talking about, who's dead?"

I got myself under control and felt disgust at my outburst, but it was too late to play secrets. "It's time to come clean, Penny, to stop the games. I'll tell you something you don't know. Berrigan's not in there. He's dead. He was shot in a park in Balmain the other night. I know because I was there, in fact the police think I did it. Now I'll tell you something you *think* I don't know. Ricky Simmonds is in that garage."

I heard the quick intake of her breath and felt her stiffen beside me.

"How did you know?" she said softly.

"I wasn't sure until I checked at the cafe. You saw Noni and Berrigan alright. You also saw Ricky. I didn't think you'd go through all this just for revenge on Noni. Ricky's your obsession—which is worse luck for you."

"Why?"

"Remember you told me he seemed to be looking for someone, a young man?"

"Yes."

"He was looking for his father. That's alright, nothing wrong with that. But who do you think it was who got shot at Bare Island? Who do you think shot him and why?"

176

She was silent and another voice cut in from behind us.

"Don't let it worry you, Penny."

We turned together, he held the rifle steadily on the centre of my chest and it wasn't far away, not a fraction of a second away. My gun was in the car, light years away, the binoculars were on the staircase where I'd put them when I spotted James's car. He was standing with his feet nicely spaced in a clear spot. I was off balance on a pile of rubble. Penny stirred beside me. The rifle didn't waver but his voice was sharp and menacing.

"Easy, Pen, easy. I don't want to hurt you."

"But you will if you have to," I said.

"That's right, mister. I got nothing to lose now. I been waiting for you. Saw you last time—who are you anyway?"

"Let's go inside and talk about it." I tried to get balance and a better foothold but I was kidding myself. There's something about a couple of feet of rifle barrel and the black hole at the end that stiffens your muscles and throws your hand-eye co-ordination to hell. I just stood there. All I could do was talk.

"We have to go inside," I said. "You can't shoot us here. How's James? How's Bert?"

He ignored the remarks and made his decision.

"Go out through the back door and up to the fence. I swear I'll blow your head open if you try anything. Sorry, Pen, you too."

We went. The yard at the back of the shop was a rubbish heap—bottles and deadly missiles by the hundred—but I believed he'd do what he said and I tried to look as innocent as a man on a golf course. The back fence was missing palings and there were plenty of places for a person to step through it.

"That's far enough," Ricky snapped. "Perce!"

He yelled the name again and the man I'd seen before came out the door carrying a sawn-off shotgun, double-barrelled. The stock had been cut back too and was wound around with black insulation tape. It wasn't for rabbits.

"Get through. You first, Pen. Nice and easy."

Penny slipped through and I bent and followed her. This brought me to within a few feet of the man with the shotgun. He was fiftyish and every day of it showed in his face which was lined and creased like an old boxing glove. His body was thick, still strong-looking but with the mark of thousands of measures of alcohol on it. His hands seemed to be shaking slightly and that was even more frightening than Ricky's steely strength. I shot a look at James's car. It was dusty and travel-stained; its bright cheerful yellow was dimmed but still incongruous in the surroundings. I wondered what had brought the owner here and how he was coping; how his stagey manners were standing up to the real-life situation.

I half turned and spoke to Ricky who'd come through the fence with the rifle still nicely poised for use. I nodded at the car.

"Why's he here?"

"Christ knows." It was the first indication that he wasn't in total control, with everything figured out. Maybe that was a good sign, maybe not. I told myself it was. Perce moved aside and we went out of the fading sunlight into the near night of the workshop. Before we went inside I saw close-up what had disturbed me during my earlier, apparently incompetent, surveillance. By the door there was a cut-down oil drum with a crank handle sticking out of it. A cloud of flies buzzed around the metal shaft and the top of the drum.

I wasn't prepared for her; I'd chased her up and down the coast and looked at her picture and talked to a dozen people about her, but I still wasn't ready for the impact of her. She was taller than I expected, leaning against Bert's workbench, and somehow more vivid. Her hair was a dark blond tangle and she had one of the most passionate faces I'd ever seen. The high cheekbones were startling and the mouth was a wide, sensual slash. Her face was pale with the imprint of tension and lack of sleep. Her eyes were dark, shadowed pools. She was wearing a white dress, street-length and cut very low in front. It was spattered all over with something dark and I thought I knew why the flies were gathering outside. She took a few steps toward us as we came into the garage and her movements were like something from an adolescent's daydream. I could understand the depth of Penny's hate and the quality of Madeline Tarelton's feeling about Noni. She wasn't a woman's woman.

If she was a man's woman she certainly wasn't Saul James's. He sat on a chair a few feet away from Noni. He had on his usual beige outfit and his beige look. The girl washed him out completely; his eyes were fixed on her as she moved, but you had the feeling that he could disembowel himself there and then and she wouldn't notice.

"Well, well, well. Little Penny the La Perouse picaninny." Her voice was husky, edged with tiredness and maybe fear, maybe something else. "I always said you'd end up with a nice white man. Who's your handsome friend?"

The remark seemed to be directed at Ricky as much as Penny, and I didn't like that one bit. She was pure trouble. Penny glared at her but didn't speak. I broke the silence.

"Hello, Noni. Hello, James. Everything under control?"

James raised haunted eyes and looked at me.

"No, it's not." He pointed to the younger dark man. "He's going to kill us."

I studied Ricky in detail for the first time. He was several shades lighter than Perce, hardly darker than a Latin. His face wasn't heavily influenced by Aboriginal ancestry either. It was craggy rather than fleshy and his ears stuck out a bit. A few gloved fists had hit and moved it around but hadn't diminished the intelligence and character in it. Not that it was a nice face. It was a dangerous face and it scared me more than a little. He wasn't tall, I had that on him, but right then I'd have traded a few inches for my Smith & Wesson.

"I don't think so." I tried to make my voice sound calm

and confident although my throat was dry and my tongue felt like a bit of old rope. "He only kills when he has to and there's no point in killing any more people. Three's enough. Where's Bert?"

Noni let out a high laugh that cracked and ran down to a sob. "Ricky didn't kill *him*—I did." Her eyes flew off to the shadows near the front door, past the truck which stood near the middle of the floor, over the pit. Ricky didn't say anything or move, he just kept that rifle steady. I went over and looked down at the shapeless heap on the floor. I twitched back the hessian covering. Bert's heart wouldn't trouble him any more. Nothing would. The side of his head was caved in; a dark, soggy-looking mass like molten chocolate covered it from above the ear to the collar of his shirt. It hadn't been done with just one blow of the crank handle, or two.

Penny shot me a look that could have been triumph, then the impact of the whole thing reached her.

"Who did Ricky kill?" she said softly.

"The boy at Bare Island, to give him the cover for this big play." I waved my hand to take in all of us, including Bert, and the truck. "Only it's gone a bit sour, eh, Ricky?" I turned to look at the older man.

"How about you, Albie, who have you killed today?"

He put the shotgun down, leaning it on the running board of the truck which was an old Bedford, and began to roll a cigarette from makings he kept in a tin. He glanced across at Ricky.

"Might have ta be you," he growled.

Ricky looked puzzled, glanced at the man smoking and then stared at him as if trying to find answers to a hundred questions in his face. Noni was standing by the bench, only a few feet from me now, and running her hand over the smooth, artificial surface of the airline bag. The money bag.

"You'll never spend it, Noni," I said quietly, "not now."

"Shut up," Ricky snapped. "Fuckin' shut up. You can't tell the bloody future. We'll spend it, we'll go . . ."

"You won't go anywhere, even if you got this rig fixed up." I pointed at the Bedford. "You're blown. There's half a dozen people in Sydney know about you now. How far do you think you'd get, you and her? You'd have to live in a cave, what good would money be then?"

Ricky was looking agitated. He shifted the weight of the rifle in his hands and looked speculatively at me. It was dodgy talking to him like that. If he felt too hopeless about his prospects he might feel like going out in a welter of blood. Why not? I wanted him desperate, off balance, but not crazy desperate. I had to offer him something.

"I suppose you might get away somehow. Up north you could get a boat perhaps. Risky as all hell . . ."

Ricky clutched at it. "We'll make it. Shit, there's boats leaving Australia all the time. We'll make it."

"I don't understand any of this," James wailed, "not a word. Noni, you can't go off with this . . . killer. I love you, you're mine . . ."

The words must have sounded ludicrous, even to him. Noni let out a hoot of derision. She spun around and advanced on James waggling a finger in his face.

"Poor Saulie," she crooned, "poor baby Saul."

It didn't throw James, he must have been used to it.

"You're sick, Noni," he said sharply. He'd said it before—maybe it had worked. Not this time. She broke into a crazy, jerky dance.

"Ricky, oh, Ricky baby," she sang, "we'll go to Thailand, we've got enough money there for a thousand fixes, ten thousand fixes, big fixes, lovely fixes."

James put out his hand as if to steady her, help her down from her perch, but she slapped at him, skittered away. She slammed into the side of the truck and crumpled, sliding down to the oily garage floor. James moved toward her but Ricky's rifle came up sharply.

"Leave 'er," he rapped out.

James stopped and looked helplessly at me. I shook my head gently.

"She doesn't understand," I said. "She thinks she's in it with him but she isn't. He's got no use for her."

"I still don't understand all this," James said. He seemed less pathetic, sensing that his nursemaid role might have a little longer to play. That'd be enough for him. I looked across at Penny but it didn't seem to make any difference to her. She was looking at Ricky in a way that chilled me. It evoked a memory and I placed it. She was looking at him the way she'd looked at the corpse at Bare Island. For her, he was dead already. That was a pity, but probably sound judgement. I just wanted to be sure that he didn't take any of us with him on his second exit. James, frail reed that he was, looked like my only certain ally. Some knowledge might steady him. Besides, I had only one card to play and I had to prepare the game so that it would count decisively.

"Since we're all here, more or less, and nobody's going anywhere until night time, I might as well tell it the way I see it." I raised my eyebrows at Ricky. "OK, Ricky, you're the one with the gun and the money?"

"Watch him, Rick, he's a smartarse," Perce said. "I'm going to finish off the wiring." He started to get into the truck. The Bedford had been spray-painted grey and bars had been welded onto the front of it. A light metal frame had been welded up over the tray and I could see a couple of petrol drums on the tray just behind the cab. A tarpaulin that looked big enough to fit over the frame was lying on the floor beside the truck.

"I've got a couple of bottles in my car, Albie," I said. "Be a bit warm but . . ."

He got down and looked at Ricky. "Jeez, Rick, I could use a drink."

"No," said Ricky. "Why do you keep calling him Albie, mister?"

"That's his name, Albie Simmonds."

"Percy White's my name, smartarse."

"You can call yourself Joh Bjelke-Petersen for all I care, but your name's Albie Simmonds and you robbed a bank in 1966 with Joseph Berrigan."

"I knew it," Ricky said softly. "I knew you was him."

"It's bullshit," Albie muttered. "I didn't know Berri-gan."

"He ever let Berrigan get a look at him, Ricky?" I asked.

"No, no he kept right out of the way."

"Berrigan would have known him, even after all this time. There's a woman in the hospital here that knows who he is."

Albie's sullen face showed some interest.

"You see 'er? How is she?"

"I didn't see her, the girl did."

He turned toward Penny, the shotgun forgotten, the rifle forgotten, everything forgotten but the woman. I was seven feet from the shotgun. I'd have to step over Noni who was slumped down by the running board. I looked at Ricky. He was angry and puzzled but he wasn't careless. I'd never make it.

"I saw her," Penny said. "She isn't well. She was badly hurt but she thinks there's something else wrong with her. From the look of her she could be right. I'm sorry."

He shook his head and climbed into the truck.

"How long, Perce?" Ricky asked.

"Coupla minutes."

Not long, not long enough. Noni pulled herself up and limped over to the bench. A handbag was lying beside the airline bag and she reached into it and pulled out cigarettes. When she had one lit she struggled to regain the arrogance that was ninety-nine per cent of her style. It was a real struggle and she didn't quite make it.

"What's that about Ricky and me?" she said shakily. "What would you know about it? Who the fuck are you anyway?"

"He's a private detective, Noni," James put in.

"Don't tell me you hired him, baby? Not to get little me back?" She tossed her head and puffed smoke. She was still trying.

"No, not me, your father."

"Him. Fuck him."

Oh, Ted, how much sharper than a serpent's tooth it is.

"He cares about you, Noni," I said quickly. "With the trouble you're in, he's your only hope. Ricky'll drop you off at Oodnadatta crossing."

"No, he wouldn't," she said wildly. "He wouldn't."

"He's been planning to from the word go. Look, I'll tell you how it is. Ricky was looking for his father. Some kids who get dumped are like that, can't think of anything else." Albie quietly got out of the truck and stood listening. Ricky made no move to interrupt me so I went on.

"He found out a bit, got a line on his father and Berrigan and the bank job. Then he met you and found out that you were connected with that Macleay scene. I think he probably had the kidnap idea planned first but I can't be sure. When Berrigan contacted you Ricky saw it as a chance for the bank money if it was still around. He killed the boy at Bare Island to give himself a cover. God knows where he found him, and he stuck close to you and Berrigan, up here and back. When there was nothing doing on the bank money he hit on the idea of Berrigan fronting for the kidnap. You put Berrigan up to it, Noni, at Ricky's suggestion. It worked, more or less, and he killed Berrigan. I know I didn't because I fired low—ballistics will prove that—but Ricky didn't care. He reckoned he had enough red herrings dragging around to get clear."

"What about his father, how does he come in?" Penny asked quietly.

"He'd kept out of Ricky's way for years, then he heard that Ricky'd been killed. He checked at the morgue and knew it wasn't him. My guess is that he came in on it just because he thought Ricky would make a balls-up of it—which he has."

Penny started to cry quietly and Ricky looked at her amazed. For the first time the rifle wasn't ready for instant use. I was encouraged. This seemed to be the right tack.

184

"You had it alright there, mate," I said, "but maybe it's not your fault, maybe it's inherited."

He swung the rifle on me, but carelessly. I could see the black hole wavering and his eyes weren't any steadier. "What the fuck do you mean?"

"Albie, Perce, whatever you want to call him, he denies he's your father, right?"

"Yeah, but . . ."

"Let me finish. Did you know he was on with the Baker woman, the one Berrigan bashed?"

"No. So what?"

"After Berrigan went to jail for raping Noni, so it was thought, Albie here and Berrigan had a meeting and a bad falling-out."

"So? Berrigan found out Perce was fucking his woman."

"No, other way round."

"I don't get it." The rifle was all over the place. Soon . . . soon.

"Albie isn't your father. Berrigan told him who was."

Ricky shook his head. He took one hand off the rifle and brushed it over his face as if it was covered with cobwebs.

"No. No . . ."

"Right. You killed your father in the park, Ricky."

Now! I jumped him and nearly made it. I pushed at the rifle and swung my foot at his crotch but he was strong and young. He went back and fended me off with a sweeping lift of the rifle. It caught me in the mouth and I went down. Everybody had moved—Albie bent for the shotgun and his foot caught it and he fumbled, getting it near the trigger guard—he was bent over it and he took both barrels in the face. His face disappeared and blood erupted as the gun's roar was still filling the garage.

Ricky took in the full horror of the man collapsing, faceless, and he made a leap for the cab of the truck. Noni screamed his name, snatched up the bag and clawed her way into the truck. Ricky had the thing started and revving and he drove it straight through the doors. The truck went thump, thump as it passed over Bert and the doors splintered like matchwood. Then here was a big empty space where the truck had been and Penny was frozen like a statue. Blood had rained on her, drenched her.

23

I got up and went past Penny, out the back door and through the fence and the shop. The Datsun started like a dream and I swung it around in the quiet street and headed off after the throbbing, roaring truck. I scrabbled on the seat beside me and got the gun out of the parka as I drove. I put it on the floor on the passenger side. That way I'd have to think for a second or so before I could use it. The gun made me feel better. It shouldn't have but it did.

We were in a wide street and the Bedford was bucketing along ahead of me scattering the few cars around in front of it. They pulled over to the sides of the road haphazardly and I had to drive dodgem style to avoid them. A man jumped out of his car and made flagging motions. Maybe he wanted to make a citizen's arrest, make a hero of himself. I cursed him through some broken teeth with all the foul vocabulary I had picked up from school, army, pub and married bliss. He jumped clear. A quick look in the rear vision showed me what I should have expected—a yellow Mini burning along behind me just close enough to be a nuisance.

The truck was blowing thick, rich, blue smoke but going well, heading west, into the sun. We thrashed past the houses and the shops and the factories where people were pursuing their legitimate and illegitimate ends. We slewed around the corners and I could see the petrol drums bouncing just slightly on the tray of the truck; they were anchored well enough and were giving the Bedford stability. It had a big, strong engine for pulling loads and now it was just pulling Ricky, Noni, a hundred and five thousand dollars and the fuel. I could catch it, but Ricky drove like an angel and I couldn't pass him. We left the wide, sealed road and got onto a thin ribbon of bitumen flanked by ten feet of gravel on each side. The wheel base of the truck could hold the bitumen but Ricky moved off and on it just enough to throw up a screen of dust and slow me down.

The road started to climb and wind and I could get a look ahead as far as a hundred yards; the sides of the road were baked clay now and Ricky threw up less dust. Twice vehicles came from the other direction and Ricky barrelled straight at them, forcing them off the road. For a minute I thought the shape I could see up ahead of us was just another citizen, then the Bedford picked up speed and seemed to be driven with some mad purpose. I strained my eyes and was able to make out the distinctive shape of a police wagon. Ricky drove straight at it but the wagon veered off the road onto some cleared space and I could see the driver fighting to turn the thing as the Bedford rocketed by.

I braked and the cop was back on the road and giving the wagon all he had. It was probably the most excitement he'd had in years. The pace picked up and I stayed a bit back of the police vehicle, letting him do the work. James stayed back of me. The cop was pushing Ricky to the limit and I caught a glimpse of the Bedford swaying as she went round a bend, then we were on a long, straight stretch, climbing hard.

The grey truck dipped on one side and started to go into a slide. Ricky fought it and stopped the thing from turning over but he went into a sideways spin that took him off the road and ran the front of the truck into a clay embankment. I braked and stopped fifty yards short of the truck. The police wagon shot past and the driver plastered rubber on the road getting it to stop. Two cops jumped out and started to run the thirty yards or so back to the truck. I heard a sharp crack and they stopped, turned and raced back to the wagon. I got out of the car after grabbing the Colt and saw Ricky on the running board sighting along his rifle. With a shriek a bullet whipped off the hood of the wagon.

One of the cops rested a rifle on the mudguard of the wagon and opened up. A window shattered in the cab and Noni climbed down and started to run back toward me. She dropped the airline bag in the first stride and half-turned back for it. I screamed at her to keep coming and sprinted toward her. I reached her and thumped her hard onto the road. We were twenty yards from the truck when a bullet went into the petrol drums. A thousand heavy guns went off and a fiery wind blew over our heads. My eyeballs were scorched when I raised my head to take a look—the Bedford was a dark, ghostly shape inside a bright, dancing ball of yellow and orange fire.

James was standing beside his car and I lifted Noni up and half-carried her back to him. She collapsed into his arms and started to cry into his shoulder. He lowered her into the car seat and crouched by her, stroking her hair and murmuring in her ear. I started to walk toward the cops when one of them dropped to one knee, brought up a pistol and pointed it at me.

"Drop the gun," he yelled.

I looked at my hand, the Colt was still in it. I dropped it and came on.

Petrol had leaked from the truck and the ground around it was a pool of fire, somewhere in the middle of which was the money. Pity. One of the cops was inside the wagon frantically using the radio; the other held his gun shakily on me while I talked. He let me show him my documents but he was too nervous to take in much of what I said. I tried to keep out of direct line of the pistol while reinforcements arrived. What had happened on the road was going to take some explaining. Other things would taken even more explaining. It was going to be a long night.

24

It was. They bundled us into police cars and took us into town. I told them about the garage and who Noni and James were. They let Noni clean herself up a bit but she needed much more than a bath, she needed a lot of expensive medical treatment. I hoped she wouldn't talk too much but she let James protect her and she scarcely said a word. With luck, I thought, I'd be able to get her out of this and back to her father fairly clean. Maybe that wasn't letting all the cards show but I recalled what someone had once said to some cops: "Until you guys own your own souls, you don't own mine. Until you guys can be trusted every time and always, in all times and conditions, to seek the truth and find it and let the chips fall where they may—until that time comes, I have the right to listen to my conscience, and protect my client the best way I can."

That's how I felt. The cops sure as hell didn't seem too concerned about an incinerated black man and another the same colour with no head to speak of. That's how I thought I'd play it, but Penny threw a spanner into the works, or tried to.

They picked her up in the garage. When she came to see us in the police building she'd washed the blood off and was wearing some kind of policewoman's smock. They'd told her about Ricky. It didn't seem to touch her. Then she told me that she'd given the cops who came for her something to take with them and be careful of the fingerprints—a crank handle. Her eyes glittered maliciously when she told me this. Noni was within hearing but it was wasted on her. She was burying herself in James's warm solicitude, a good beginning for the attitude she'd have to take up when all Ted's money started working for her.

It was very complicated and I didn't help by refusing to tell them anything until the lawyers got there. Cy Sackville came up the next day and some smoothie Ted got to handle Noni's part in it. Sackville spoke for James, too, but he was pretty much in the clear. The cops didn't like it one bit. There was nothing in it for them but trouble. They tried to stick me with various things from conspiracy down to dangerous driving, but their hearts weren't in it and Sackville brushed them aside. Penny they didn't even hold and she stayed for a few days with relations in town, then she left without contacting me.

The lawyer took Noni back to Sydney and I never saw her again. I heard later from Cy that Ted's lawyers had headed off any charges connected with Bert's death. The crank handle held her fingerprints alright but she claimed that Bert had tried to rape her. If his body had been in the state it was when I saw it, the coroner might have wondered how many blows with a crank handle to the head it took to prevent a rape, but the truck wheels had passed over Bert's head, front and back, making a mess that no one could interpret. I was pretty sure she'd been in on the kidnap idea with Ricky, but there was no way of proving it and it wasn't in my interest anyway.

I saw a fair bit of Saul James in the few days I spent in Macleay straightening things out. After they pried him loose from Noni he seemed to have no direction, no purpose and sort of attached himself to me. I asked him about his part in the play.

"Gone," he said wryly. "The understudy was too good, he filled in on the first rehearsal I missed and now he's got the part."

"Tough."

He shrugged. "I wonder what will happen to Noni?"

"Overseas trip if I know Ted. She's no loss to you, James."

He looked hurt.

"At least there's one consolation. It didn't cost you any money."

"I thought the money was burnt?"

"It was, but I wrote down the serial numbers of your share, you'll get it all back."

He looked at me as if I'd betrayed him instead of saved him five thousand dollars. I'd denied him his little bit of martyrdom.

I finally got clear of the cops and of James. I flew back to Newcastle, played games with some more cops and got my car out of their clutches. Someone had washed it by mistake while it was impounded and it was with pride that I drove it back to Sydney.

That took me back to the let-down that follows cases like this one. I mooched into the office and screwed up circulars and paid a few bills in anticipation of Ted Tarelton's cheque. I sat around at home reading novels and writing a report on the case. My .38 came back from the Balmain police. Berrigan's case closed. I heard from Grant Evans that the Macleay cops were glad to have the bank robbery off their books. They hadn't revealed any of this pleasure to me.

Three days went by like this, slowly and with little ends of the Tarelton case being tied up. Ailsa's return was imminent—there was that at least to look forward to. I was at home in the middle of the day in the middle of the week when the phone rang. I put my book down and looked at it reluctantly. I answered it reluctantly. My stomach lurched when I heard the voice on the other end. For a fraction of a second I thought it was Ricky Simmonds.

"Hardy?"

"Yes. Jimmy Sunday?"

"Right. You sorted it out—Ricky and Noni and that?"

"You could say that. It's over anyway. Who told you?"

"Penny."

"Oh, how's she?"

"Alright. You see Jacko's fight with Rosso's coming up on Friday?"

I hadn't seen; I'd pushed the whole Aboriginal-Italian business away into a corner of my mind, a worry corner but a corner. I associated it with the Tarelton business and that was cleared up. Besides, no one would pay me for interfering in Coluzzi's plans. I was a mercenary wasn't I? That reminded me, Ted Tarelton hadn't paid my account yet.

"Umm," I said.

"We're ready to move."

"What does that mean?"

"Trueman's been at Jacko, you know, hinting he might have to take a dive. Jacko's played it smart, let Sammy think he'll co-operate. Probably will, not for sure, you know? He's not stupid, Jacko."

"I never thought he was," I grunted. "Where does that get you?"

"Coluzzi's got a bundle on Rosso. Too much to lay off."

I felt relieved. Well done. "Good, you've got him then, provided Moody can win."

"Oh, he'll win. Shit, you should see him, sharp and hard, he'll kill him. He scared me when I saw him sparring, he's that good."

Sunday knew what he was talking about. I respected his judgement in matters pugilistic, but he was undercutting my relief. Why was he telling me this?

"That's great Jimmy. I'll be there, I'll see you. Tell Ted Williams I'll get the tickets I promised him."

"Hold on Hardy, we need your help. We want Coluzzi's balls, not just his money."

"Oh?"

"Fuckin' right. He's for it and you're going to set him up for us. You can contact him can't you?"

I said I could. I didn't want to, but I could.

"OK. Tomorrow night at Trueman's."

192

"What do I tell him?"

"Tell him the niggers are organising and they want some of the action. Make him think he can tie up the Moody-Rosso fight. That'll bring him."

"What are you going to do?"

"Kick the living shit out of him."

I suddenly felt insecure, old, in need of a rest. "Look, have you gone into this? I mean Coluzzi's a professional, they don't leave things to chance."

"We've been tailing his heavies for days. We've got 'em all pinned. Jacko'll be safe. There'll be a small party going on in Newtown tomorrow night too. Just a small do—a few cops might feel like coming along though."

That was persuasive. They obviously meant business and weren't going to let me off. "OK, I'll contact Coluzzi and get back to you. You'll have plenty of people along? Those Italians aren't soft."

"Don't worry. Tell him nine o'clock."

I hung up, made a cigarette, got a drink and thought about it. Siding with Sunday against Coluzzi was like backing the Apaches against the cavalry, but something was working inside me. I could have ducked it, could have pretended that Coluzzi wouldn't buy it, got out of it some way. But I thought of the two men dead in the unfriendly town up north and the girl who'd seen too much pain and blood at seventeen. They hadn't taken a trick in the whole mess. Noni was on her way to London, or wherever, and I was due a big cheque. I hunted around for the card, found it in some unwashed clothes and called Coluzzi.

I got a female Italian voice on the other end and then a long, long wait. When Coluzzi finally came on the line his voice was soft and guarded.

"I've been wondering about you, Mr. Hardy, what do you know?"

"Hello, Coluzzi. I've been out of town, up north with the black people."

"So?"

"Maybe you've got problems, maybe not. The Aborigines are organising themselves a bit. I don't think they'd be too keen on your idea of fights betweens blacks and Italians, not the way you see it anyway. They'd like to see their boys coming out on top once in a while, or twice in a while."

He didn't say anything, forcing me to go on.

"I've met their top man, Jimmy Sunday. He wants to talk to you about a deal.

"What deal? I don't need a deal. Why should I meet him?"

"Well, I'm just passing this on, you understand? He says he can arrange the result of the Moody-Rosso fight. That's to show his good faith."

There was a pause while he considered it. When he spoke again it was with all the straightforwardness of Lucrezia Borgia inviting you to dinner.

"That's interesting, very interesting. Maybe I better meet these people. Where and when?"

I told him. He didn't sound happy but I said that was all I'd been given. He said he'd be there and rang off.

It left me edgy, without diversion. Ailsa wasn't due in until the next day. A postcard told me that. The rest of the mail was just waiting to be waste paper and I obliged it. I wished I'd asked Sunday about guns. I hoped there wouldn't be any guns. I wished Penny would come to see me but I knew she wouldn't. I wished the fight would be called off; I read the last couple of days' news reports on the fighters. They were both in great shape, both going to win, according to their trainers, both going to be world's champions. Moody had made the better impression in training. He was comfortably favoured to win. Coluzzi must have got good odds on his money. I called a man I knew and got fifty dollars to win thirty-five on Moody. Then I worried. What if Coluzzi knew the man I knew? What if the man I knew told Coluzzi? I drank and smoked and worried. Then I thought the hell with it. I'm a private detective, I'm tough. I can be stupid if I want to be.

I called Harry Tickener and we insulted each other for as long as we could stand it. He had tickets for the fight and was going himself. He agreed to leave two for Ted Williams at the paper and to meet me at the club with two for me.

"Ailsa?" he asked.

"I hope so."

"Good. I expect to have company, too."

"That's nice. Do I know her?"

"Your name's never come up."

"OK, be mysterious. I'll see you there."

"You won't be able to miss us."

That was a good exit line. I wondered what it meant. Harry sounded happy. Good. If Harry could be happy maybe we could all be happy.

25

Twenty hours later I was happy. Ailsa flew in around eleven and we went straight back to her place and to bed. We got out of bed an hour later for something to eat and drink and then back again. After that session I smoked and we picked up the pieces. Her tan told the story of where she'd been and she filled me in on the progress of her interests in the Pacific. The picture amounted to good news and more good news. I told her I was glad about it and she scrutinised me for the irony in such remarks that usually sparks off our fights. It wasn't there. The heart had grown fonder. I told her about the Tarelton case and promised I'd take her out to dinner when I got the cheque.

"Oh, that reminds me," I said. "I'm taking you out tomorrow night if you're free."

"Good, where?"

"The boxing."

"Ugh, no thanks—horrible."

"Harry Tickener'll be there."

"Harry's nice but still, no."

"I think he's got a girlfriend."

"Really, that's interesting. Who?"

"I don't know, and if you don't come tomorrow night I'll make sure you never find out. I'll break it up and you'll never know."

She yawned. "Who cares."

"I gather you're not coming?"

"Right. Come and see me afterward."

We wasted the afternoon a bit more and I left. I went home and played with my pistols for a while; I cleaned them and loaded them and checked their actions. Then I wrapped them up and put them away. I'd bought some cut price Scotch and I sampled it just to see whether it was a bargain. Not bad. Quite smooth. Of course the first drink can be misleading so I had a second. I thought I detected a metallic taste so I had a third. I was mistaken about the metallic taste. It was good smooth whisky that needed drinking without any judgemental attitudes in view. I had a fourth in a calm, purely objective frame of mind.

I ate something and showered and dressed myself in the clothes I'd worn to break into Sammy's gym some nights before. I took the papers I'd removed then from the hiding place and stuck them in my pocket. I thought again about the guns and compromised by putting the Colt into the clip in the car. The Celica had gone back to the Tareltons soon after my arrival back in Sydney. I had a mind-flash image of Madeline Tarelton as I climbed into the Falcon. An unscrupulous, despicable person would ring her up some time and find out just how much her husband didn't understand her. But an unscrupulous, despicable person wouldn't be driving to Newtown for a showdown between ethnic minorities, and he wouldn't be haunted by the eyes of a dark girl standing stock-still while blood rained on her.

I was nervous and early, much too early. I drove into town and down to the Rocks to kill time. The Opera House billowed up like bedsheets in a high wind. North Sydney was canopied by purplish cloud, but the sky to the east was a pale powder blue. The stratosphere was in two moods like me; my satisfaction at the conclusion of the Tarelton case, messy though it was, was tempered by the threat of the events ahead. I parked and wandered up through the city which gradually emptied around me. By eight o'clock there was only a thin line of traffic made up of people snapping up the last parking spots for their night on the town. Nine-tenths of the city was asleep and the remaining tenth was only fitfully awake in those oases of light where celluloid was spinning, liquor was flowing and there was money to be made. I went back to my clean car and drove to Newtown.

I parked half a mile from the gym and walked through the streets. Any one of the couple of black people I passed could have been Sunday's confederates, or none of them. It seemed to me that Coluzzi was a brave man to agree to a meeting in this territory. I'd have insisted on neutral ground. The thought bothered me as I walked along. Coluzzi was totally professional to all appearances and this was a bad move. I scouted around the gym looking for signs of trouble but everything was as quiet as a synagogue on Sunday. I walked back to my car and took out the gun. The door to the building was open and I took the stairs as quietly as I could. On the stars the stale smell of tobacco smoke and the reek of sweat blended into a threat of mustard gas. The place whispered of tension and danger. It was a good place not to be.

I pushed open the door to the gym. The bulb over the ring was glowing, making a sickly greyish patch of light in the centre of the room. My feelings of threat and danger became more intense; I felt as if I were walking into an ambush prepared especially for me. Still, I went. I took a couple of steps into the room and strained my eyes at the darkness that hung in every corner. There were no sounds, no movements. I looked again at the ring, this time with eyes that had grown used to the gloom. What I'd taken for shadow at first glance now didn't look like shadow any more. It had shape and bulk but it was very still. I moved quickly across to the ring and climbed through the ropes.

Jimmy Sunday lay there with his eyes open, staring up into the bulb the way no living eyes could. He was wearing a polo-neck sweater and jeans. The rolled neck of the sweater was soaked with blood and blood had seeped through and run in a trickle across the canvas floor. I crouched beside him feeling sad and sick and furious with myself. Every instinct should have told me that Sunday would be out-matched coming up against Coluzzi. I had known that, but I'd let myself be persuaded otherwise because I was being easy on myself. I'd dramatised my own self-sacrifice of siding with the Aborigines and ignored the objective facts—that they didn't have a chance. I had the resources to do something about it, I had the cop contacts, or I could have headed Coluzzi off, somehow. But I hadn't and this was the result.

Death does different things to different faces. I'd seen my father dead and ready for departure in a funeral parlour; his skin was painted, a thing unimaginable in life. He looked like a waxworks dummy and my mother just said "It isn't him" and we went away. She didn't even cry.

Death in the raw, violent death, is different again; I'd seen the evil stamped like a stencil mark across some dead faces and innocence blooming on others. In death Jimmy Sunday looked younger than he had in life and I was reminded that I'd thought him young when I'd first seen him at a distance. The scars from boxing and boozing and living had been almost erased and his brown skin was smooth and taut. Somehow that made it worse. I closed his eyes and went away. There was nothing else to do, not there.

I left the gym and walked back to my car with my shoulders hunched and the pistol tucked into my waistband. I felt an urge to use it on Coluzzi or one of his apes but at the same time I recognised that as the immature and useless impulse it was. When I got home I had a drink and poured another, then I called the Sharkey number. When Rupe came to the phone he was nervous. When I identified myself he was hostile. I told him that Sunday was dead and asked if he had any family. There was a silence before he spoke.

"Yeah, sort of. A woman and a kid, not his, but same thing."

"Did you know about the plan to move against the Italians?"

"A bit, not much. I wasn't gonna be in on it. Too fuckin' old. But I heard Jimmy was gonna give the word at lunchtime today, but no one seen him since last night. Where'd you see him?"

I told him and he said he'd send someone over there.

"Who done him?" he asked.

"I can't prove it, Mr. Sharkey."

"Ah, what the fuck does it matter. You got anything else to say?"

"No. Just that I'm sorry."

His answer was the sharp click of the connection being broken. That did wonders for me. I sank some liquor and poured some more. The glass suddenly felt as heavy as lead, full of reproach. I set it down and started working through my little red book of telephone numbers. My first call was to Grant Evans. The second, back to me, was from a policeman in Macleay. My next call was to a security organisation in the city. I followed that with a call to Major Ian Mahony who was head of the security firm that guarded Macleay hospital. I had to give him references in the constabulary and the military. They seemed to satisfy him and I got an interview arranged with him for the following morning, in Macleay. I poured the liquor back into the bottle and went grimly off to bed to prepare myself for my busy day.

My last conscious thought was that I had put the finger on Jimmy Sunday for Coluzzi.

26

Busy is right. The radio alarm woke me at six o'clock. I came swarming up out of a dream in which I'd been fighting a ring full of people with my bare fists. I must have set my jaw resolutely in the dream because it was aching like fury when I got out of bed. I made coffee and swilled down aspirin and caffeine tablets. The coffee was stale, this case had dragged on and I'd neglected my domestic necessities. I promised myself some fresh coffee and clean sheets when I'd done what I had to do. I had a shower and let the water play on my injuries, a split scalp and battered knuckles, both beginning to heal. I had lost two teeth, knocked out clean, and another was very loose. That wasn't such a bad score except that I was still waiting for the cheque to justify them. Today, I'd be on my own time, the way to go out of business someone once told me.

I drove to the airport through a clear, mild morning. The traffic seemed to acknowledge the clemency of the day by parting in front of me and staying back to allow me through. As before, there was no crush for the flight to parts north. I handed in Penny's unused return ticket and my unused Newcastle to Sydney section plus some cash and got a return ticket to Macleay. I had no luggage, no guns, no hand grenades, just my bright, sharp wits and my tarnished old soul. I bought the papers and a copy of *Ragtime* and boarded the plane. The papers told me everything that was going on in the country around that time which was nothing; *Ragtime* gripped and held me like a new lover and I didn't lift my face from it for the whole trip. I knew what I was going to do in Macleay. I didn't have to think about it any more.

I got a taxi into town and arrived at Major Mahony's office punctually at nine-thirty which was just as well. Mahony was a Britisher in his fifties. His face spoke of hot parade grounds and long nights over the bottle in the mess. He was bulky behind his mahogany desk. Pink scalp showed through thinning silver hair but he still had a few good, bullying years in him.

"You come well recommended, Mr. Hardy," he barked, "but you ask a lot. Convince me."

It was an old tactic and the only way to confront it was head-on.

"What do you think of drugs, Major—hemp smoking and things like that?"

He glared over the pipe he was stuffing, a big black job that looked fit to roast a quarter pound of shag.

"Hate it. Degenerate. Catch any of my people at it and out they go."

"Precisely. That's why I'm here. If you co-operate with me it'll help to close down a drug-growing and distribution point in this part of the country."

He grunted and puffed at the pipe.

"Hemp you said?"

"Hemp certainly, but you know where that leads."

"Do I not. I was in the Middle East for long enough—people lolling about, pansies . . ." He broke off choked, I suspected, by his excitement, but he coughed as though the tobacco smoke had caught in his throat. I followed up quickly.

"All I need is access to the woman, ten minutes alone

with her, then the services of a stenographer for a few minutes.''

"Sick woman, Mr. Hardy, very sick. I checked with the hospital this morning. She's dying.''

"Does she know?''

"Yes, they told her. She insisted on knowing. Does that alter your plans?''

"No.'' I could have added "on the contrary'' if I'd intended to be perfectly frank with him, but I didn't.

"I suppose it can't do any harm considering the circumstances,'' he mused. "The woman might be glad to perform a last service.'' He looked at me enquiringly.

"I think she will.'' I hated myself for indulging him in his pompous humbug, but I had no choice.

"Very well then.'' He picked up a pencil and scribbled a note. "Take that to the operations desk outside and you'll get what you want.''

I stood up and assumed as respectful an attitude as I could without saluting. I don't think he'd have minded if I had saluted.

"Thank you, Major. Great help.'' We shook hands. He managed to turn the gesture into a condescension for him and a privilege for me.

I went out to the office where all the work was done and handed in the note. A tired-looking man with red-rimmed eyes lifted a phone and spoke briefly into it. I looked around the room. There must have been ten or more telephones and the walls were covered with maps of Newcastle and Macleay and other towns in the area with red-headed drawing pins sticking in them. I waited five minutes before a young woman in a white blouse and blue skirt came into the room. The weary man nodded at me and she walked across and stuck her hand out.

"I'm Pam Henderson. Mr. Hardy, is it?''

I shook the hand and said it was. She picked up a notebook from one desk and slid a portable typewriter out from the cupboard. She was all business. Her hair was drawn back and well pinned. She wouldn't waste a second of a working day fussing with it. She collected a set of keys from a hook by the door and we went out to a car yard behind the office building. She got behind the wheel of a big Valiant station wagon and had the car out of the yard and heading down the street while I was still fastening the safety belt. She parked in a reserved bay outside the hospital and marched up the front steps with me trotting along behind her. She was just what I needed; if I'd had an assistant like her I could have sat in my office and thought up wisecracks. I could just turn up for the denouement and make sure the client had the name right for the cheque.

The hospital reception desk stayed her for maybe five minutes and the ward sister for about three, then we were inside Trixie Baker's room. I summoned all my courage and spoke to my companion.

"I won't need you for a few minutes, Miss Henderson. Please wait outside close by."

She spun on her heel and went out. I breathed a sigh of relief and approached the bed. Neither the appearance of the Baker woman when I'd found her at the farm, nor the desiccated voice on the tape had prepared me for the head on the pillow. Flesh had fallen away from her bones and she looked mummified. I couldn't remember what colour her hair had been when I first saw her, but it was white now, snow white. Her eyes were open but they were filmed over with pain, or perhaps morphine. I hoped it was the latter.

"Mrs. Baker," I said softly. "Mrs. Baker, how are you feeling?"

The pale eyes widened a little and the creases beside them deepened.

"Bloody awful, but not for long. Who're you? Doctor?

"No, I'm a detective. My name's Hardy. You've heard of me."

"I have, from the darkie. I seem to be able to remember everything just now. Too much, really, too much. What do you want, detective?"

"Some help, Mrs. Baker. Some help for Albie Simmonds in a way."

The smile that spread across her ravaged face was almost sweet.

"Oh Albie. He was a dear, Albie. How is he?"

"I'm afraid he's dead, Mrs. Baker. He was shot. A friend of his is dead too and that's where I need your help."

The information didn't trouble her. Somehow she'd acquired some strength in her last hours. I felt guilty about manipulating her.

"Are you a religious woman, Mrs. Baker?" I asked.

She let out a short, breathless version of the cackle I'd heard on the tape.

"No, no, not a bit. Wish I was, then I could think I'd be seein' Albie soon, couldn't I?"

"I suppose so."

"But it's bullshit. Things are so bad, so rotten, there couldn't be a God, not a nice one like they say. Why, anyway?"

I explained to her. It took some time and I had to repeat myself. She kept slipping away into some state that telescoped the last fifty years of her life. Things I said triggered memories and resentments and she lived through some scenes the meaning and content of which only she could know. It was her way of facing death and I couldn't deny it her. In the end she agreed to do what I asked. I called Henderson in and she took down the statement in shorthand, typed it up there and then and Trixie signed two copies.

I took the pen from her skeletal fingers and stepped back from the bed. Her hand fluttered on the coverlet and I bent down to hear what she said. Her voice was very faint.

"All gone now, eh? Albie, Joe Berrigan, me soon. What about Noni? What happened to her?"

"She missed out on all the trouble. She's got problems though, she's on drugs."

"She'll be alright. She'll die old and rich."

It sounded like wisdom and I treated it as such, nodding and saying something in assent. A soft sigh came from her and her eyelids came down. I jerked up alarmed and Henderson glided up to the bed. She took the stick-thin wrist in her strong brown hand and laid fingers across it. After a few seconds she put the arm down and raised her fingers to her lips. We went quietly out of the room.

"She's asleep but it can't be long," Henderson said professionally.

"Are you trained?"

"Five years, army nurse."

"Your typing looks alright, too."

"Business school. Graduated first-class."

"You should be doing more with it."

"Are you making me an offer?"

I backed away physically and verbally. She'd be running things within a week, telling me what jobs to take and how I could increase my fees.

"No, sorry, I'm in a very small way of business."

She sniffed and drove me to the airport. It wasn't the worst of my rides out of Macleay but it wasn't the best either.

I read *Ragtime* in the waiting lounge and finished it on the plane. I kept it with me to give to Ailsa. On arrival in Sydney I went to Cy Sackville's office, talked to him for a while and left the papers plus several others I signed myself. Cy wasn't wearing the suit I'd seen in Macleay, in fact I'd never seen the suit before. Cy probably had more suits than I had fillings. Still, I liked him and promised to pay him before Christmas. He waved the promise aside which was probably wise.

I left, taking note of how to furnish an office with taste and style. There were only two problems: one, I'd never be able to afford it and two, if by some chance I ever could, this decor would be out of fashion. Difficulties . . . difficulties . . . On the drive home I considered what I'd done. The papers I left with Sackville were sworn statements by Patricia Baker, widow of Macleay, made in the belief that she did not have long to live, that Aldo Coluzzi was her partner in the marijuana-growing business, supplying capital and arranging distribution. Two other men, Carlo and Adio, surnames unknown, were mentioned as agents.

It wasn't much. It probably wouldn't even stick, but the papers would go in to the Drugs Enquiry Commission that was sitting just then and it wouldn't do Coluzzi any good. He'd get a mention in the press with luck and there'd be some investigation of his business affairs. I calculated that there should be something in there for auditors and tax men to chew on. At the moment there might be a deportation order in it. I'd settle for that.

As for fat Sammy Trueman, he was going to lose money and the best fighter he'd ever had.

27

Prizefighting is in the doldrums, of course. I can remember when the big stadiums in Melbourne, Sydney, and Brisbane did a roaring trade a couple of nights a week and stories on fighters pushed the politicians off the pages of the newspapers. That's all finished; the big stadiums are closed and pulled down mostly and the big crowds assemble for football and to see androgynous pop stars who are millionaires at eighteen and dead of drugs by twenty-five.

The Moody-Rosso fight was being put on at a League's club in the eastern suburbs, a great barn of a place designed to park as many cars as possible and accommodate as many bars and poker machines as possible. Living near it must be hell. The club had put on a good front for the fight; there was a big red banner with the fighters' names on it draped over the main entrance and a few old-time pugs were on hand to lend colour. Still, nothing could disguise the fact that the place had been designed for a softer generation. This place smelled of money. The stadiums smelled of sweat and piss.

I parked the Falcon and went up the steps into a lobby furnished in what might have been Elizabeth Taylor's taste when she was a girl. It was all scarlet and gold and the mirrors seemed to me to have a slimming effect. Most of the members thronging through to lose their money could use it. I scouted around for Tickener but he wasn't there. I was, as usual, neurotically early. Passages led off from the lobby to bars and entertainment rooms which were off-limits to non-members.

There was a bank of poker machines standing by one wall and I shook out some change and started dropping it in and pulling the lever. The machine devoured the money like a Venus fly trap taking nourishment. I turned around and almost had to grab the lever again for support. Tickener was walking toward me and beside him was the six-foot redhead I'd seen at the newspaper building. They came up and I summoned the strength to move away from the machine. The reporter's face wore a half-moon grin; I could have sworn he'd grown an inch or two. That still left him a few inches short of the redhead.

"Cliff, this is Toni Blake. Toni, Cliff Hardy."

I admired her. She was wearing black harem trousers with gold high-heeled shoes and some sort of beaded, lacy top; the slim arms, completely bare, were creamy, not one of your freckled redheads. I tried to keep my eyes off the cropped hair and treat her like a normal human being.

"Hello," I said. It sounded weak so I said it again. Then it sounded stupid so I gave up.

"Going to be a good crowd, Cliff," Tickener said heartily. He was enjoying my reaction, as he had every right to. I'd taken the mickey out of him more times than was fair. The girl took hold of Tickener's arm enthusiastically, the way you handle a good bottle of Scotch.

"Let's go in and get a drink," she said thrillingly, "the auditorium's this way."

Harry kept up manfully and I tagged along, trying to get my mind off her swaying, queenly gait. I failed. Harry flashed the tickets and we went into a room a couple of hundred feet square with bars along three walls. It was filled with rows of metal chairs and the boxing ring was set up on a three-foot-high stage in the middle of the floor. The place would have held about three thousand people which, even with tickets at five to ten bucks each, doesn't amount to much of a gate. There were television rights, though; the crew had set their gear up around the ring and heavy cables snaked across the auditorium floor. A couple of hundred people were already there, some sitting down but mostly crowded around the bars. I saw big Ted Williams over in a corner with Rupert Sharkey. They both held schooners of beer and looked depressed. I nodded at them and they returned the nod guardedly. I wanted to go over and talk to them, tell them what I'd arranged for Coluzzi, but I didn't. It wouldn't have helped. There were a fair number of Aborigines in the crowd, maybe a quarter of the people were dark, and this proportion held as the room filled up.

People parted in front of Toni and we walked down what was virtually an aisle to the bar.

"My shout," I said. "Toni, what will you have?"

"Triple Scotch," she said. "I'll have just the one drink all night."

"Harry?"

"Beer," Tickener said. "Middy."

"You'll have to give that up if you're going to hang around with me," the girl said. "It makes you fat and gassy in bed."

"Scotch," said Tickener.

"Three triple Scotches."

We took the drinks over to our seats which were in the ten-dollar section with a clear view and just far enough back to keep your neck comfortable. Tickener asked me about Ailsa.

"Wouldn't come," I said. "She doesn't like the fights."

"I love them," Toni said.

"Why?"

"They're exciting, primitive."

"What about the blood?"

"I don't mind that."

Oh, Harry, I thought, you've got your work cut out here.

"What do you report on?" I asked her.

"Politics mostly."

That figured.

The lights went down and an announcer as wide as he was tall pulled over a boom mike and started his spiel. I glanced across. Tickener and Toni were holding hands. There was a rush through the doors and a lot of noise as people took their seats. The announcer heaved himself out of the ring and the first of the two preliminary bouts started. The four-rounder was between a pale, crop-headed boy with heavy shoulders and a thin Aborigine whose arms seemed to hang to his knees. Their styles were completely different and didn't mix. The crew-cut was a rusher and flailer and the dark boy was a fancy stepper with a neat straight left. They did no damage to each other and the fight was a draw. Two white men came up for the six-rounder, a heavily tattooed six-footer and a chunky guy who assumed a crouch while the referee was giving him instructions. This fight was over in five seconds; the tattooed man tried a left lead and the croucher came up under it and clouted him with a right he'd brought up off the floor with him. The tattooed man folded like a butterfly's wings and the big body sank gently to the floor. The referee raised the arm that had done the damage without bothering to count over the fallen one.

That brought Rosso and Moody out early. I realised that I'd nearly finished my drink. Tickener and Toni were whispering and had barely touched theirs. The seat beside me stayed empty until the announcement of the main event began, then I was aware of a huge bulk beside me and a cracked, hissing voice.

"Gidday, Hardy, can I use this? Can't see a fuckin' thing from back there."

"Hello, Jerome. Sure, it's vacant. My woman wouldn't come." I don't know why I said that but Jerome laughed.

"Mine neither. Reckons she seen enough fights when I was at it. Cunt of a game."

Toni caught the word and glanced across sharply. I made muted introductions and a wave of beer breath swept across us as Jerome responded. He had a glass in his fist and raised it as an ex-welterweight champion took his bow.

"Woulda killed him," he said.

Under the savage glare of the TV lights Rosso looked ugly, dark hair fuzzed on his arms and shoulders like fur on an animal and his skin was mottled. He wasn't tall, about five nine, a real natural middleweight with terrific strength in his arms and thighs. He looked as if he could go all night. Moody looked better. His skin was glossy under the lights and he was better proportioned with the meat and muscle better distributed. If I'd been his manager I'd have been a bit concerned about him. He looked as if he might grow into a light-heavyweight, the disaster division where there's no money to be made unless you're wasting to get in against middleweights or giving away pounds to heavies. But he looked good tonight.

The announcer didn't hold the action up too long. He tried a joke in Italian which got booed by a section of the crowd and then he gave it up and waddled away. The referee was Tony Bourke, a better than useful lightweight in his day. Trueman crouched in Moody's corner, whispering in the fighter's ear. He mimed a low punch and combination and the young Aborigine nodded. He clamped his teeth around the mouthguard and jumped up off his stool. I heard a sharp intake of breath from Toni as Moody skipped across the ring. But the Italian started the business by rushing Moody into the ropes and trying a clubbing left which Moody took on the glove.

The Aborigine had no trouble in ducking under Rosso's follow-up right swing and propping him with a straight left as he moved back into open space. That was the pattern of the round; the shorter man rushed in, bullocked his opponent to the ropes and tried to smash him with short, clubbing punches. Moody jabbed him. Moody took the points for the round but there was something a bit supercilious about his style; his shots stung the Italian and made him look clumsy, but they didn't hurt or frighten him or sap the strength in his body.

Ross's handler had smooth silver hair like Rossano Brazzi and a ring with a big, bright stone in it glittered on his finger as he waved and jabbed in the air in front of his fighter. Trueman and someone who looked like the dark boy with the withered leg worked quietly and efficiently on Jacko and there was little conversation in the corner.

In the next two rounds Rosso tried to cut Moody off and slam into him in confined sections of the ring. He managed to hem him in a few times but he couldn't do much when he got there. Moody tied him up quickly and Bourke broke them and the Aborigine was off again, not dancing exactly, just moving in and out quickly and precisely and scoring with long lefts. His timing was good but not perfect. Rosso caught him with a few heavy body swings that had more power than they should have, given Moody's evasive abilities and speed. But the Italian was way behind on points when they came out for the fifth.

It wasn't a good round for Jacko. He seemed to have tired a bit and looked apprehensive. I couldn't help wondering if the fix was in, somehow. Moody took a couple of punches that he should have slipped easily and Rosso roughed him up badly in a clinch. The crowd noise went up a couple of notches. The Italians felt that their boy was getting on top and the Aborigines weren't happy at all. No one was neutral

211

and the change of fortunes in the fight affected everyone. I could hear the rustle of money as bets were put on and laid off.

Moody looked a little distressed in his corner after the round but Trueman's style hadn't changed at all. The sixth started out much the same as the last round with Rosso aggressive and clumsily effective. Rosso brushed Moody's left lead aside as if it was a cobweb and slammed in a hard clean right to the midsection. Moody felt it and responded with a cuffing, playful-looking left to the side of the head. Rosso ignored that and bored in to land a short, jolting right near the Aborigine's heart. There was a commotion behind me and I turned to see Ted Williams on his feet with beer slopping out of a schooner.

"Do him for Sunday!" he roared.

The punch or the shout transformed Moody. Maybe it was both. He seemed to settle into a firmer stance and loom over the Italian at the same time. He swayed out of reach of Rosso's next swing and speared a hard left into his face. He followed that with a crisp right; it was the quickest punch combination of the night and Rosso faltered. He missed with a roundhouse drive at Moody's head and Jacko came in shifting his weight slightly and sliding into position for the perfect punch—his whole body flowed in behind a short right that took Rosso on the chin and destroyed him. Moody's shoulder hardly moved and the punch wouldn't have traveled a foot. Rosso's knees sagged and he collapsed like a ruptured bag of cement. The darkness was in and wrapping around him before he hit the canvas.

It was the sort of end-of-fight you read about rather than see, maybe like when Dawson finished Patrick or Burns knocked out O'Neill Bell. Everyone was standing up shouting and people were turning to each other asking if they'd seen it. Toni towered up there, her eyes like saucers at the ring. I could feel the excitement in Tickener beside me. Jerome, on the other side, was hustling. He brushed men aside to get to others and I caught a flash of his brown fist in the air, full of money.

I'd made money, too, but it was the kind of moment when money doesn't mean anything. I'd invested a lot of emotional capacity in the events leading up to this and the moment was sweet. I finished my drink and felt the euphoria of the blacks around me catching hold and sweeping me up. My face creased into a smile and I was standing there foolishly taking in the scene like a stoned-out hippie. Suddenly the euphoria washed away and the alcohol warmth inside me died.

Five rows away Penny was standing beside a tall Aborigine. She was wearing a flame-red dress of some satiny material that touched a fetishistic nerve inside me like a dentist's drill going into tooth pulp. A poplin trench coat was floating out around her shoulders; it was too big for her; someone else's coat, and her eyes were shining and the flash of her white, chunky teeth was a stark, erotic signal. She moved her head a fraction, saw me, and looked straight through me. I stood still, empty and cold, and the fellow-feeling I'd had with the blacks around me ebbed away and I was back where I'd been before—alien, excluded and hostile.

Jerome said something to me and I grunted in reply. I started to move off and found Tickener by my elbow.

"Great fight, Cliff," he bubbled.

"Wonderful," Toni said.

"I don't know," I said blankly. "I think Sands would have been home sooner."

A while later I was driving to Mosman to see Ailsa, but I didn't expect the visit to be a good one. My head was too full of the images of women: wild ones, rushing to the edge; ambitious ones with their toe-holds for security showing in their eyes, and the young ones with the illusions being scrubbed off their faces by the long days and nights.

About the Author

Peter Corris is a former academic turned journalist, thriller writer, and jogger. Born in Victoria, Australia, he is now an enthusiastic resident of Sydney, Australia, which has provided the inspiration and locale for THE DYING TRADE, WHITE MEAT, and his upcoming Cliff Hardy mysteries.

CONSPIRACY
INTRIGUE
MURDER

From **Fawcett Books**